THE
LAST
GOOD
PLACE
of Lily Odilon

THE
LAST
GOOD
PLACE
of Lily Odilon

S A R A   B E I T I A

flux™
Woodbury, Minnesota

First Edition
First Printing, 2010

Cover design by Ellen Dahl
Cover images: tree © iStockphoto.com/Yellowboat Studios;
    woman © iStockphoto.com/Vladimir Piskunov

Flux, an imprint of Llewellyn Worldwide Ltd.

Library of Congress Cataloging-in-Publication Data
Beitia, Sara, 1977–
   The last good place of Lily Odilon / Sara Beitia.—1st ed.
      p. cm.
   Summary: When seventeen-year-old Albert Morales's girlfriend Lily goes missing and he is the main suspect in her disappearance, he must deflect the worries of his angry parents, the suspicions of the police, and Lily's dangerous stepfather as Albert desperately tries to find her, with her sister as his only ally.
   ISBN 978-0-7387-2068-5
   [1. Runaways—Fiction. 2. Stepfathers—Fiction. 3. Sexual abuse—Fiction. 4. Mystery and detective stories—Fiction.] I. Title.
   PZ7.B38865Las 2010
   [Fic]—dc22
                                                            2010019112

Flux
Llewellyn Worldwide Ltd.
2143 Wooddale Drive
Woodbury, MN 55125-2989
www.fluxnow.com

Printed in the United States of America

For Paul

One

7:45 p.m.

Albert Morales sits on the curb with his head down between his knees, trying to breathe. He waits for his heart to stop pounding so they can get moving again. Olivia Odilon is nearby, just across the street—a slim shadow concealed by the dark arch of a restaurant entryway right next to an empty newsstand. Albert looks up briefly and sees her eyes across the way, two shining chips of glass reflecting the harsh glow of the streetlight. Albert doesn't really believe in God but he prays anyway, in a sweaty ecstasy of desperation, that he won't have a full-on asthma attack. Now that he needs it, the inhaler he uses on very rare occasions is several hundred miles back, sitting on top of his dresser along with, as he recalls, his only necktie, the MP3 player he'd received for Christmas, about three dollars in change, and a snapshot of his girlfriend Lily. Lily, who also happens to be long gone.

No point thinking about that.

After a moment he tries a tentative breath, then, finding that he can, he pulls another one down into his lungs, exhaling gratefully and taking in another deep drink of air.

It's good.

It's difficult, but he pushes the panic he's feeling out of his mind, instead concentrating completely on catching his breath. He can hear Olivia's feet scraping impatiently at the pavement like a restless animal. He lifts his arm and raises a finger to let her know he just needs another moment.

Albert opens his eyes and sees a small something between his sneakers in the gutter. Without thinking, he reaches down to grab whatever it is, and comes up with a damp matchbox in his fingers. He shakes it. Empty. On one side is a tiny picture of woman wearing a sly smile and not much else; Albert flips the box over and sees that it comes from a place called the Alibi in a city called New Salisbury.

"Whatcha got there?"

He looks up and sees that Olivia has crossed the street and now stands in front of him. He tosses the empty matchbox up and she catches it between her hands. "From some bar or strip club, I guess."

She reads the thing, then laughs softly. "Wish we had an alibi right now?"

He stands, not answering. "I think I'm okay now. Let's go."

The two of them set out again, down the deserted street on their way to Lily.

TWO

The Kogen house, tucked away at the end of quiet Myrtle Avenue, stood dark. Avoiding the streetlight that shone like a spotlight on the black road and sidewalk, Albert sprinted across the Kogens' front lawn and down the narrow side yard. His shoes crunched on the frosty grass. It was a cool, clear February night and he wished he'd worn a heavier jacket, or at least a hat. Shivering, he stepped carefully into a flower bed and inched his way up to the window, lifting his hand but hesitating, drawing out the moment of anticipation before he would see her again. Then he was rapping the glass with his knuckles, two long bursts and three short ones. A second later, a light went on in the room and Lily lifted the sash. It was just after midnight.

"Hey," Albert whispered, his breath a shimmering ghost between them.

"Hey," came Lily's voice from inside. Then she leaned out the window and gave him a long, warm kiss. "Come inside, quick."

Albert ran his tongue over his lips and tasted cherry lip balm from her mouth. He lifted himself through the low window expertly, having sneaked into her room this way several times in the weeks since that wonderful and unbelievable day when Lily had smiled at him at school and he'd found the courage to actually speak to her.

Her bedroom was warm and smelled like sandalwood, and was lit only by a lamp with a gauzy orange scarf she'd draped over the shade for mood.

"So," he said, like one of them always did, "what do you want to do?"

"I think you know," she said, closing the window after him and drawing the blinds quickly, covering the ghostly reflection of her room in the window glass. She kissed him again, a brief peck this time on the corner of his mouth, and asked, "Why didn't you just come to the door? My parents won't be back from Philly until Sunday and Liv is staying the weekend with Kate's family at their cabin. We have the house to ourselves."

He shrugged, the corners of his mouth twisting. "Coming in through the window is more exciting." His heart fluttered like a bird trapped in his rib cage, but he kept his voice pretty much steady. He wanted to grab her hand, just for an excuse to touch her.

Lily's face was tilted downward and her eyes darted up to Albert's from under her long eyelashes. When she smiled at him, it was a crooked, sexy smile that caused him actual physical pain when he looked at it too long. From one corner of the room, he couldn't take his eyes off her— from the hair escaping from her loose ponytail to outline her face in little waves, to her long, pale neck, to her pretty butt rounding out the back of her jeans, to her bare feet with chipping teal paint on the nails. He was amazed at how he could be so delirious over someone he didn't even know existed a few of months ago.

Breaking into Albert's thoughts, Lily turned to him and said, "What are you looking at?"

Without thinking, he said the first thing that popped into his head. "You should be naked. All the time." Even as the words tumbled from his mouth he knew he shouldn't have said it, that she would misunderstand. "I just mean, you're beautiful."

"Idiot." But she blew him a kiss from where she'd finally sat herself on the bed. She stretched over to the nightstand and turned out the lamp, and then the room was black. "Why don't you come over here?"

He heard the bedsprings creak as she shifted her weight, and a second later, she was next to him and had hooked a finger into the waistband of his jeans and pulled him away from the window and onto the bed with her.

The few seconds that the window had been open had made the room cold, and they hurried under the covers. The sheets were cold as well, and as Albert pulled the top one up he noticed a light soap smell, like they'd just been washed. He pressed his mouth to hers and then their arms and legs were tangled in each other and the blankets, making it awkward to take off their layers of sweaters, shirts, socks, jeans—everything that kept warm skin from skin.

Albert felt clumsy, like he was moving too fast in the dark, but Lily didn't act like she minded. It wasn't long before he stopped worrying about it.

The next time Albert looked over at the glowing green face of the clock, it was almost two. They'd dozed off with their arms around each other. He'd startled himself awake, very aware that the little time they had was slipping away, as always, and that he couldn't just sink into pleasant sleep for the rest of the night. Before dawn, he would have to dress and slip back into the cold and run home before his parents were up and around and noticed he was gone.

Somehow sensing his wakefulness, Lily stirred in his arms. He was lying on his back and she was nestled in the crook of his arm. He shivered, but all the covers were in a pile at the foot of the bed and he didn't want to disturb her by reaching down for a blanket. Instead, he tightened his arm around her. Burying his face in her hair, he whispered "I love you" into the top of her head.

"Huh?" she breathed, half awake. "I love you, too."

They were silent again, and Albert had almost dozed off when he felt the bed jostle and the bedspread slide off. Opening his eyes, he saw Lily's dim outline, wrapped in a blanket with one arm snaked out, feeling around the side of the bed for her clothes.

"Are you awake?" she whispered.

"Yeah."

He waited for her to continue, or to at least lie down, but she just sat there. He sat up, too, suddenly more awake. "Did I do something wrong?"

A wheezy little laugh escaped her. "Not at all. It's just, I don't know. Sometimes I feel weird. Like just now, when I woke up."

"Weird? You mean, like, since your accident?" Albert knew that Lily had had some kind of accident about eighteen months ago, with an injury that had included a couple months in a coma and months more of rehab that she was still working on. In fact, the whole town knew about Lily's accident, and Albert had heard about it soon after starting school here last fall; before he'd even met the girl, he'd been familiar with her reputation.

"Yeah. I lost months around that time, big chunks they say I'll probably never get back."

He remained silent, waiting for her to continue, knowing she wasn't done.

She went on, "But sometimes I think I *am* remembering things, and it's a sneaky kind of coming back. Sometimes I don't know if these ideas are dreams or memories. Mostly it's impossible to tell which is which. It really sucks." She sniffed.

"Are you crying?" Albert asked, putting his arms around her tense body. "What's wrong?"

She slid to her feet from the edge of the bed, slipping out of the embrace. "I mean, I've just been feeling... weird...and I wanted to, I don't know, throw it out at you. See what you think." She began pacing the floor, wrapped in the coverlet. "Only I don't even know how to put it into words. There's just something on the edge of my brain, something trying to get my attention. But I can't quite see it, you know?"

"I'm not sure I understand," he said. "But I want to. Why don't you tell me what it is?"

"I'm trying!" she said, her voice loud in the stillness of the dark room. Then she said, "I don't want to scare you off. I'm tired and confused and the middle of the night just screws with my head. Forget it."

He tried again to pull her back down to the mattress, back into sleep with him, but she resisted. "Just say whatever you're thinking, even if it doesn't make sense," he told her.

"I want to." She finally found her clothes. "Hey, I'm thirsty. I'll be right back—" But she cut herself short.

He lay back down. "We can talk all night if you want," he said through a yawn. She left and he thought he heard her say something at the door, something that began with *I need*, but it was so soft and then she was gone. And soon, so was Albert, back into sleep.

Awaking with a start for the second time that night, Albert sat straight up in bed. He was confused for a moment, finding himself in a bed that wasn't his own. Then the sleep fog cleared and he remembered where he was, and why. Shivering, he leaned over and pulled a blanket from the foot of the bed up and over himself. He couldn't have been asleep long, he thought, because Lily wasn't back from the kitchen. He looked at the clock, then figured he'd give her a couple more minutes before he went after her and dragged her back to bed for the few more hours they could steal before it was back to their daytime lives, apart.

Another sharp jolt went through his brain and he looked at the clock again. Now it read 4:53 a.m. It had been almost three hours since Lily had gone to get a drink. He rubbed his eyes. Had she come back and he'd forgotten? Was she in another room, brooding or maybe even crying, resentful that he hadn't stayed awake long enough to come looking for her?

Cursing to himself, Albert jumped up and scrambled around in the darkness for his clothes. Before he'd even finished shimmying into his 501s, he was pulling on his sneakers and slipping through the bedroom door into the hall. Though he knew the house was empty save the two of them, habit and some superstition kept him from calling Lily's name out loud.

The kitchen was dark when Albert went in, and it was empty. The only signs that anyone had been there were a Coke can sitting on the island and the squeak of his own shoe rubber on the tiled floor. He sighed as he turned to leave the kitchen to begin a room-by-room search—something was bothering her and she wasn't going to make this easy. It was hide and seek, and apparently Albert was "it." His stomach knotted with anxiety and he felt guilty for feeling irritated with her.

A peek into the living room and then the den showed the same empty scene as the kitchen, so Albert went back to the bedroom, where there was still no sign of Lily. Both his nerves and his exasperation grew as he left the bedroom again to search the rest of the house. Twenty minutes later he was back in Lily's room, seated on the edge of her bed— still alone—bewildered and unsure of what to do next.

He was pretty positive now that Lily was not here. It occurred to him that maybe she really was hiding from him, but as soon as he thought it, he rejected the idea as absurd. Anyway, why would she hide from him in her own house? But there was something going on. He'd looked in every room, flipping lights on and off in each one, including the bathrooms and bedrooms and even the basement, then he went back through them all again to check under and behind the furniture, too. By the time he was making his second round through the house, this time faster and louder, he wasn't worried anymore about making noise— he called her name as he searched for her in the unfamiliar rooms.

Back in Lily's bedroom again, after coming up with nothing, he tried to figure out what to do next. She just wasn't here. And to complicate things, dawn was coming fast and he was left with this problem and no time or ideas on how to solve it. As he was putting this together, his irritation was slowly dissolving into a vague fear.

Albert was pulling on his jacket so that he could take his search to the yard and the neighborhood, if he had to, when it occurred to him that he'd overlooked a room: the garage. For some reason it was the arrival of this idea—a vague picture of the never-before-seen garage had popped into his head—that stoked his fear. If she wasn't there, either, then he would have to face the fact that the problem was a big one.

Following up on what was his last idea, Albert was in the kitchen moments later, where the house and garage were connected. He fumbled with the lock on the door to the garage and stepped into the coolness, his feet echoing on the concrete floor and the faint smell of motor oil hitting his nose. When he found the wall switch with his hand, harsh fluorescence stung his eyes.

As he'd already known it would be, the garage, too, was empty. Lily's car was gone.

Three

9 p.m.

"Are we crazy?"

"Yes," Albert says through a bulging mouthful of grayish, greasy, fast food hamburger. He swallows. "But I don't think your stepfather or MacLennan—or the cops, either—have left us much choice there, Liv."

"Don't call me Liv," she says automatically, but without much force. She picks up her own burger, which only has a couple of small bites taken from it, then drops it back on its slick paper wrapper. "It's amazing how fast everything can go to crap, though, isn't it?"

Picturing the last time he saw Lily, the way the night had started and the way it ended, Albert nods.

"It's only been two days, but it feels like we've been

gone for years," she adds. "And Lily—it's as if she's been gone forever."

"We're going to fix this," he insists. Even in the short time they've spent together, he's found Olivia's almost constant pessimism a drag. It's true that things have gone to crap, and quickly, but if he lets himself dwell on it too much he's afraid of becoming too overwhelmed to keep going forward. "We're all she's got." *And she's definitely all I have,* he thinks, *or else I'm likely to end up in jail for murder.*

"Right. So neither of us has much of a choice. We have to try to find her, even if—"

"Never mind the note she sent us—"

"—you, she sent it to *you,*" Olivia interrupts.

He ignores her, knowing that this is a sore point with her, continuing, "And never mind that we have to find her because she's the only proof left of what really happened, that we have to get to her before your stepfather does. Not to mention that if we can bring her home it will prove that she's alive." He stops, his voice beginning to rise toward a shaky squeak.

"Please," Olivia hisses, though there's no one at the neighboring tables. "Keep your voice down!"

He drops his voice to just above a whisper, but doesn't stop hammering at his point. She needs to hear it—*again and again,* he thinks, *and again, until she gets it.* "He's looking for all of us, because the three of us are the only ones who know what he did. So we don't have a choice—we have to find her and make sure she's safe, and we have to do it without getting caught."

Then they are both quiet, blending into the background of the too-bright, too-quiet fast food restaurant. Both of them are worn out, catching snatches of sleep when they can, and Albert has a lost feeling. The brightness makes him long for a nice, dark place where he might curl up in deep, dreamless sleep until everything is over.

"Eat, why don't you?" he says roughly, gesturing at her uneaten food. He's seventeen and barely weighs one hundred and fifty pounds, so he's aware that trying to get all paternal and commanding with this girl he's only known well for about a week is pretty much a joke. They're the same age and both juniors, and though she's kind of a runt, besides being the younger sister, it's not like she would take orders from him; she probably wouldn't take orders from anyone. Knowing this doesn't stop him. Their cash flow is low and the girl needs to eat something. He feels protective of her because she's Lily's sister, but also because she doesn't have anyone looking out for her, doesn't even think she needs it. He can't guess what's around the next corner, or how bad it will be. Better to face whatever it will be with a little something in the stomach.

"What are you smirking about?"

Albert realizes he's actually smiling. "I was just thinking how my manly interior dialogue sounds a lot like it's coming from my great-grandmother Hawl."

Olivia manages a thin smile. Albert studies her face, a pale smear under the fluorescent lights, fringed by unnaturally black hair. They're sitting across from one another in bright yellow molded plastic benches, the kind that are attached to the table between them. They've ordered a burger each and taken their tray around the corner, away from the doors and the main window, and away from the homeless man digging through the trash bin near the front entrance while no employee interferes or even seems to notice, to the back of the restaurant. Their table is the nearest to the bathrooms and a bank of pay phones. Albert resists the urge to command Olivia again to eat.

"Are you about ready to go?" she says after a while. "I'm exhausted and if we don't get moving soon, I'm afraid I'll fall asleep right here."

He looks pointedly at her food, which after sitting out is pretty unappetizing, but she takes the hint and has another bite. "Yes, Daddy."

He flinches. "I prefer 'Grandma.'" He stares off into space, letting his mind wander a little. After a bit, he says, "What are we, about halfway?"

"I'd need a map to be sure, but yeah, we're probably halfway between home and Yellow Pine Lake. Why?"

He shrugs. "Equidistance."

She crumples her napkin into a ball, worrying it slowly to shreds. "That's not a word."

"Maybe not. But I think Lily would like it. X marks the middle spot on the ley line that runs between the two significant locations of the Cult of Lily Odilon. And we're its only followers."

"Vestal virgins?" Olivia suggests.

They both knew they were talking nonsense, playing some word game aimed at conjuring Lily.

"Not quite," says Albert. "Has she been talking to you about sacred geography, or was that a new thing?"

"She hasn't, no, but Lily always has a new thing. What is it this time?"

"Sometimes, late, late at night, she would just lay things on me. You know, cosmic questions, the kind that wakes you up in a cold sweat, or keeps you from sleeping in the first place." He pauses. "And this bit with Yellow Pine Lake, it just makes me remember something she said to me not that long ago, something about certain physical locations and the power of place, or whatever."

"She was—" Olivia stops, consciously correcting her tense, "*is*, full of crap. She doesn't believe in that new-agey garbage, in places of power or whatever. She ran because she didn't think she had a choice, and she went to the lake because she knew you and I could find her. The rest is just wishful thinking to give it some meaning."

"I don't blame her." He picks up the shredded napkin Olivia has dropped and turns it over in his fingers.

"Wishful thinking," Olivia says again. "It means nothing, it just *is*."

"Add it up: Kogen, the journal, the accident, her memories, the night she left—it all comes together. Or keeping with Lily's way of thinking, we could call it profane geometry." Albert knows it's crap, but he likes the way it sounds.

Olivia snorts, apparently done with the game, but he isn't ready to give up. It's all silliness, finding patterns because you're looking for them, but Albert feels like he's defending Lily, not just her quirks. "Look, you of all people should understand that sometimes people need—" But there's an interruption and Olivia is saved from hearing the rest of his speech.

The electronic chirp of her cell phone comes from her purse and they both jump, Albert giving his knee a painful bang on the underside of the table. They stare at each other. With the second chirp, Olivia shoves her hand into her bag and pulls out the phone.

"Don't answer it," he says. Maybe it's the conversation getting to him, but he's afraid.

She glares at him. "I'm not a moron. I'm just checking to see who it is."

"Wait, what if it's her?"

"It's not," she says in a strangled voice, her eyes flickering from the screen to him and back down again. "I think it's our friend the detective."

"Andersen's calling?" Albert's tongue is thick and dry, as if it might fill his mouth and choke him. "How can you tell?"

She holds the phone out to him, but he refuses to take it, like it might burn him if he touches it. "Caller ID. Heard of it?"

"Why is he calling you?"

She switches it from ringer to vibrate and drops the phone back into her purse. "You're their top 'person of interest,' and you've suddenly disappeared, and so have I. They must have figured that out by now." She sighs and rubs her eyes, hard. "I'm just going to ignore it until he gives up."

After a few more rings the phone stops buzzing, to their mutual relief. This relief doesn't last long, though, because after about thirty seconds, the phone begins to buzz again in Olivia's bag.

"Damn it," she says softly, reaching in to make sure it's Andersen again.

Albert opens his mouth to speak, but shuts it when his eyes meet a stranger's at the table behind them. Sometime in the last few minutes, a middle-aged man, alone, had intruded upon their scene and they hadn't noticed. Albert tries to remember what they'd said, wondering if this man has been eavesdropping. He puts his hand over Olivia's and gestures with his chin at the new guy.

She turns to look, then leans forward and says softly, "Meet me in the ladies' room." Without waiting for his reply, she leaves the table and heads into the short hall that splits into two doors, women on one side, men on the other. After a moment, Albert gets up and follows. He avoids making further eye contact with the man at the other table.

The restroom is a little windowless room with two stalls, but there's a lock on the door. Olivia turns the deadbolt and presses her back to the door like someone is out there planning to knock it down.

Albert leans against the sink. "Why are we hiding in the bathroom?"

She gives him an irritated look. "It was so quiet in there, and even with the ringer off, the buzzing on this thing is loud. I just didn't want that guy to get suspicious, or take a good look at our faces."

"Yeah, there's nothing suspicious about going to the bathroom together."

"Shut up, okay?" She holds up her purse, which is buzzing again. "Think. What are we going to do about this?"

"Ignore it? Turn it off?"

She slaps herself on the forehead. "Turn it off! Why didn't I just turn it off?"

Albert doesn't know, but since in his panic he didn't think of it either, he doesn't say anything. "I still don't get why he's calling. Does he think we're just going to give up, turn ourselves in?"

"Maybe he thinks you're holding me captive, another victim of your bloodthirsty rampage," Olivia says.

"That's helpful. Really."

"It's reflex." She looks sorry.

"Maybe he's not expecting either one of us to answer. Maybe it's something else entirely." Albert chews his lower lip, thinking. "What do you know about tracing?"

She just looks at him.

"I mean, cell phones run through satellites, right? Can't they do a thing—is it triangulation?"—he grasps at barely remembered ideas—"where they use your phone's coordinates to pinpoint where you are? Can they trace our location that way?"

Olivia pulls the phone out of her bag, turning it off mid-buzz and dropping it on the counter by the sink. "I don't know! Is that real? Can they really do that?"

"I think they can." He doesn't actually know for sure, but he's afraid, a sensation he's getting used to.

"Does it even have to be on, or connected, for them to do that? What if they already did?"

They stare at the phone as if it had suddenly grown fangs.

Then Albert says, "We should get rid of it."

"Agreed."

"Where?"

Olivia points to the trash bin next to the door, over-flowing with paper towels. "Why not there?"

After they make sure the ringer is off, they wrap the little device in paper towels until it's an unidentifiable ball of paper refuse, then Albert takes off his coat, pushes up his sleeve and reaches into the can of he-prefers-not-to-know-what and buries the balled up phone in the middle of all that trash.

"Well, thanks, Lil. I sank pretty much all of my cash into that stupid phone," Olivia says when Albert is done burying it. "That model cost me twenty bucks extra, and it has an MP3 player…" She shrugs, but her eyes sweep the trash can regretfully as she does. "So we should probably jet."

Grossed out by digging in the garbage, Albert washes his hands and up his arm with hot water and a ton of soap, trying to do it fast. "I'll get you the money for a new one. Let's go."

Just then the door thumps and there are several insis-tent raps on it, more like pounding than knocking. Albert accidentally splashes water all over the counter and Olivia lets out a little scream. "What the hell is going on in there?"

a gravelly female voice demands from the other side. "Open the damn door!"

Olivia struggles to undo the latch, and the door flies open and into her the second the catch comes undone. The form of a woman—not old, but definitely a lot older than her teenage coworkers behind the counter—fills the doorway. She glares from one to the other with narrowed, darting eyes.

"I'm sorry," says Olivia. "We were just…" But she doesn't know how to finish the sentence she's begun.

The woman saves her the trouble. "Out," she commands. She points at Albert. "You too, Romeo. I know what you little freaks do in here."

"No, you've got it wrong," says Albert. Olivia kicks him to keep him from going on.

"Save it!" says the woman. "Just get out of here before I call your parents. Bet they'd love to know what you've been up to in a public restroom. This is a family restaurant!" At this point, everyone in the place—which is just the man at the table, the homeless man still digging in the trash, an old couple seated near the front, and the two people behind the counter—is looking at them as the woman leads them to the front exit.

In the parking lot, Albert zips up his coat as he walks. "Come on. She's watching us." He points at the bright front window. In fact, the faces inside are all turned to Olivia and himself.

"I wish we had a car." She gestures up as they begin to

walk. "Look at how clear the sky is. It's going to be cold tonight."

Whether they're rested or not, cold or not, frightened or not, it's time to move, and quickly. The idea that Olivia's cell phone might be tattling on them is unsettling, and they both want to put as much distance as possible between themselves and the thing. So leaving the bright glow of the restaurant's neon sign, they head back into the night, following the dim line of the black highway. They each keep their own thoughts to themselves, letting out only faint puffs of breath in the cold, the roadside scrub crunching under their shoes.

Four

She was really gone.

Even after awaking alone in the house and seeing the empty garage for himself, Albert couldn't believe that Lily would just take off without saying anything to him. He spent the next couple of hours searching her neighborhood on foot. He tried to go unnoticed as he spiraled farther and farther from her house down the sidewalks and alleyways, not sure what he was looking for except some sign of Lily. The darkness had turned dim gray, which meant dawn wasn't far off. When he found no trace of Lily or her car, he went back to the house—her house—and back to her room. He kicked off his shoes and sat on her bed, pulling the blankets up around his shoulders. He wasn't sure what to do next, and he couldn't shake the nightmare feeling that he was moving through dense fog in a dream scenario that made no sense.

It would've been nice, he thought, if this were just a very realistic nightmare, something he could wake up from. People didn't usually disappear like that—there one minute, gone the next. He kept coming back to his certainty that Lily would not have left him alone in her house, now a trespasser instead of a guest, confused as to what had happened and feeling like he was at the edge of some disaster. He wanted to lie down and fall asleep again, so he could wake up with everything back in place and the nightmare over, but his heart wouldn't stop thumping. He was too aware of the seconds and minutes slipping by until he would have no choice but to do *something*.

Then Albert had another thought. He hadn't yet tried the simplest thing—getting an explanation from the girl who was causing all this anxiety in the first place. Feeling hopeful for the first time since he'd awakened in the empty house, he shrugged off the blankets and left Lily's room to find the phone. He remembered seeing one in the kitchen and he sprinted through the house to reach it. Probably just a misunderstanding, he told himself, relief already pouring in as he dialed Lily's cell. He was sure now, already starting to feel stupid for panicking, anticipating her voice on the other end of the line. She'd gone out for doughnuts or for some other slightly crazy whim; she was probably already on her way back and when she saw him she would be unable to understand his distress and probably laugh at him for being so worried over nothing. Her unpredictability, the way she gave in to her impulses, was part of what drew him to her—there was nothing boring about her.

Does it take several hours to buy doughnuts? asked a voice in the back of his head, but Albert stubbornly shut it down.

The phone rang several times and then went to voice mail. Albert hung up without leaving a message. Just as he disconnected, he thought he heard a sound from somewhere in the empty house. Curious, he dialed Lily's cell phone again, slowly making his way back to her room as it rang and rang without answer. It was still ringing when he got to Lily's room, and by then he had the *brr-click* of the phone ringing in one ear, and the faint tinny tinkling of an electronic ringtone in the other.

Albert hung up, then dialed Lily's number a third time, dropping the handset on the bed and letting it ring. Listening hard, he moved around her room, tracking the sound of the familiar electronic ring until he found Lily's bag on the floor in the corner. Her cell phone rang from inside it.

He picked up her bag and dropped it on the bed, then hung up the telephone. The house was still and silent again. Feeling guilty, he dumped out the bag's contents. A bunch of Lily's junk rattled out and settled into the folds of the blankets. What Albert saw was what he figured were the usual things found in a girl's bag, but the sight of her phone and her little pink fuzzy wallet made his heart pound for some reason. After a moment of just looking, he picked up Lily's wallet and opened it. Inside was her driver's license and six dollars.

"Why would she leave without her phone or her

purse?" Albert asked aloud of the room. As if the strong sense of her presence, among all her things, might be enough to force an answer.

If this had been a hypothetical situation, a what-if and what-would-you-do kind of thing, Albert would have said that of course she wouldn't leave without any of the basics like her license and money. But she was gone, her car was gone, and everything else, including her boyfriend, was still here. So the fact was, no matter how improbable: she *had* left. And he was completely in the dark as to why.

Now Albert finally noticed that the sun had fully risen and it was actually surprisingly high in the sky. It was morning, early for a Saturday but very late for him, since he still needed to get back home and into his room without being seen by his parents.

So he had a decision to make.

Sitting there with Lily's empty bag and its contents, junk that had taken on extra weight, in his lap, Albert decided that sneaking home, and soon, was the only reasonable thing he could do at the moment. If he could just get into his house and into his own bed until at least noon, perhaps things would work themselves out without him while he slept off a bad night.

He pushed away the little voice in his head that was now shouting *Find her! Tell someone! Something's wrong! Something's bad! She's gone!* He really wanted Lily to just be cutting loose because her mother, stepfather, and sister were out of town and she had a bit of temporary freedom.

And you know that's all it is, he thought, slamming the door on the worry-voice that had been tormenting him.

If he told someone ... and who would he tell? What would he say? If he raised some alarm about her, it would only get Lily into trouble when she showed up again, with no clue about the way she'd made them worry.

If Albert was honest with himself, he didn't want to cause trouble for either Lily *or* himself, or worse, trouble between them because he'd overreacted. He wondered if Lily was trying to start some trouble, and his irritation began to elbow out his worry again as he was leaving the empty house. It was as simple as walking out the back door and shutting it behind him, but the thud of wood on wood and the click of the latch sounded so final. Once through the door, he made his way home by side streets, cutting through a few back yards.

Hadn't he known something like this was going to come up, sooner or later? Lily was sweet and smart and he was crazy about her, but he knew she had a wild streak. He hadn't been in town for two weeks before he heard the stories going around George Washington High School—and one story in particular. Lily's version of this story was called "The Bad Thing," and it was a short story because she remembered very little of it. The legend, though, went by the longer title of "That One Time Lily Odilon and Some Other Juvenile Delinquents Broke into Lily's Step-Dad's Dental Practice and Lily OD'd on Laughing Gas and Almost Died." This second version was surprisingly short on juicy details (since no one who'd been there had come forward to share them), but even so, the popular version of the story had an ugly, gossipy sting.

He could kind of understand why her parents kept their thumbs on her, but he felt guilty for the thought. She probably thought the same about him and his strict parents. Both of them had done things in the past to burn what trust their parents had in them, and both of their parents seemed unwilling to let them earn the trust again. Though maybe Lily wasn't trying very hard.

By now Albert was almost home and tired of the struggle going on inside his head. He wished that Lily would finish her little joyride or whatever and just call him. He promised himself he wouldn't even be too much of an ass to her when she finally *did* call. He would be willing to let the whole thing go—unlike their parents. Forget it like a fading nightmare, if only she would pick up a phone and call him.

But he was still unwilling to share his worry with anyone else. The fear of what the consequences might be if he let his worry send him like a baby to the adults kept him in check. He was afraid Lily would dump him for being a pansy if he ratted her out and ruined her fun. Still, until he heard from her, it was like holding his breath. He wasn't sure whether he was doing the right thing.

A few minutes later, Albert was letting himself in through the back door of his own warm, silent home, being careful not to make a sound. He was thankful that at least his parents didn't seem to be awake yet. He was able to creep to his bedroom and into bed. He dropped his clothes in a pile on the floor and pulled the covers over his head, wanting to think of anything but Lily but unable to push her out of his brain. Within minutes, though it would've seemed impossible, he was dead to the world.

Still, he had to wake up eventually. The rest of the weekend was unbelievably long as Albert waited for the phone to ring and for Lily to put him out of his misery. But she never called; his vague fear kept growing even though he didn't know exactly what he was afraid of. Mostly he stayed in his room, unable to focus on his homework or pay attention to the TV, just staring at the ceiling or out the window, waiting. It sucked.

Monday morning was the worst day yet. As Albert stumbled around his room getting ready for school, he couldn't believe the new week had somehow arrived without Lily. And he still wasn't sure if he should say something to someone. As he walked alone to school, it was harder to convince himself that Lily was off on some weekend joyride. Her parents had to be home from Philadelphia by now, and her sister from wherever Lily said she'd been, and they would find that she had gone. Albert was now sure that something was very wrong.

So, unable to leave it alone, he aimed his path toward Lily's house instead of straight toward school. He thought he could see some activity from a block away, and when he got closer, what he saw sent a jolt of alarm through him. He felt an irrational desire to bolt in the opposite direction before anyone saw him. Mostly, Lily's house looked the same as it always did, except that there were two police cruisers parked outside and people standing in the front yard on the frosty grass. Giving in to panic, Albert quickly turned the corner and began heading back in the direction of the school. He looked over his shoulder and saw Lily's mother and sister standing a little apart in the yard. They seemed to be talking to a cop, and Lily's mother seemed to be crying.

Albert didn't remember arriving at school or much of anything that happened all morning. All he could do was obsess about what might have been going on at Lily's house. That is, until things got worse. The tipping point—when everything went from vague to a horribly real, actual situation—was right around the time Principal Gherdt pulled him out of third period U.S. History.

Crouching down next to Albert's desk while the whole class stared at them, Mr. Gherdt said in a loud whisper, "Some gentlemen want to speak with you, Mr. Morales."

Albert had no choice but to follow Mr. Gherdt out of the classroom and down the empty halls to the school's main office. The principal walked a few paces ahead, and Albert noticed for the first time that the man walked like he had an itch he couldn't scratch in public. When they went through the glass doors, the secretary behind the counter glanced up at them and did a double take, and Albert hated that other people knew something about him before he did. Gherdt led Albert through the main office and down a short hall into the small conference room that the guidance counselor used as a place to "rap" with troubled students. Just as Albert was wondering if he and Mr.

Gherdt were going to "rap," he saw that the room wasn't empty. Besides himself and the principal, there was Mrs. Patel, the guidance counselor herself, and two men Albert had never seen before, one tall and one not, both wearing droopy sport coats. The four adults looked at Albert silently as he came into the room, and Albert saw Gherdt and one of the men exchange a look. The two men were standing against the far wall as Albert and Gherdt lingered just inside the door. Only Mrs. Patel was seated—at least sort of, with one haunch resting in a pretend-casual way on the edge of the desk.

Gherdt pushed Albert into the room and closed the door behind them. "Take a seat," he said, gesturing at the plastic chair in front of the desk.

Albert sat as he'd been told, and asked, "What's going on?" He knew this had something to do with Lily. He hadn't cheated on any tests, hadn't stolen anything or gotten into a fight—there was nothing else it *could* be.

One of the men said, "We're hoping you can tell us that, Mr. Morales."

The guy addressing Albert was the taller one, who seemed older than the other guy. He wasn't super-big, but Albert noticed prominent muscles on his forearms where his jacket sleeves were pushed up, and his neck was thick. He looked like a guy who never hit the gym, but instead got his muscle from his daily activities. Some big dogs had the same look.

"This is Detective Andersen," said Gherdt, "and his colleague, Officer Demiola. They're here—"

"Thanks, Principal Gherdt," interrupted Andersen. To Albert he said, "We were hoping you could answer a few questions about a"—he cleared his throat—"chum of yours. I gather you're close with a senior named Lily Odilon?"

"What's happened? Is she okay?" The words fell from Albert's mouth.

Andersen raised an eyebrow and took a step closer to Albert. "I'll tell you, kid, we're not sure she is. Mind if I ask you a few questions, see if we can't shed a little light?"

"Um." Albert didn't know what to say, because he didn't quite know what was happening. He cleared his throat, but still found no safe words.

Turning to Gherdt, Mrs. Patel spoke up. "Vernon, don't you think we ought to call this boy's parents? They should know their son is being questioned by the police at school this morning." Even with what she was saying, there was a fair amount of the usual pep in her voice.

Before Gherdt could reply, Andersen said, "That's a good idea, ma'am."

"Both your parents at work?" Gherdt asked, on board because the cop was on board.

"Yes. But my mom works in town, so it'd be better to call her." He was babbling, not really knowing what was coming out of his mouth but knowing it was coming out too fast. Something about this guy's pale, expressionless eyes turned him into a scared little kid. That, and Albert wasn't used to talking to cops. "They'll have to page her, though, so she might have to call you back." Still babbling.

"That's fine," said Andersen, crossing his arms over his

chest. "Do you folks mind going into the other room to do that? I'd like to chat with Albert here while we wait—if he doesn't mind."

Albert did mind, but he said nothing. They were all looking at him again, so he nodded.

Gherdt and Mrs. Patel left the room with Detective Demiola, who was saying as he shut the door on Albert and Andersen, "I have a few questions for you folks about Miss Odilon…"

"Lily's a friend of yours?" asked Andersen once he and Albert were alone.

"She is," said Albert, his voice coming out weak. "More than a friend. I'm her boyfriend."

"When was the last time you saw her?"

The guy didn't worry much about putting a guy at ease, Albert decided. "Friday night, or I guess actually Saturday morning. It's a long story."

"I have as much time as you need."

Albert squirmed in his chair. "Sure, but shouldn't I wait until my mom gets here?"

Andersen sat down on the couch and tented his fingers, merely looking at Albert.

"I mean," Albert went on, "am I being questioned? Am I in trouble for something?"

"I'm just trying to understand. You're not under arrest for anything. What do I have to arrest you for? We're just talking because it looks like something bad could've happened to your girlfriend and I figure you want to help. You do want to help?"

"I want to help. Maybe you can tell me what happened to Lily? I haven't heard from her since … the last time I saw her, and I've been kind of worried."

"Why would you be worried?"

"I don't know." This was true; at least, he didn't know how to explain the uneasy way he'd felt when he'd woken up in Lily's bed with no Lily.

Andersen scratched his eyebrow, saying, after a pause, "Okay, but if you were so worried—for whatever reason— why didn't you tell somebody?"

"Her parents were out of town, and Lily—she gets funny ideas in her head sometimes and does unusual things."

Andersen pounced on this. "What kinds of 'unusual things'?"

Albert wished he'd said nothing. It was too hard to explain. "Nothing bad, just … she's just a free spirit or what-ever. You can ask anyone who knows her."

"We intend to."

"I didn't want to get her in trouble." It sounded stupid when he said it out loud.

"That's not the real concern here." Andersen leaned forward, catching Albert's eye. "Let's start with you telling me about the last time you two were together. Go slow and don't leave anything out."

Albert tried. He filled Andersen in on the entire chro-nology—starting with crawling through Lily's window Friday and finishing with being led out of class by Mr. Gherdt just a short while earlier. Andersen let him tell his story uninterrupted, then made Albert go through the whole story again, this time questioning things—asking for clarification here, more detail there. Sometime during the second telling Andersen had stood again, listening with his back to Albert, as if this would give him some different perspective on the same story. He paced the small room as Albert spoke and the detective's hovering made Albert nervous—which, Albert suspected, was the point.

When Albert had finished his story the second time, Andersen took a seat on the couch again. He was perched on the edge, though, not relaxed into the cushions. His expression was hard to read, and Albert wasn't sure if the detective thought he'd done well or not.

Then there was a cursory knock on the door and Mrs. Patel was poking her head into the room without waiting for an invitation to enter. "Mrs. Morales just called back. She'll be here in ten."

"Fine, fine," said Andersen, motioning for Mrs. Patel to leave. When the door closed again, he said to Albert, "Like I said, we're just talking here, and I appreciate your willingness to cooperate. I'm going to ask your mother to bring you down to the station tomorrow so you can give me your statement. Officially. That is, if you're still feeling cooperative."

"I'll do whatever I can to help."

Andersen looked at him. "Nothing about your story you'd want to change?"

"I told you everything I know, everything I remember," Albert insisted. "It's not a story. It's the truth."

"So your story will stay the same when I tell you we found Lily's car an hour ago?"

Blindsided. "Her car? What about *her*?"

"What about her?" Andersen was looking at his phone, like he wasn't that interested in Albert anymore.

"I mean," said Albert, aware that he was raising his voice but seemingly unable to stop, "if you found her car, where is Lily?"

Albert stood, as did Andersen, who said, "Are you curious about what we found?"

The room felt hot and Albert felt like he was suffocating. "Why don't you just tell me?" he demanded, his voice even louder. "Is she stuffed in the trunk or something?"

The cop put his phone back in his pocket, saying, "The car was left at Meyer's Drug in Middletown, parked around back with the keys still in it." He didn't appear troubled by Albert's outburst. "The store owners called it in, said it had been parked there since yesterday. No sign of the girl. But the drug store is on the edge of town, not far from the highway or the dump. We have a search crew out there looking."

Albert felt the blood drain from his face, and he struggled to understand what these words meant. He was saved trying to figure out how to ask when the door opened. He looked over and saw that his mother was there. She gave him a frightened looked, but it was also a hard look and a disappointed look, too. She was flanked by the other cop and Gherdt. Andersen went to her and they exchanged a few low words Albert couldn't fully make out; Andersen's sounds were firm, while Albert's mother was unusually tame.

Albert stood like a dumb animal, looking at his shoes and lost inside his head, until someone drew him from the conference room and dropped his backpack into his hands as the five of them made their way down the little hall and into the front office.

The cops left immediately, without another word to Albert or his mother. Gherdt seemed like he had more to say to Mrs. Morales, but when one of the secretaries told him she was patching a call through to his office, he left with one irritated backward glance at Albert. And though Albert had never thought the guy particularly liked him, the suspicion he thought he saw in the principal's expression gave him a rude jolt. This guy saw him every day, had even joked with him in the lunchroom before and had never had to discipline him. Albert's stomach clenched, and he wondered what exactly they all thought he'd done and how they could think he was that kind of person. Still, he felt like he should have been expecting this reaction somehow; whenever an adult acted mistrustful of him, he always began to believe he must somehow deserve it.

With the principal gone, this left Albert with his mother, who was looking up at him with her own hard-to-read expression; the school secretary, who was trying to pretend they weren't there; and Mrs. Patel, who had returned to hover the way she always did.

Mrs. Morales glanced pointedly at Mrs. Patel, then turned to her son and put a hand on his cheek. "You look

pale and your skin is clammy," she announced. "I
ing you out and taking you home."

"I'm fine," he said, embarrassed. He was suspicious of
her concern; past experience had taught him to suspect she
was hiding some rage, too, at being called away from work
to deal with trouble at her son's school.

His mother was still inspecting his face. "You look like
you're going to faint."

At this point no one in the room was even pretending
not to listen, and Albert felt like the secretary and Mrs.
Patel were now staring at him, waiting for him to collapse
or do something interesting. He agreed to leave with his
mother just to make it stop. He'd had enough scrutiny for
the day.

The ride home was quiet, and tense. Albert's mother
kept her eyes on the road, not giving even a sideways glance
at Albert; as for Albert, he put his hands in his lap to stop
them from shaking and stared out the window until they
pulled into the driveway at home.

"I want to explain—" Albert began, once they were
home and standing in the kitchen. It was really important
that he make her understand, but he didn't know which
words could do that.

"I don't want to hear it," his mother said curtly. "If it's
about why you were out in the middle of the night, well,
I'm not stupid. I don't like it and I thought we raised you
better, but…" She trailed off. Her mouth was a thin, hard
line. "I guess I'll hear the whole story tomorrow when you
talk to the police." She paused, adding, "As for the rest of

it—I know you didn't have anything to do with that girl disappearing."

That girl.

Albert didn't trust himself to speak. He left the kitchen and went to his bedroom, shutting the door softly. His mother hadn't stayed home with him on a school day since he was eleven. Though he was in his room and she was on the other side of the house, thankfully leaving him completely alone, knowing she was there at all—that she was thinking about him—was a weight. And though she was as sharp with him as usual, her show of motherly concern, something he hadn't seen much of since about the time he'd turned twelve, was disturbing. For the past few years, he'd become used to their relationship's two gears: the nag and fight gear—the one where he screwed up and she harangued him about it, and the tolerance gear—where they pretty much ignored each other as long as Albert didn't do anything to set her off. Today's mom-ishness seemed like a bad sign, like when there's a death in the family and everything is subdued.

At the thought of death Albert shook his head, as if he could physically knock the thought of death—especially death and Lily—out of his head.

Kicking off his shoes, he stretched out on his bed. His eyes were wide open and he stared at the dusty popcorn ceiling. He saw old dust turning brown-gray and a cobweb in the corner. The drabness reflected the way he felt. Drab and trapped, too, like some pathetic little bug in that spider web. His mind kept chasing after Lily. He couldn't help thinking that if he'd somehow been able to hold her really tight, he could've pressed the wildness that must've possessed her that night right out of her body. He saw it squeezing out of her like a sigh. Maybe then she wouldn't have bolted.

Albert turned over onto his stomach. What had Lily been up to that night? He went through various reasons, ranging from running to the store for turquoise nail polish to a sudden desire to see the sun rise over the landfill, but he couldn't settle on one that felt like it might be *the* reason. He kept coming back to the question without an answer. The only thing he was dead certain of was that the road things were traveling on now was not the one Lily had intended when she got up in the middle of the night and slipped away. She was wild, but not cruel.

So whatever had to follow scared the hell out of him.

He felt a hot, dense unhappiness lodged somewhere between his throat and his chest. It might have been relieved by tears, but he couldn't cry. Not that he *wouldn't*, but he just wasn't able. So the knot got bigger and more difficult to stand.

Sometime later, Albert awoke to the gloomy mid-afternoon. He was still lying on his stomach. He experienced a sleep lag right after he opened his eyes, where he knew something was wrong but didn't remember what. He'd been so awake the last he remembered, he was surprised to find that he'd been sleeping for—check the clock—two hours. The image of Lily's face surfaced in his mind, and he let out a soft groan. He rolled onto his side and closed his eyes again, trying to sink back into a protective layer of sleep before his brain began its pointless picking, picking, picking at a problem he could do nothing about. He knew it was weak, but he needed a little more time to pull it together. So much had happened so quickly.

More hours later, Albert's dad got home from work and came into his room. He sat on the edge of the bed and Albert sat up, still dopey from sleeping the day away.

"Your mother told me about ..." He gestured vaguely. "About your girlfriend. You want to talk about it?"

Albert didn't, but it didn't matter, since he was pretty sure his dad was actually hoping they *wouldn't* have to talk about it. His dad didn't go for talking about stuff, especially the big stuff, *especially* if feelings were involved.

Echoing his mother, his father said, "Your mother and I know you didn't have anything to do with her going off."

"Her name is Lily. And no, I didn't, if you're asking."

"Of course I'm not," his father said, his tone a warning. "She's a sweet kid, she is, but I'm not sure she's the best influence on you, given your history."

"Dad—"

Albert's father gave him a rough pat on the shoulder. "The fact stands that she's gone off somewhere, and the police are involved, and you're involved, too, because you were sneaking around when you should've been at home. And so you're grounded until we get this sorted out."

"Why?" Albert protested. It was automatic. He wasn't actually surprised.

"I would think it would be pretty obvious—you've

defied our rules and managed to get yourself in what looks like a hell of a lot of trouble. Apparently we need to keep a closer eye on you, because your judgment isn't great."

"My judgment is—"

His father waved an impatient hand. "I'm sorry about … Lily, and I truly hope she comes home safely to her family. But you were out when you shouldn't have been, against our rules. That's bad enough. If she doesn't show up soon, it's all going to get much worse. Do you understand the trouble you could be in?" His voice was soft, but very serious.

"I don't care." It wasn't like it mattered.

Albert's father gave him a pitying look. "For what it's worth, I know how it feels with that first love, how you think you're never going to get over it."

"Dad, please," Albert said, and he could feel his face get hot as he tried to keep his temper. The hot prickling in his skin didn't go away until his father had sighed, heaving himself from the edge of the bed, and left.

Albert skipped dinner—the idea of pork chops and mashed potatoes with his parents and the giant elephant that was Lily's disappearance in the room made Albert's stomach clench. No one came to call him to the table. Instead, he forced himself back to sleep.

When he next lifted his head from where it was buried in his pillow, it was just after seven. He had about fourteen hours before he had to face the world again. Covering his head with his pillow to block the familiar sounds of his parents eating dinner—dishes clanging, the small black and white TV in the kitchen tuned to the local news, the sounds of their muffled conversation—Albert closed his eyes.

What is the matter *with you?*

Albert tried to roll off his stomach and open his eyes, but he was in that sort of sleep paralysis state, at the line between dreaming and waking. He recognized the voice as Lily's. He tried to open his mouth to speak, but he couldn't do that either.

I'm impressed with your handling of this situation, she said in his head. Wry, as she often was. He felt her weight on the edge of the bed. *It's good to know that* this *is what you're like in a crunch.*

It's been a rough day.

The ghost of a chuckle. *Tell me about it.*

Now he imagined his hand snaking out from under the covers, searching out and finding hers. Giving it a squeeze. *Where did you go?*

But apparently the conversation was over. Soon he went deeper into sleep and there were no dreams there.

———

"We have a statement from the neighbors that places you at the scene the night Lily disappeared."

They were in a small cinderblock-walled room at the police station downtown, a bare little office with a high window, not the grim interrogation room Albert had imagined from too many *Law & Order* reruns. He squirmed in the hard plastic chair that Detective Andersen had pointed him to after leading him, alone, from the front desk down a hall to this room. Albert's response to the detective's remark that was really a question was a frustrated, "I already said I was at her house that night. I told you that yesterday."

He'd gone through the day with his mind all muddled, and now he was an hour into giving his official statement, and it seemed like the interview was turning, in a not very subtle way, into an interrogation.

Andersen looked down at some papers on the table in front of him, like he was consulting notes. "Both Mr. and Mrs. Fermacelli say they were awakened sometime around two a.m. by loud arguing—a male and a female voice— which they both say was coming from the Kogen house. The racket came to an abrupt halt several minutes later. Mr. Fermacelli states that he, uh"—Andersen looked at his paperwork—"'couldn't stand it' and went outside to look around. He saw no one, but states that he saw a car driving away that he believed came from the Kogen driveway and which he also believed to be Miss Odilon's vehicle." Andersen stopped, watching Albert for a reaction. "Did you and Miss Odilon argue?"

"Argue?" echoed Albert, bewildered. "No. He's mistaken. I never left Lily's room until later, when I realized she was gone. I didn't hear a car, and I didn't hear any arguing." He looked down at his hands, his words hanging in the air. The overhead light gave off a low buzz.

"Was there anyone else in the house?"

"Like I told you," Albert said, "it was just us."

"Dr. Kogen, in his statement, said that he's witnessed several arguments between you and his stepdaughter."

"I don't know why he'd say that. I've only met the guy, like, twice!" Albert rubbed his eyes until little stars burst behind his eyelids. "Why would he say that?"

Andersen ignored the question. "You ever been arrested?"

"No." Which was technically true.

"Ever been in trouble?"

"No." This, on the other hand, was a lie.

"Tell me something. I have two witnesses who heard arguing, another witness who claims you and the girl were known to argue, and you yourself admitting to being the last person to have seen her. What would you think if you were me?"

Albert knew it looked bad, whatever *it* turned out to be, but he wasn't about to say so. The air seemed to go out of the little room.

Andersen pressed on. "Are they all lying?"

"I just don't understand why her stepfather would say that."

"So *he's* lying, is that it?" Andersen's eyes were a flat gray-blue and when they met Albert's, they were cold. "Perry Kogen is a friend of mine. I've known him for years. I've known you for about ten goddamn seconds. You'd better level with me, and right now."

"I *am*," Albert insisted, cringing at the way his voice cracked. He kept picturing Lily's empty car. "I've told you everything I know." He looked around the windowless room, and he was afraid. He was afraid of the cops...afraid for Lily...afraid something big was happening.

Andersen's eyes flashed before they went dead calm again. He sighed. "Let's go through your story again, from the beginning..."

Five

*T*he burger joint they've hurriedly left is on the outer edge of town. Now they're about a mile down the road from its neon sign. The way is amazingly dark and has the feel, to Albert, of absolute wilderness. They're only a couple days' walk from home but the environment is really different: the scrubby trees and brush Albert has gotten used to since moving to Little Solace are gone, replaced by tall pines that are just shadows in the gloom.

Olivia leads and they walk in silent single file. Whenever they hear a car coming, the two of them crouch down, as still as possible, until they have the road to themselves again. After the car passes, they continue walking. It's become routine. Occasionally they hear an owl's hoot or a rustle deeper into the trees, but these night noises are part of the background and after a while, they stop jumping at every sound.

Lulled by their rhythmic steps, Albert lets his mind go off on its own and he stops worrying about what they're doing. This marching, the back of Olivia's coat a few paces in front of him, the smell of pine and frost in the dark, the thunder in his cold ears of his blood pumping, and his own heavy breathing, are all that he knows. There is just the present.

Gradually the trees that have choked the road thin out. Soon there is open meadow on either side of the highway, sloping down to the forest. Albert looks up at the clear dark sky, imagining what little heat there'd been during the day escaping into the perfect glittering night. He feels small and adrift, like he might lose his gravity and float off into cold space.

Olivia's practical voice cuts the silence. "We have to get off the main road," she says, her breath coming out in a cloud of cold vapor. "There's no cover here." She turns to Albert and points to the tree line across the flat grass. "There."

"How are we going to follow the road from that distance?" he asks.

"I haven't been this way in a while, but I remember a set of train tracks this side of the trees. If we follow the tracks, that should take us into the next town. I'm pretty sure the rails go the same way, and we won't have to worry about cars spotting us."

"Naw, just about getting run down by a train. Or murdered by hobos out in the woods."

Olivia's wry smile is very faint in the dark, but Albert can hear the mockery in her voice, a darker echo of Lily that gives him a twinge. "I'm not worried about it. It's too goddamn cold for anyone to be out tonight. Besides, I don't think it's that far, honest. Just over the next little rise, I think."

They set out across the open field toward the dark shadow of the pines, and this time Albert insists on leading the way.

"Just in case," is all he gives for an explanation. He's serious about the hobos.

The ground slopes unevenly and the distance over it is longer than it looks. But as Olivia had predicted, just this side of the trees is a raised line of railroad tracks stretching off in either direction, parallel with the road.

Olivia eyeballs the slope up to the tracks. "Think we should cross over to the other side, closer to the cover of the trees?"

"No," Albert says. "No one is going to see us so far off the road in the dark. It's probably safer if we stay on this side."

"Safer...?"

He doesn't want her to know how jumpy he feels and how much he doesn't want to disappear into the choking black of those trees. So he says, "I think it's better if we can see the highway."

For once, Olivia doesn't argue.

The train tracks actually do parallel the road for a while and they're able to cover a lot of ground by following them. As they walk, they see a couple of cars in the distance but they don't bother hiding, confident that they're far enough away to be invisible. They stop when the highway and the tracks seem to branch off from each other—the road taking a gentle curve to climb a rise and cut through two low hills; the tracks barreling straight ahead through the darkness and, it looks like, into the hill itself.

"Now what?" Albert says. He wishes he has something to drink and makes note of it for when they get to the next town, if they actually find the next town. *If* they don't spend the entire night just wandering in the woods.

Olivia uses her forearm to push her bangs out of her eyes. She gestures toward the black rise ahead. "I still think this way is our best bet." When Albert says nothing, she adds, "I don't think it's that far to the next town—Midvale or Melville or something like that. If we were standing up there, I swear we would see lights right below us."

"How sure are you?" he asks.

"Pretty. I just don't want to stick with the road and then get caught out there—picked up by a state patrol car or something."

"Okay then." It's his turn again to follow her lead.

The distance into town is farther than it looks from where they'd started, but eventually they come out of the wilderness and find themselves in civilization, more or less, just as Olivia had said they would. Looking down from the rise at the town, Albert sees it as a neon sea roaring out the names of diners, motels, truck stops, and all-night drug stores.

By the reckoning of the vague map in Olivia's head, there's a long stretch of empty highway after they pass through this town and split off north to the next one. Albert has to trust her recollection. This is all new and strange country to him—even the trees are unfamiliar. He wishes he knew the names of even a couple of them; it's frustrating, he reflects, how much he doesn't know about anything at all.

"Coffee?" says Olivia as they cut through a dark convenience store parking lot toward the main drag, which merges with the highway on the way back out of town.

"If I'm going to keep this up, yeah, I guess I could use something hot and caffeinated."

She yawns. "I'm not sure how much longer I can keep going with just a few minutes of rest here and there."

"We've been over this," he says. "We have to get to her *first*."

"I know!" she snaps. "I'm keeping company with a suspected murderer and I've probably become an accessory at this point, and a runaway besides. So don't tell me what I *need* to do. I'm *doing* it."

Albert experiences a funny moment that pretty much defines the contradictory way he feels about Olivia: on one hand, given that some of her mannerisms and facial expressions echo her sister's, being with her is comforting, like she's carrying a piece of Lily. But at the same time, Olivia is so prickly and sarcastic and hardened that the contrast just makes him miss Lily's unrealistic cheeriness.

"Fine." They're standing at an intersection. The light turns green and they cross, for no other reason but that movement has become automatic to them.

She sighs. Then, as if she can read his mind: "I'm just so tired."

As they make their way downtown, a few cars pass them but the sidewalks are pretty much empty. The wind picks up and the night becomes even colder. When Albert turns abruptly to pass through the automatic sliding doors of a twenty-four-hour grocery store, Olivia is right behind him. An electronic beep announces their arrival. The place seems deserted, with just one checker at one register counter up front and no customers. There are warm globe lights, dim, but they can still see that the store isn't very clean. The automatic door slides shut behind them with a sucking sound, and soft elevator music drifts from somewhere overhead.

The checker looks up when the door beeps, but when she sees Albert and Olivia her interest seems to die, a big yawn pulling her mouth wide.

They wander down the aisles in a weird hurried daze, and the music seems to follow them. There's no hot coffee for sale in the small grocery store, so they settle for two bottles of soda—something sugary and neon yellow for Albert, a diet cola for Olivia—and a couple of soft apples from the tiny produce department along the front side wall, opposite the doors.

The soft music coming from above switches from "You're So Vain" to the Stones' "Wild Horses." Snuffling noises are coming from Olivia, and Albert looks up from where he's setting their drinks onto the counter. He's expecting tears, but instead he's surprised to see that she seems to be holding in some fit of giggling.

"Are you all right?" he asks, totally confused.

She nods, but when their eyes meet the giggling bursts into full laughter and she covers her mouth to mute the sound, shoulders shuddering and tears running down her face. After a moment she gets control of herself, though she keeps hiccuping random giggles.

"What's the matter with you?" the clerk asks, taking the money Olivia holds out to her.

"I'm sorry," she says to Albert. "It's just that song... it reminds me of something else my sister told me..."

Albert feels his ears go red. "Yeah?"

Now she refuses to meet his eyes. "She said that when you two were... that you always liked to play this song... every time..."

The rest of his face turns the same tomato shade as his ears. "I can't believe you guys talk about that stuff."

Olivia's laughter threatens to come back. "Don't be embarrassed!" she says. "She said it was romantic. *I* think it's sweet."

"You can stop now."

She's off again, overcome with laughter. "But it's just that whenever I hear this song now... and you're right here..."

"Please shut up," Albert begs, feeling a sheepish grin crawl across his face in his embarrassment.

The clerk gives them a funny look and Albert pulls Olivia out the door in a hurry.

When they're outside, Olivia's fit passes and Albert chooses to pretend it hasn't happened. They sit on the sidewalk, not talking, huddling close for warmth, their feet in the gutter. As they drink the too-sweet sodas that they don't really want, the only sound is the fizz bubbling up from their bottles and their teeth sinking into the mushy apples. Olivia stares down at the apple core in her hand, looking at it blankly as if she doesn't know what it is, before tossing it into the gutter.

Albert studies her face in the faint light that's coming through the grocery's big front window and bathing the sidewalk. It's a tired, pale face—sharp and thin where Lily's is soft and curving. Albert can see the resemblance to Lily in Olivia, even so. He thinks how funny it is that the face of a girl he barely knows can be so painfully suggestive of a more familiar one. It occurs to him that it must be hard having Lily as an older sister—she eclipses everyone, all the time, even in her absence.

Olivia looks up and a shadow passes over her face, as if she's been reading Albert's thoughts again. She moves fast, jumping to her feet in a smooth movement and walking away from the store, crossing the parking lot.

"Hey," he says, catching up halfway across. "Now we just—" But he's cut short by Olivia's sharp intake of breath and her hand on his arm, fingers digging into his flesh right through his coat.

She swears softly.

He pries her fingers loose, asking, "What is it?"

She looks more than ever as if she's about to collapse. "I think I just saw Perry."

"What?" He looks around, as if her stepfather is at his elbow. "Where?"

She points back across the parking lot. "Over there, going into the store. I saw him through the window, as clear as anything, I swear, before he moved into an aisle and I couldn't see him anymore."

"Are you sure?" But even as he asks, Albert is moving quickly away and reaching for Olivia's arm to pull her along faster, too.

She chews a finger. "I don't know. We have to get out of here. This way," she says, directing them at a sharp angle around the back of the building and into the unlit alley behind it. Once they're obscured in the alley's shadows, they both stop.

"Did he see you?" Albert asks.

"I don't think so," she says, her legs moving again. "Or he would have come after us. Right?"

"But he must know we're here. It would be too much of a coincidence otherwise. Somehow, he followed us." Albert tries to keep his voice calm, but it's hard. "He's probably going to talk to the clerk, maybe show her a picture of us."

"Calm down. He doesn't know exactly where we are right now and that we've seen him." Olivia takes his hand and begins to run down the alley, pulling him along and glancing back over her shoulder. "Come on. We can still get out of here before he catches up."

Spurred by a shot of nervous adrenaline, they run deeper into the alley's dark interior and away from the bright lights of the main roadway.

For the first time since they'd left home, Albert is actually glad there's an expanse of wilderness standing between them and the next town. The thought of it makes him feel somehow safer...they'll be concealed in the dark instead of so obviously lit by streetlights and the other lights of a town at night, where there are so few places to hide.

Once they reach the end of the alley, Albert and Olivia keep up a steady pace, staying in the shadows and snaking in a roundabout way toward the north edge of town. It starts to rain, cold, slushy drops that drip off Albert's tingling scalp, down his neck and under the collar of his coat. He's instantly cold to the core. "I hate him," he half pants, half whispers as they crouch in someone's back yard, making sure the coast is clear before moving on.

Olivia hears him and says, "Not as much Lily does. Or me."

"I'm not so sure," he says, but the words are soft and Olivia has already darted away. He follows.

Six

"Let's go," Lily said, slipping her hand into his and pulling him toward the sidewalk in one effortless motion.

It had only been a matter of days since Albert and Lily had become whatever they had become. Boyfriend and girlfriend, Albert guessed was the way most people would put it, but the words lacked a sense of the significance he felt when his mind settled on Lily. "Joined at the hip" was what his mother had already said, more than once and kind of snidely, with a distasteful pursing of her lips after the words were out. Albert would have been okay with being joined to the soft curve of Lily's hip. As it was, though, he was still getting used to the new pleasure of Lily's small, cool hand in his.

Albert wanted to ask her what the hurry was, but he also wanted to give Lily a chance to tell him on her own. So he let himself be pulled away from the school grounds and toward

Lily's car. The final bell was still ringing in his ears. He always went along when she pulled him toward something, from the very first time she gave his hand that impatient tug. At first, he followed her because she was a girl, a girl who for some reason dug him. But then he broke through the novelty that she was A Girl and found Lily there. And then … well, he was hooked within days, and with even the smallest crook of her finger she could get him to follow.

"Where are we going?" he asked at last. With Lily you never knew, and she had a way, at least for Albert, of making the most ordinary crap seem exciting.

She gave his hand a squeeze, not meeting his gaze, her mouth twisting into a small, secret smile. "Does it matter?"

"Not even a little." They fell silent and she led him through the rowdy, roaring sea of high school students who had also just been set free from school for the afternoon.

Once the sidewalk ended and they were stepping off the school grounds, Lily slowed her pace. Albert walked next to her, his arm draped over her shoulder, very aware of her arm snaked around the small of his back and resting on his hip.

"Where's your car?" he asked after they'd walked about a block.

Lily pulled her arm away from his and waved to a girl crossing the street up the block. It looked to Albert that the girl in the distance looked away when Lily waved, after giving a sort of half-hearted salute in return. "What?" Lily said, looking from the girl to Albert. "Oh, I'm parked around the block. I couldn't really pull into the school lot when I'd skipped all afternoon. Be a bit conspicuous, you know?"

Albert opened his mouth to ask yet another question, then closed it when he couldn't decide which to ask first. Finally he asked, "Who was that girl?"

"My sister." She pushed a strand of hair behind one ear. "She tries to pretend she doesn't know me."

"Why?" But he was only asking because he figured he should.

Then they reached Lily's car, which was parked at the curb in front of a little yellow house. She keyed open her door, saying, "Don't you want to know why I ditched this afternoon?" Then she was in the car and Albert had to wait for her to reach over and unlock his door.

He slid into the car, picking up the thin thread of the conversation. "Well, yeah. And anyway, why didn't you bring me along to wherever it was? I could've used an excuse to get out of school today."

She pulled the car away from the curb and onto the road with a jerky jackrabbit leap, and didn't see that he was laughing at her. Swearing, she swerved to miss a parked car. "I just got my car back not too long ago. After physical therapy, my mom made me take the driver's test again—just one of the many things I got to relearn after my accident, like writing and using chopsticks. Except I guess I'm still getting the hang of the driving thing. If I ram someone with this car, I'll be back to where I was after all the stuff that happened—walking or bumming rides."

The accident. He knew a bit about that. He also knew that Lily was all over the place today and seemed almost physically incapable of sticking to one line of thought or producing a straight answer to the questions she raised.

"Not having a car sucks. So how did you—" He stopped mid-sentence, backtracking before she could swerve off on some other verbal tangent. "You still haven't finished telling me where you went this afternoon, or where we're going."

Lily stuck out her lower lip, glancing briefly away from the road in order to give him completely fake, sad, puppy-dog eyes. "You're not pissy with me, are you?"

"Not really." It was infuriating, how she tried to mellow him out—and how it always worked.

"Good," she said, stomping on the brakes to barely avoid running a stop sign. "I decided to cut this afternoon at the last minute. I didn't plan it. I went to a couple of places, which is where I found the thing I want to show you. But you have to wait until we get to my house."

"Your house?" he echoed.

She glanced over at him and rolled her eyes. "Don't worry, no one's there. And it's no big deal, anyway. I wasn't planning on playing bondage games in the living room."

"Damn. Better luck next time, Albert my man," he sighed in a stage whisper.

She just laughed, a happy sound.

The house was empty, as Lily had said it would be. Albert wondered briefly where the sister might be, but forgot about the sister almost as soon as the thought came into his head. Once they were inside, Lily made a big production of hustling him into the basement to wait. While he sat in the afterthought of a room—just a couple of dusty sofas and a couple more dusty armchairs, a cabinet TV that was as old as his parents, and discarded stuff that hadn't yet made it to a donation box—Lily ran back upstairs.

"It's actually in the car," she called down to him. He heard the garage door open and shut a moment later, then again, a moment after that.

Beaming as she came down the stairs again, she handed him a big cardboard square. "Look what I found."

He looked. "It's an old record," he said. She seemed to be waiting for more, so he added, "Cool. I didn't know you liked vinyl."

"Not just a record. Charles Trenet." The name was soft and boneless as it rolled off her tongue. "It's not an original single or anything, but it is a really early Columbia LP. I found it at the Goodwill for a quarter, and it doesn't have a scratch." When he didn't say anything, she added, "Do you know how much this would cost on eBay?"

"No," he said. "A hundred bucks?"

She grinned as she pulled a blanket off a big rectangular mass that turned out to be one of those cabinet stereos with the turntable and speakers all inside. She flicked the power switch on and the speakers crackled. "More like ten, but still."

She held out her hand, expectant, and Albert carefully pulled the record from the cardboard sleeve and then its paper jacket, handing it to her like an operating room nurse hands a scalpel to the surgeon.

"Where'd you get that thing?" he asked, meaning the ste-reo system.

She tucked her hair behind her ear and blew some invisible fuzz from the needle. "It was my dad's."

Albert looked around the gloomy basement. "Why doesn't he let you put it in the living room, or at least your bedroom?" he asked. "This place is like a storage unit."

She looked confused for a moment, then her face showed understanding, as well as a rare scowl. "You mean Perry?" she said, saying the name with contempt. "He's not my dad. He's my mother's husband. My dad hasn't been around for, god, more than ten years. He just left behind this dinosaur stereo system, maybe a few other things, when he took off. I always liked it, so I brought it with me when we moved in here. Neither my mom or Perry wants it junking up the house, so I keep my records down here and I play them when they're not home."

"I'm sorry," Albert began, not really sure what to say.

"I don't care," she said. "Now just be quiet a minute. I'm going to play 'La Mer' for you, and you're going to love it."

Lily lowered the needle to the spinning disk before dropping herself into a chair. Albert leaned against the wall, his arms folded across his chest, the record sleeve still in hand. At first there was just the rhythmic scratch of the vinyl as it rotated under the needle, then he heard a man's voice singing what seemed like a vaguely familiar tune, though the words were in what sounded like French and so he couldn't understand them. It was a pretty, wistful little song, with soft vocals and instruments that made Albert think of old radios not tuned right and old people's houses. He wasn't sure he liked it. Anything with a fuzzbox and a monster drum kit was more his taste.

"So," Lily said, once the final scratchy note had sounded and all that was left was the whispery hum of the needle on vinyl again. "Isn't that gorgeous?"

"Awesome."

"Are you just saying that because you think I want you to like early twentieth-century French pop music as much as I do?" Laughing to herself, she unfolded her legs and rose from the rust-brown sofa, going to the turntable and lifting the needle arm gently from her new find.

"Yes. I mean, no. Why would I do that?"

She gave his arm a playful punch. "Because you're just goopy over me," she said, kissing her finger and pressing the finger to his lips. "So goopy, in fact, you'll even pretend to like Monsieur Trenet just because I do."

"Goopy?"

She laughed again, her mood so good it was almost disturbing. It seemed to Albert to hint at one of the manic upswings he was already able to see coming. "Totally and completely goopy. Liked a melted ice cream cone. And everyone knows it."

He glanced down at the record sleeve in his hand, the words "Long Playing Microgroove" catching his eye. "What 'everyone'? I don't know everyone. I don't know anyone. No one at all knows I'm melted ice cream gaga in love with Lily Odilon."

"Not no one," she said, taking the album from his hand and

placing it on top of the record player. She took his wrists and drew his arms around her.

"I would tell the world if I could," he said, feeling how dorky a thing it was to say as he was saying it. He kissed her forehead to cover his embarrassment, murmuring again, "The whole damn world."

She smiled up at him, her eyes sparkling. "The world doesn't care."

Seven

By the time the tenth shoulder slammed into his in passing in the school halls and the hundredth pair of eyes sent venom his way, Albert stopped taking it in. Not that he didn't notice each time he caught a shoulder blade, but it was as if his body had absorbed all it could and was done working the same information over and over again. He just shrugged a tired mental shrug and pushed on like it hadn't happened. Some of these came from people he'd thought were okay—who he thought didn't hate him, at least—but apparently that was one of the may things about which he had been wrong.

That was Tuesday.

By Wednesday, news of Lily's disappearance and her abandoned car was not only all over school but the biggest topic in town. The local news stations kept showing footage of the cops surrounding her old 1989 Toyota Corolla, as it sat calmly in an out-of-the-way parking lot west of town "like a little dog waiting patiently for its master's return," as one reporter described it. Ugh. Albert couldn't stand to look at the pictures and always made sure to be out of the room when his parents watched the six and ten o'clock news on TV.

"No evidence of a crime" was the phrase the helmet-haired anchors kept repeating and the newspapers printed in the story's daily migration farther back in the pages.

"No evidence of a crime." It was a phrase that Albert held on to against the fact that he didn't know what *had* happened.

There was nothing that proved Lily had run into some violence, nothing—in spite of the argument the Kogens' neighbors claimed to have overheard—to make anyone think Lily had taken off for any reason but her own. Albert finally realized that this was not the story people wanted to hear. He felt like everyone was waiting for a body to turn up so they could hear about a nice, juicy murder mystery starring a hometown Wild Girl and her boyfriend, The New Guy in Town. So they could say they knew someone who knew someone who went to the same school as the girl, or who had the same hairdresser as the girl's mom. They wanted some good shots for the evening news and the front page of the paper—meaty stuff, not just Lily's empty old car without even a smear of blood. Albert almost felt guilty just because people seemed to suspect he'd done something.

Everyone—not least of which, the cops—seemed to think Albert knew something about what had happened to Lily.

And man, he wished he did.

After the long and miserable days at school were over, Albert hurried home to hide, and when his parents came home from work, he avoided them, too. His heart pounded every time the phone rang, and his fear was that it would be Lily's parents, calling to demand he tell them what he knew—or worse, some catastrophic news coming from the other end of the line, something he didn't even dare name. And everywhere he went, he felt watched. He was sure the police were keeping tabs on him, and every day his father kept shooting angry glances, through a crack in the closed front drapes, at a van parked across the street.

Albert felt claustrophobic and alone. He wished there was someone he could actually talk to about it. But when he'd moved away the few friends he'd left behind had all gradually dropped him, and his best friend from what he thought of as "back home" was overseas, no longer his high school buddy Chris but an enlisted man. He hadn't seemed able to make any new friends in this town, a situation not likely to improve under the circumstances. He couldn't talk to his parents, either—he hadn't confided in them about anything important since he was a pretty small kid. They loved him, he knew, but they had a narrow idea of the way things were supposed to be done, and neither of them had approved of his getting involved with Lily in the first place.

"That girl is too fast for you," his mother had said

after the first and only time he'd brought Lily to meet his parents.

"She was in some trouble last year," his father had added, "and I've heard she has problems. You don't need that. Find someone else to go out with."

Albert had wanted to knock their heads together, and wondered if Lily's parents were saying the same kinds of things about him to her. But he dealt with his parents' nagging like he always did: he clenched his jaw and kept his mouth shut—at least, whenever he could manage it. After the fun little conversation with his parents, he avoided mentioning his new girlfriend to them whenever possible.

So it turned out that Lily's disappearance was solid proof to Albert's folks that she meant nothing but trouble. As Albert dragged himself through the week following her vanishing act, he knew he was in deep trouble because of it. Yet when he wished for someone to talk about it with, he wished first for Lily. Whatever happened, he couldn't help that.

He couldn't sleep at night, and getting out of bed in the morning was almost more than he could pull off. Whatever people thought he knew about Lily, he knew nothing after the moment she'd left him alone in her bedroom the night she'd disappeared. And not knowing was awful. But even worse was the tidbit that the cop, Andersen, had given him—that the neighbors claimed to have overheard Lily arguing with someone just before she drove off. It was driving him crazy.

Because if the neighbors were right and they had overheard an argument, it hadn't been between Albert and Lily. And if Lily had been one half of the argument, then there had to be someone on the other end.

That was the person the cops needed to find.

Albert couldn't help wondering what would have happened if he'd been the one to overhear the shouting instead of the neighbors—who were apparently nosy enough to listen, but not concerned enough to check it out or even just call the cops. Or if Lily's bedroom had happened to overlook the driveway instead of the other side of the house. Or if he hadn't slept through whatever had happened.

What might have been different?

Sluggish from lack of sleep and what he guessed was depression, Albert found himself zoning out in misty fantasies where the what-ifs were wiped out and he rushed in to save Lily from whatever, or she returned home safely—either way, there was always a storybook happy ending. The fantasies only made him feel worse when he came back to reality. Then, at other times, he tried to imagine where Lily actually was now, but he never got too far in this before his heart began a painful, uneven thumping. He stopped paying attention in his classes or to anything else. He didn't have time for the present; he was obsessed with the might-have-been and the what's-to-come. And he kept waiting for some signal from Lily that would finally put things right.

So Thursday at noon, Albert didn't even notice that there was something brewing in the lunchroom until it was already happening and he was at its center. A senior he recognized but whose name he didn't know reached under the lunch tray Albert was carrying and slapped it up out of his hands. Brown gravy splattered Albert's face and the front of his shirt, and the tray itself landed with a loud crash in a wet pile of the stuff it had been carrying. The sound of the plastic tray landing was deafening; the entire lunchroom went still when it clattered against the concrete tile floor.

Dazed, Albert looked down at the floor and his ruined lunch, then up at the guy who'd done it. He was very aware that everyone seemed to be staring at the two of them. Then he saw that they were not alone in the center of attention but surrounded by a bunch of other guys, mostly seniors, at least half of them muscle heads from the baseball team. His eyes and the eyes of the tray-slapper met. Then Albert lost the contest and was the first to drop his gaze, settling it back to the vaguely meat-and-potato-shaped mess at his feet. The silence in the lunchroom stretched on, and Albert's only thought was to wonder how he would ever travel from this side of the moment to the other.

"Oops," the guy said. All his friends were laughing, though the rest of the room was still quiet. "Need a hand?"

Albert just looked at him. *Dave Jensen*, he thought, the name suddenly popping into place. *This guy's name is Dave Jensen.*

"Sure you do. Here," Dave Jensen said, dumping the food from his own tray onto the floor. "Guess you'd better clean that up."

"Go to hell," Albert muttered, dropping to one knee

and trying to scrape up the mess from the floor onto his tray.

Jensen moved closer and ground Albert's hand under his sneaker. "What was that?"

Lubricated by gravy, Albert's hand was easy to slip out from under the guy's foot, though not before his knuckles cracked painfully. He stood up. "What's your problem?"

"I think you know what my problem is."

"Yeah?" Albert flicked his hand, and a tiny wad of gravy and mashed potatoes landed on Jensen's cheekbone, right under his eye.

The guy shoved up his sleeves to expose his alarming forearms and stepped closer to Albert. "This is going to be fun."

Something came loose in Albert's head, and just like that, he didn't care if these guys beat him bloody as long as he hurt somebody first. His bony, long-fingered hands balled up tight and he was already anticipating the satisfaction he would feel when his fists started pounding this guy's face. "You do whatever you have to do," he said, "and so will I." All the while he was thinking, *One good hit to flatten his nose or bust up his eye. I just want to feel something break before he kills me.*

"There are at least half a dozen cops hanging around this place these days," Jensen said softly. He was smiling. "But I don't see any of them here now. So if you want to go, killer, let's *go*."

"Stop it!"

They both turned to the source of the voice.

It was Olivia Odilon, Lily's sister and a girl Albert barely knew.

"Why don't you stop acting like a Neanderthal?" she said to Jensen. "We all know you can kick his ass. Good enough, okay?"

There was a tense moment when Jensen turned his attention to Olivia, but she just stood there, almost like she was bored, until Jensen rolled his eyes and walked away. He said something rude, something no one but his buddies could hear, and they laughed at whatever it was.

Albert felt like he should say something. It was humiliating to be bullied like a third-grader and then defended by his girlfriend's little sister. But he was saved from having to come up with something to say to her because she walked off in the other direction, now that she'd chased Dave Jensen and his jock squad away from Albert.

At the same time, someone had apparently gone for a lunch lady, because by then she and the janitor had arrived to find Albert and the gooey mess at his feet. The spell of silence was broken by the arrival of the two adults, and gradually the room was buzzing with normal chatter and a little something extra. Albert felt bad leaving the mess for someone else to clean up and he was too embarrassed to face walking through the lunchroom anyway, so he bent down and tried to help scoop the mess into the janitor's bucket.

The lunch lady pushed him aside impatiently. "Just get out of the way, will you?" she said in a voice that was gentler than her words. "It's fine."

The janitor winked at him and jerked his head toward the exit.

Albert straightened up, unsure of what to do now. There were at least fifteen minutes until the next class period. He saw Olivia still standing a few feet away. The corners of her mouth were turned up in some kind of smile, but she didn't look happy. She looked tired, he thought, maybe as tired as he was.

"Come with me," she commanded when their eyes met.

Not knowing what else to do, he followed her through the lunch room. "Where are we going?"

She ignored his question until she stopped at an empty table on the edge of the large room and plopped herself down in a chair. She hooked another one with her feet and pushed it out for Albert. "I'm going to give you half my sandwich," she said.

"Thanks." He took what she offered—peanut butter and banana—and ate it in about three bites. "I guess I owe you two, now."

"Gawd, you stink like old spaghetti," she said, wrinkling up her nose as she picked at her half of the sandwich.

"I think it was pot roast," Albert said, looking down at the wet brown stain soaking through his shirt.

"Don't you have a shirt you can change into before next period? You look like you wiped diarrhea on yourself."

"Lovely."

"Seriously," she insisted. "You'd better find something, because they're not going to let you into class like that."

"Okay, okay," Albert said. "I think I have a sweatshirt in my locker."

She went back to eating her sandwich and they were quiet.

After a bit, she said, "I love how those guys stand up for my sister *now*. You should have heard some of the crap they said about her after the accident. Even Pat, who I thought was different than that. Some of them were there, everyone knows, but no one came forward and no one helped her. They were her friends, until they weren't." She paused. "Lily told you about her accident, right?"

This girl didn't waste time dancing around what she wanted to say, Albert had to give her that. "That's not what she called it, but yeah." Albert knew about what Lily called "The Bad Thing That Happened" because she'd told him about it on their first date, since, as she'd put it, someone else was bound to tell him about it if she didn't first.

Olivia rolled her eyes. "Well, she didn't mean to over-dose on nitrous and end up with severe brain trauma, right? So it *was* an accident, no matter how it started. Par-tying or whatever."

Albert was acutely uncomfortable. He barely knew Olivia. They didn't have any classes together, and he'd only been in their house a couple of times when he was actually supposed to be there. On those rare occasions, he'd gotten the feeling that Lily's family didn't approve of him any more than his family approved of Lily. He could barely identify any member of Lily's family, he'd seen them so little. Of all of them, only Lily had made an impression.

"I wonder..." Olivia began. She was staring off into space as if seeing something that wasn't there. "I wonder if Lil is just off on another patented Lily Adventure. You haven't known her very long, so you don't know how it is with her."

"How is it with her?" he asked, too sharp.

Olivia sighed. "You really don't know, dude. Ever since we were kids, things would be going along, nice and normal, and then out of nowhere, she'd have to shake things up. Like she couldn't stand the quiet, you know? Her randomness is actually pretty predictable anymore. But our parents won't listen to me. And Jesus, you should hear what they say about *you*. So, what do you think?" she asked Albert. "Do you think Lily's just jerking us all around?"

"I...I don't know," he said, which was true. Then something in her face made him add, "But I don't think so. I think it's something more."

"Yeah?"

He shook his head in the negative. "You don't think I...?"

"No. You're not that guy. It's totally obvious."

"Thanks," he said. "You're the only person who seems to think so."

Olivia sighed again. She looked as if she wanted to ask another question, but she didn't break the silence. A few moments later, Albert couldn't stand it anymore and left to go find a dry shirt. He looked back once at Olivia, and she was staring off into space again.

When school was finally over, Albert left the grounds at a sprint. He felt like a coward but he wanted to get a head start, just in case Dave Jensen was looking to finish what he'd started at lunch.

Once he was clear of the school and pretty certain no one was following him, he slowed his pace from a jog to a shuffle. The late-winter wind was sharp as a knife. He was sweating from the jog and the cold didn't bother him, except in his lungs. He worked to control his breathing. The street he walked down was quiet and empty and his footsteps echoed dully on the pavement. There were no places with this kind of almost-perfect silence back in his old town, and even now, almost six months after moving here, he was still getting used to it. But today the silence and solitude was a relief. Behind him was hostility and accusation at school, and in front of him was his claustrophobic house, where they all mostly pretended to each other that none of this was happening. But of course it was all he thought about, and here on the empty street, he could think about it without distraction.

Still, even shuffling as slowly as he was, eventually Albert found himself on his street and in front of his house. He grabbed the mail from the mailbox and went inside, planning to start his homework instead of giving in to the now-constant desire to just go to bed and forget everything. In the still house, Albert dropped the mail on the dining room table and leaned his backpack against the table leg.

He looked at the clock. There were still a couple of hours before one of his parents came home from work. Two short hours left in which he didn't have to act some role.

He sat in one of the chairs and pushed aside a pile of the table's constant clutter of papers and bills and unopened junk mail, clearing a spot where, theoretically anyway, he might actually do his homework. He pushed today's mail in the other direction to keep it from being eaten by the older pile. As he did so, something caught his eye, and he focused his attention on the stack of envelopes he was shoving aside. He ruffled through them with his fingers until he'd found the one that had interested him.

The envelope itself wasn't anything special—just a dull white rectangle, the blue crisscross of the security lining bleeding through just a little, like veins under a paper skin. There was no return address, but he recognized the small black handwriting addressing the envelope simply to "Albert."

He slit the envelope with his finger and saw that there was a postcard inside. He plucked it out and held it up. On the front was a grainy photograph of a large, freestanding arch with a city behind it. Yellow, bubbly letters cried "Greetings from St. Louis" along the bottom of the picture. It wasn't a remarkable postcard at all, except that Albert had seen it before.

The last time he'd seen it, it had been tucked into the frame of the mirror over Lily's dresser. A souvenir, he thought he remembered her saying, that she'd picked up years ago on some family vacation.

Turning the card over, he saw a folded piece of lined notebook paper clipped to it. He unclipped and unfolded the paper to see more of Lily's dense, back-slanted hand-writing.

His pulse raced as he read:

A.—

I'm in a hurry and I don't have a lot of time to say what I need to say. I don't even know how much I can say. Who else might be reading your mail?

First off, I want you to know that (a) I didn't plan to leave that night and (b) I'm okay for now. I know they're looking for me, though, so I don't know how long I'll stay that way.

After the bad thing, I didn't remember anything that happened—the days before it or the months after and obviously not the accident itself. But I've started to remember now. Mostly about Perry. And this is the thing: he knows it. I don't know how, but he does.

The night I left, he thought I was alone in the house, so he came back with bad ideas and I had to get away from that asshole. He didn't know you were there, so at least I knew you were safe. If he knows now that you were there, he might think you know other things, too. What I'm saying is, Perry's dangerous. Please believe me.

I didn't know what to do the night I left, but I'm going to the last good place. Don't tell anyone—when they come for me they'll believe him over me and there won't be anyone left to protect me.

I need time to figure out what to do next. I'll try to stay there and wait for help as long as I can (should the Machine of God decide I deserve it).

Love,

L.

It was a halting, odd little letter. He read it several more times, quickly at first, but then more carefully, trying to understand what she was circling around so indirectly. With each read he hoped it would make more sense, but it didn't. His heart continued to thump, and he tried not to think about what would have happened if one of his parents had seen the envelope first.

He tried to understand what she was trying to say to him. Perry had come for her that night, thinking he would find her alone—and then what? It had been loud, a fight over something...something connected to the break-in and Lily's accident, maybe, and loud enough to wake the neighbors...and then she'd just vanished.

Albert had the realization that Perry Kogen was the only person who knew, at least in part, what had happened to Lily. He knew more than anyone else about it, anyway. He knew, yet he was letting people worry and search for her and think the worst.

Kogen was sitting on some pretty damn relevant information, Albert thought to himself as he held Lily's letter gently in his fingers. Sitting on it while Albert was twisting in the wind without a clue, getting questioned by the police, his parents fielding phone calls from the local newspapers and the local TV stations, too, all wanting their take on the Lily Odilon story.

But putting the Kogen question aside for a moment, at least this note showed that Lily was okay for now. In trouble, but okay.

Still, Albert was disturbed by the thought of Kogen's secret knowledge, as well as by Lily's grim, cryptic tone—which was maybe her intention. He turned the letter over and over in his hand. If Kogen really was still angry with Lily over what had happened, and really was after her now because of it, maybe he should take this to the police. Even though Lily would object. But she had made it explicitly clear that she didn't trust the authorities to protect her from her stepfather's anger. And there was no question but that Albert would believe Lily's take on things. If she said she was in trouble, she was in trouble.

That last conversation with Detective Andersen came to his mind. *I've known him for years. I've known you for about ten goddamn seconds.*

So for now, Albert wouldn't trust the cops, either. He definitely had no reason to. What he needed was time to think it over before he decided what to do. Perhaps Lily's paranoia was catching, because suddenly Albert was almost afraid the police were going to burst into the dining room right now, confiscate the postcard and letter as evidence, and grill him about every word until they found Lily and delivered her to her worried family. Her mother. And her stepfather.

Still, Albert had a few questions himself that he wished he could just ask Lily right now. What had gone on between Kogen and Lily the night she'd left, what was Lily afraid he would do if he found her, and what could Albert do about it? He had no influence over Lily's "Machine of God," and he had no idea how to help her, though help seemed to be what she was asking for, in her Lily-esque way. He wondered if Kogen ever got violent.

I'll wait for help as long as I can... He understood now the fact he'd been trying to ignore since this mess had started: it was up to him—not the police, not her parents—to help Lily.

Albert folded the paper in half again and tucked it and the postcard back into the envelope, smoothing the flap as he thought about what to do. For now, he knew he had to hide Lily's letter away somewhere, somewhere his parents wouldn't see it, until he had a chance to think and come to some decision. At the thought of his parents, he looked up at the clock in a sudden jolt of panic—and he saw that less than fifteen minutes had passed since he'd arrived home from school. It just felt like a lot longer. His parents wouldn't be home for a while still, yet he couldn't shake the idea that in an amazing bit of bad luck, one of them would arrive home early today and somehow just know something was up. He knew he was broadcasting guilt as much as if he were standing in the dining room with a carton of cigarettes and a stack of porn. For his sanity, he needed to hide the lifeline Lily had thrown him right now.

Even under the weight of its responsibility, holding the envelope from Lily gave Albert some small comfort. He was holding a physical link to her, and that, at least, was proof she was still there. For the moment.

By the time Albert reached his bedroom, some of the initial shock had worn off. He went to the small bookshelf that ran along one wall under the window. On the front edge of the shelves were random stacks of CDs and books and papers; behind them, his childhood books were still in neat rows, buried and untouched for years. Kneeling in the careless jumble of dirty clothes and more books and CDs on the floor in front of the shelf, he read Lily's letter over once more, then pulled his old copy of *Treasure Island* from the back of the shelf and tucked the envelope inside. He wished for the thousandth time that he had just one person he could talk to.

Then he thought about the way Olivia had studied his face at lunch, as if she'd been trying to read something there.

Eight
Midnight

Olivia is certain that Kogen is following them, even after they're past the city limits and back out into the black wilderness that borders the highway. Albert is doing his best to convince her that she's wrong, but he can't change her mind. Olivia's constant glances behind them, and her gasping double takes every time a twig snaps or a car buzzes past them, are beginning to work on Albert's nerves, too, until he himself starts to believe Kogen just might be on their trail.

For his sanity and hers, Albert keeps reassuring Olivia that it's impossible, that Kogen hasn't seen them, and that she's probably mistaken about even seeing the guy at all. And as he keeps talking her down from her panic, he hurries them both on as quickly as possible.

Which isn't actually all that fast. First, it's too dark to see very well where they're going. Besides that, they're moving so far from the highway—at Olivia's insistence—that the ground is uneven and littered with sticks and rocks and gullies that trip up their feet, tired feet that are already dragging. Albert's so tired he feels like he might doze off while he walks; from the droop of her shoulders, he figures Olivia is feeling the same way. The whole thing reminds him of a story he once read about a guy—his own age, he seems to remember—who entered a walking race. The rules were simple: whoever kept walking the longest, won. Anyone who stopped walking was shot or killed or something. He can't remember what the point of the race was—why the kid had entered the race in the first place, what prize made it worth the danger. But once you were in the race, the point was incredibly simple: to keep walking until the end, or else. There was no turning back, no backing out.

Albert's meandering train of thought is interrupted when Olivia trips over a fallen branch at his left and, losing her balance, falls. She curses under her breath and stays on the ground. Without a word, Albert reaches down and pulls her up by the elbow, and they keep walking. And as they do, they continue to look over their shoulders every time they hear a bat fly overhead, or the wind rustling a tree branch.

It's midnight and they're in the middle of nowhere, not even sure they're right about where they're going, with cops behind them and maybe in front of them, too—and Albert feels like he can't judge anymore if they're doing the right thing. Going to Lily *seemed* right a few days ago—Lily herself is the only evidence left, and they have to get to her before Kogen does or things are going to get even worse for all of them.

But he can't help doubting. *Is this all pointless? Can we even find her?*

Are he and Olivia crazy to think the two of them, alone, can fix the mess surrounding Lily?

Yet Albert also knows there's nothing else to do but at least try. And so here he and Olivia are, heading on foot upstate in late winter like a couple of fugitives, hiding their whereabouts from the cops and their families. They're both scared, and they're in a hurry, and they're dying for just a few hours' rest.

But like in the story he's remembering, the only thing to do is to keep walking, or else.

The steady effort of walking warms Albert, and, lulled by the rhythm of their steps, he slips into a mixture of memory and daydream about Lily.

It was November and Albert and Lily were at the reservoir, wrapped together in a denim-squared comforter and leaning against the back of her car, pulling in air that tasted of frost but was still a few weeks away from the real thing. They were parked in some empty afterthought of a picnic area on the high side of the dam overlooking the low water. The sun was a hard, cold ball of light in the gray sky and they'd just kissed each other for the first time.

So clear is the memory, Albert can almost smell the

burned fields and frost in the air and the warm cinnamony scent of Lily's skin.

Her hand found his under the blanket and gave it a squeeze. "So how do you like living in Little Solace?" she asked.

"I hated it when we got here," Albert said. "But I'm starting to think I was completely wrong."

"Really?"

He leaned down and kissed her on the temple, a new privilege that felt exciting and weird at the same time. Her face was pointed down or he would have tried for her lips again. "Being here gives me a jittery, trapped feeling—like I just have to run or I'll suffocate. You ever get that feeling?"

"Yeah," she said. "I'm kind of known for that. That, and breaking and entering."

He laughed.

She shifted her weight and leaned against him. He put a shy arm around her shoulders. She said, "I don't even remember that night. I only know what they told me—that I broke into my stepfather's office and almost burned it to the ground. I've lost a lot of memory of what happened before that night, too … there's just this blur, then a long blank space, and then it picks up a few months after everything happened. I don't even remember why I was there, or who I was with."

"Does it matter now?" he asked. He felt her body stiffen.

"Maybe. I feel like maybe it does, yeah. There's … something … just kind of hovering on the edge of my mind, and I can't quite catch it." She looked up at him and smiled a wet-lipped, wide smile that reminded him of his dirtier thoughts. "I wasn't always the girl everyone gossiped about, you know."

"That's hard to believe."

"I know, right? But before my mom got remarried, it was just her and Liv and me. I know I'm romanticizing it or whatever, but life was pretty good then. That's how I remember it, anyway. Like every summer, the three of us would go to this dinky little cabin on Yellow Pine Lake and spend, like, all of August there." She went on in a dreamy voice. "I remember that even in late summer it was always windy and cloudy at the lake. Liv would stay inside when it got rainy, but I wanted to be outside all the time, so when she was too much of a wuss to come outside, I'd go off on my own. Then I started to like it better that way, when I would be by myself for a while. One time that last summer I went off alone when Liv and my mom were sleeping. I found a secret place and stayed there all day, just exploring. I remember I had this sandwich and I fed it to some fish and some birds. By the time I left to come home it was almost dark and my mom was super pissed at me for making her worry. Liv made me show the spot to her later, but I never went there again."

He could imagine such a place. "Sounds awesome." His words came out wistful.

She laughed. "Didn't you ever have a place like that?"

When he was younger, they'd hardly ever left the city, and definitely never stayed at a lakeside cabin during the summer. "Not really. I didn't have any brothers or sisters to hide from, anyway. I wish I had."

"A summer place, or a sibling?"

He shrugged, but he sometimes wondered what it would be like to have a brother.

"By the next summer, our mom was remarried and it wasn't just the three of us anymore. We moved out of our house and I—" She stopped, giggling nervously. "Never mind. It'll sound stupid."

"Say it," he urged.

"Okay, but don't laugh. I just never felt like I belonged in this new idea of a family. I wanted it back the old way. You know how little kids are—I didn't want a new dad. After that, we didn't go to the lake anymore, either. It was the last good place, before everything changed."

"Maybe someday we can go there together," Albert said. It came out corny and awkward-sounding and he felt like a moron when he heard the words in his ears.

But she seemed to understand the way he meant it. "Maybe," she said. "Maybe we'll find a new good place that's only for us."

And then she kissed him and he was glad, after all, that he'd said it.

Nine

"Why aren't you eating your dinner?"

Startled from his daydreaming, Albert looked up from the plate where he was slowly deconstructing a broccoli-and-ham quiche with his fork. "I am eating it, Mom."

She dropped her fork onto her plate and pressed a hand to her forehead, like his words caused her actual physical pain. "You haven't taken three bites. What's wrong with it? You like quiche!"

"*Nothing* is wrong with it," Albert said, struggling to keep his voice mild. "It's good. I guess I'm not very hungry."

She gave his father an impatient look when he made the mistake of looking up from his own plate. "Luis? Are you going to say anything?"

"You're upsetting your mother," Albert's father said. "Stop playing with your dinner and just eat it."

Lily's letter was all Albert could think about. When his father had arrived home from work first, Albert's books were still sitting in the neat pile he'd made on the dining room table when he got home from school, and his homework was still untouched. Ever since then, Albert had been under the observation of one parent and then two, right up until dinner was put on the table. Now, hoping to get them off his back, Albert stuffed bites as large as he dared into his mouth, barely chewing before swallowing. He only choked once. He was hoping to excuse himself as soon as he'd eaten enough to satisfy his mother. While he chewed, his mind turned to the letter hidden between the pages of Robert Louis Stevenson and the melodrama of the message Lily had sent him.

"Albert?"

He was jerked out of his thoughts again to see that his mother was staring at him in an irritatingly demanding way. "What?" he said, still trying to keep the impatience from his voice, if only to avoid a lecture on manners to go with the lecture on proper dinner consumption.

"I asked how your day was," she said. "Luis?"

"Quit staring off into space and answer your mother," his father said.

Albert thought about his day: getting tripped in the hall before second period, suffering the super-fun lunch tray disaster, getting a D minus on a geometry pop quiz, and, oh yes, finding something sticky and putrid and definitely dead in his locker at the end of the day, thoughtfully placed on the gravy-stained T-shirt he'd left there after lunch.

"It was fine," he said.

He had a stomachache and a headache and a heartache, and now he also had some kind of mystery dumped in his lap … one where the stakes were very personal. But he was seventeen and almost six feet tall, and if he mentioned problems he was liable to get a sardonic "aren't *you* a dainty little orchid" from his father—a remark he'd been chastised with for as long as he could remember, one he'd had the gist of long before he understood the joke.

"It was fine," he said again, adding "this is good" through a mouthful of food, gesturing at his plate with his fork.

This turned out to be the right answer, and having given it, Albert was allowed to withdraw back into himself. As long as he remembered to eat his food. Not just allowed to withdraw—encouraged. Sometimes he wondered if his parents felt as trapped with him as he felt with them. The older he grew, the more strained their little family became. As far as his parents were concerned, the only right way to be was the way everyone else was. They wanted him to join a team, to dress like a "nice young man," to keep his hair trimmed, to smile and remember people's names, to never admit to being anything but happy-go-lucky. To never admit to feeling doubtful or afraid or unhappy. A good son was someone they could brag about but who kept politely in the background and would never give them headaches. He'd been assured once—patronizingly, by an arty old aunt who lived in New York and still dyed a magenta strip into her hair—that this was normal, but he wished he had a brother or a sister, at least, to even out the sides.

Albert's relationship with Lily had been a threat to his parents' perfect two-against-one dynamic. Before, Albert had never had anyone who was automatically on his side—but Lily was, always, about whatever. In the first few weeks they'd hung out together, his parents somehow never managed to remember Lily's name, and they often found reasons why she couldn't come to the house and even more reasons why Albert couldn't go out.

That didn't stop him from seeing her, of course; it just made it harder. But the fact that it was difficult was also somehow exciting. And when he'd realized how strongly he felt about Lily, Albert had also realized that there were far better things to strive for than pleasing one's parents.

He and Lily never did anything that would've sounded exciting if reduced to a list on paper, but it *was* exciting, anyway. And weird. Love—Albert was soon sure that he was in love with Lily, no matter how much his parents hinted that they knew what *that* was all about, even if *he* didn't yet—was a weird experience. From almost the first time they were together, they could talk about everything—the big things like life and death and love, and smaller things like the music they liked or the movies they dug. They laughed over things only they thought were funny, and it was like they'd always known each other. He felt like himself with her—but smarter and surer and realer, in a way he never did at home.

"Why don't your parents like me?" Lily had asked him after about a month. She'd dropped it right out of the blue while they were sitting in her room one day after school. "Is it the sex thing?"

At this point, Albert and Lily hadn't actually gotten to the sex thing. "Well, if you think that would help…"

She'd punched him. "I just mean, you're their only kid, their baby, and they're probably not that comfortable yet with the idea of some girl showing up and metaphorically making you into a man. Forcing them to deal with the fact that you're not their little boy anymore and all that crap."

He'd kissed her for a long moment, liking the idea of all that crap. She'd pushed him away, looking at him as if she actually expected an answer. He said, "Who cares?"

She'd frowned, not letting it go. "Be serious!"

"I *am* serious. When I'm with you, that's all there is. Like right now, I'm pretending that I don't have to be home in the next twenty minutes and that we have all the time in the world. I don't want to talk about my parents."

"You know I'm right," she'd said, wrapping her fingers in his and looking at their hands.

"The thing with my parents and you is, like, a turf war. They don't want anyone else to mean anything to me. They don't want me to think more of you than of them."

"Thank god you're their son and not their daughter," she'd laughed, the crease between her eyebrows finally smoothing out. "They'd have you in a veil and a chastity belt. And good thing for *my* parents I've already set the bar so low. 'Lily's not in jail? Super!'"

"Don't say things like that."

"So you *do* like me the best?"—as if she didn't already know the answer.

Albert did like her the best, and he could see that it drove his parents nuts. They told him he was too young to know his own heart, that he was too young to be so set on the first girl he'd been serious with, that they'd only known each other for such a short while. Sometimes he recognized the truth of what they said, but he never admitted it to them.

Because even if they were right, even if he was stupid, it didn't matter.

On a normal weeknight, Albert would have hurried through his dinner so he could get away—either borrow the car to go see Lily, or shut himself in his room and talk with her on the phone for hours at a time. On a normal weeknight, his parents would be grumbling and banging on the door, sometimes yelling, and usually riding him, too, about whether his homework was done … On a normal weeknight, Albert and his parents sure wouldn't have been having such a deadly slow and polite dinner.

They're probably enjoying this, was Albert's thought as he scraped the last rubbery bit of egg and pie crust from his plate and into his mouth. *They don't care where Lily is or wonder what might have happened to her. They don't want to hear about it from me—all they want is for me to cooperate with the police and get it over with fast. And forget about her.*

"Did you hear me?"

He looked as his mother and realized that she'd been

talking to him yet again, and yet again he'd missed it. *Damn.* "No. What?"

She shook her head, really irritated now. Her voice shook a little. "I wish just once that we could have a pleasant meal in this house. I really do."

"You know what I wish?" Albert said suddenly, the words coming out loud and abrupt before he knew he was going to say them. "*I* wish you'd ask me how I'm doing and actually want to hear the answer." He thought of the sideways call for help Lily had sent and the thought prodded him to go on. "*I* wish you'd say something about Lily."

"Don't start," his mother said, her diction becoming emphatic and her tone shrill, like it did when she was working herself into a real temper. "We've been walking around on eggshells all week, trying not to upset you. Have we pressed you about your chores? Have I made you clean up that disgusting pigsty you call a room? Have I mentioned how much I *detest* that vulgar shirt you're wearing, even though I've asked you a dozen times to get rid of it?" She paused for a breath. "And I should know you wanted to talk about Lily? I would think that's the *last* thing you'd want to talk about!"

"Whatever," Albert muttered, knowing he was pushing his luck.

She wasn't done. "Not to *mention* the position it's put you in! Have you forgotten being questioned by the *police*? Have you forgotten that you were out *sneaking around* when all of this happened?"

"All you care about is how things look!" Albert shouted before he could help himself.

"That's about enough out of you," his father said, and this was as far into the debate as he was usually willing to go. Two red patches had developed on his cheeks.

Albert pushed his chair back from the table and stood up. "I'm going to my room."

They ignored him, which he took as a frosty signal that he was totally and gladly excused from dinner.

At the last moment before his fingers left the edge of his bedroom door, Albert resisted the urge to slam it shut behind him. He went over to the tiny TV on the desk across from his bed and turned up the volume high enough to hear, but not so much that it would be distracting or grounds for an angry pound on the door. After a moment, he swept a pile of CDs from the chair at his desk and carried the chair over to the door, jamming it under the doorknob as quietly as he could. If his parents tried to come in without knocking they were going to be pissed, but at least they wouldn't get the door open in a hurry.

A chill worked its way from his scalp, down his back, and all the way through both his legs, as Albert finally did what he'd been dying to do: he went to the bookshelf and shook Lily's envelope from its hiding place. The little paper rectangle fluttered to the floor, the envelope and the postcard coming apart as they fell, and the letter landing a little apart with the writing side up. The fragment *but I'm going to the last good place. Don't tell anyone* caught his eye.

He hadn't understood this line when he read it, but like a switch flipping from off to on, it made sense to him now. Suddenly he was sure he knew where she was—sort of, anyway. "The Last Good Place" wasn't just some metaphor, but a real place from the last happy summer of her childhood. He imagined her there, hiding like a scared rabbit, probably trying to decide whether to stay put or keep running...and if to run, where to find her next hiding place.

The image of Lily as a frightened animal was an unpleasant one, and Albert blinked, as if this would erase the picture from his head.

His brain working, he stretched out on his bed with the letter in his hand, staring at it. He wasn't even reading the words anymore. He had them memorized. The paper was a talisman, as if staring at it long enough would give him an idea.

A plan.

The TV droned. Random sounds from the other rooms in the house, a voice or a door or a toilet flushing or steps in the hall, made Albert's pulse race. He set the letter on his pillow and went over to check that the chair was wedged firmly under the doorknob. Then he sat heavily on the edge of his bed and rubbed his face with his hands. Something bothered him as he tried to put together, in some meaningful order, Lily and her accident and her stepfather and her disappearance. He couldn't quite see the whole picture.

He ran over the facts as he understood them. About a

year ago, Lily ran with a party crowd and they frequently got into minor trouble—they were caught smoking, ditching school here and there, and once got busted at a kegger and cited for underage drinking. One night, for some reason, they decided to do something different and break into Lily's stepfather's dental clinic—not too difficult, since Lily knew where to get the keys and the alarm code—and huff some laughing gas. Obviously things got a little wild at some point, based on the destruction found later: files dumped, broken glass, instruments scattered.

What the cops put together from the scene, since Lily had no memory and none of the other kids had stepped forward, was that Lily had OD'd on the gas and her friends, probably in a panic, had left her. It was lucky for her that someone had seen the light through the plate-glass windows and called the police. The police called Lily's stepfather and they all arrived on the scene to find the office wrecked and empty, except for an unconscious Lily. Later, at the hospital, the doctors informed Lily's parents that in addition to the damage from the gas, she'd hit her head on the way down and had "some pretty awesome head trauma," as Lily put it later to Albert.

"I was a veg for nearly four months," she'd told him, as if this was a normal thing. The only good thing about it, she said, was that her stepfather had declined to press charges against her for the break-in and the major damage.

Then after her release from the hospital, Lily had cleaned up her act. She ditched the old crew and was working through a couple of kinds of rehab and giving her senior year of high school a second shot.

By the time Albert moved to Little Solace, the story had mellowed from juicy gossip to a local legend along the lines of "Don't you know the deal with *that* family?" The Morales clan had first heard the story from their Realtor when Albert's parents were buying the house.

Then Albert had met Lily, and they were happy ... and then Lily split without warning, maybe because she and her stepfather were still not OK about the break-in after all this time, and they'd had a fight, and she was afraid.

Sighing because his head hurt, Albert shut off the TV and the lights. In the dark, he put the letter with the postcard back in the envelope, the envelope back in the book, and the book back on the shelf, and then he unwedged the chair from the doorknob and crawled into bed.

He closed his eyes, and the lines of Lily's handwriting were tattooed on the insides of his eyelids. He wondered what Lily thought she remembered about her accident. He also wondered if she was losing her mind. Maybe the danger was coming from herself and her half-remembered lost months. Drain damage.

Except, said the part of his brain that wouldn't let him give in to the easiest explanation, *except there's the argument the neighbors overheard. The argument the police seem to think was between me and Lily but which she now seems to be trying to tell me was with Kogen. Kogen, the guy who lied about me and Lily fighting.*

Lily really was in trouble. They both were, maybe more than he had first realized.

While he slept, a plan started forming.

The next morning, Albert's parents acted as if nothing had happened the night before at the dinner table. He was too preoccupied to care, or wonder why. When it was time to leave for school, he set off in the usual direction with his backpack slung over his shoulders.

After about six blocks, when he was sure he was far enough from the house, Albert took a right where he would've normally gone left. He had a vague idea of heading toward a park on the other side of town, and a more specific idea about cutting school for the day.

It was a fine, sunny morning, an unusual February day that hinted at a spring still at least two months away. Despite all that was on his mind, Albert enjoyed the simple activity of walking with the warm sun baking the top of his cold head.

By the time he arrived at the park, Albert had come to a couple of conclusions. Neither conclusion made him too happy, but it felt good to have made any decision at all. He felt more in control now that he had a clear plan of attack. First, he decided, he needed to get into Lily's room and search it for clues. "Search the room for clues" was the way he phrased it to himself, and it felt idiotic, but there was no other way to put it when he didn't know exactly what he was looking for. He just needed something to satisfy himself that there wasn't some piece missing.

The reason he had to be sure was because of his second conclusion: that he had to find Lily, and then convince her to go to the police.

The fact that the first part of his plan was illegal still wasn't as frightening as the second part, the idea of just picking up and leaving to track Lily down. What he was thinking about was usually called "running away," although Albert felt like there were major differences between his reason for leaving and some juvenile delinquent's. Still, he doubted his parents would give a crap about how he rationalized it. The police probably wouldn't care, either.

"Doesn't matter," he muttered aloud to himself, sounding like the occasional drifters who slept in this park when the weather was nicer.

Albert sat on an empty bench, outwardly so that he could eat the apple from his lunch but really to gather his courage. He had the rest of the day ahead of him, when everyone was either in school or at their job—or seeing patients at their successful dental clinics. It was an excellent time to put the first part of his two-part plan into action and let himself into Lily's house while it was—probably, hopefully—empty. He hoped he remembered it right, that she'd told him neither her mother nor her stepfather was ever home during the day.

He should've felt faint just thinking about it, but in spite of what his father liked to say, Albert was *not* a drooping flower. He was going to do this crazy thing. He closed his eyes and was able to visualize the flat stone in the garden where he'd seen Lily retrieve the key to the house's back door. Then he saw himself with that key, slipping easily inside the empty house, stepping down the hall and into her bedroom.

Nothing could be easier.

He opened his eyes. Now all he had to do was leave this bench and go do it for real.

After several more minutes, Albert's legs got the messages his brain was sending and he stood up abruptly, hurrying back out of the park and toward Lily's house before he could change his mind. Or come to his senses.

At the far edge of the park was a duck pond, though this time of year the water was drained out and the paddleboats were all locked away somewhere until spring. At one edge of the empty pond was the unoccupied boat rental and snack shack, and beyond that was a small parking lot. There were only two cars in it. Albert had to cross the lot to leave the park. He scanned both cars without much interest, keeping an eye out for the mostly harmless panhandlers this park was know for. The first car, a beat-up orange VW Beetle, was empty. The tan Saab near it wasn't.

Albert's eyes happened to meet those of the man slumped in the driver's seat, and the shock of recognition locked their gazes.

Shit. It was the cop, Andersen.

Knowing it was probably useless, Albert ducked his head and walked faster. But Andersen was out of his car quickly and easily closed the distance between them. There was nowhere for Albert to go, so he stopped.

"I'm pretty sure school is currently in session," Detective

Andersen said when he was almost on top of Albert, by way of greeting. If he was upset at being spotted following Albert, he wasn't showing it.

Albert shrank, feeling like a naughty child. The idea that this guy had been following him—and might have caught him at something worse that ditching—made him cold all over. But trying to be cool, he said, "You mean it isn't Saturday?"

"What are you doing off school grounds, Morales?" Andersen asked, ignoring Albert's smart remark.

"I got lost," Albert said, resuming walking.

Andersen fell into step with him. "Shall I call your mommy to come pick you up at the station, then?"

Albert stopped again. "What I mean is, I was actually on my way to school."

"You're a little late. Why don't I give you a ride?" Andersen said, jerking his head back toward his car parked behind the empty duck pond.

There was nothing Albert could do but follow the detective across the parking lot to his car. It sucked and Albert didn't trust him, but it was better than having Andersen call his mother like he'd threatened to do. Once there, Andersen unlocked the car manually and held the door open for Albert, shutting it for him before walking around to get in on the driver's side.

Andersen started the car and rolled slowly out of the park and onto the main road. Neither of them spoke. Finally, Albert couldn't stand it any longer. Even though he knew this was a game and by caving in first he would lose, he asked, "How did you know I was there?"

Andersen glanced at him, then back at the road. He pursed his lips, but said nothing.

"Or was it just my lucky day?"

They were just a couple of blocks from the school now. The cop said, "Don't sell yourself short. You're a person of interest to me and my case and we're keeping a nice, cozy watch on you."

"Gee, that *is* a cozy thought," said Albert absently, his heart only half interested in goading the guy. His plan for the day had quickly gone into the toilet. Here he was, nearly back at school instead. And with the added bonus of being in more trouble with a guy who already didn't seem to like him.

"I'm not a truant officer," Andersen said, "but I think you'd better be in school when you're supposed to be in school. Don't make things harder on yourself than you have to."

Albert nodded. "I already missed my math test, so I'm good. Anyway, I like to wait until it's at least seventy outside before I start skipping hardcore." They'd coasted to a stop in front of the school. "Thanks for the ride."

Albert unfolded himself from the car before Andersen could say anything else and nudged the door shut behind him. Heading up the steps toward the wide front doors of the school, he felt Andersen's eyes on his back the entire way. He made himself walk slowly.

It was a weird feeling to know that this changed nothing: he was going to skip school again on Monday and break into Lily's room, just as he'd planned. He would just have to be more careful this time not to get caught.

Ten

12:15 a.m.

"Why are we stopping?" Olivia asks. "I recognize that gas station up there. We're almost to the turnoff."

Albert sinks to his knees, holding up a hand to tell her to give him a moment. He can't speak, because his asthma is acting up again. He's annoyed and alarmed ... this came on when they hadn't even been straining. Ignoring the slow transformation of Olivia's expression from impatience to concern as she watches him pull for air, Albert tries to concentrate on his breathing alone. The crappy part isn't just the slow constricting of his chest as he struggles for air, but the fact that the more he has to fight the harder it is not to panic, and the more he panics the harder it is to breathe. Not having an inhaler adds an extra negative psychological effect. It's as if his body knows there's no help if he can't get this under control.

"Are you okay?" Olivia asks, bending to bring her face closer to his.

He ignores her question and tries to relax, willing the bad moment to pass. After a while, it does.

"Sorry," he says when he can speak again. His voice is weak. "Give me another minute and I'll be fine."

"Take your time," she says, turning to look up the road ahead.

"It's never been this bad. Normally I only use my inhaler about three times a year. Must be the..." He gestures at the trees and the overcast sky.

"Stress?"

Not bothering to explain what he really means, Albert nods his head. *Whatever.* Then he gets to his feet. "I'm ready. Where are we?"

"I don't remember the name," she says, stamping her feet to keep warm. "But after this, we take another jog, north and east, I think. There's a turn-off, and just a string of those wide-spot-in-the-road tourist stops—food and gas and a motel, I think—before we're at the lake itself."

"You're sure about the turn-off?" Albert asks.

"I'm positive I'll know it when I see it."

"Anything more definite?" His words are kind of a croak.

"Stop worrying," Olivia offers as an answer. "If we get that far, I can take us right there."

As he waits for his breathing to go back to normal,

Albert wonders if the next town will have any kind of pharmacy. He pictures himself throwing a trash can through a window in order to steal himself a new inhaler. The picture in his mind is really vivid—from lack of sleep or lack of oxygen, he doesn't know. So clear, in fact, that he can almost see the worn countertop and the blood pressure machine in the corner of the darkened drugstore. He sees himself in the back room where the drugs are, passing over the more popular OxyContin and Valium in order to fill his pockets with names like Maxair, Xopenex, or Ventolin.

"It always comes back to a break-in, doesn't it?" Albert half laughs, half wheezes.

"Maybe we'd better rest awhile longer," Olivia says. There's a confused expression on her face. Obviously she has no idea what he's talking about; she can't, not being inside his head.

"I'm fine now," he says, still wheezing a little. "Let's just keep going."

But she doesn't think he's ready, and he's not sure she's wrong. Neither of them say anything for a while as she lets him catch his breath. Ten minutes later, they're on their way again, both silent, engrossed in their own thoughts.

"My mom is probably losing her mind worrying... first about Lily, and now about me, too."

Albert's little asthma attack has slowed them down further. They're just now getting to the town and onto what they hope is the last leg of their journey. Olivia has spoken suddenly.

Albert opens his mouth to respond, then thinks better

of it. He's tired as well as weakened now, and he doesn't feel like starting anything, even by accident.

She must have felt his hesitation because she says, "Whatever it is, just say it."

"I wasn't going to argue with you. She probably *is* worried. But I don't know her; you do. And I was just thinking that both you and Lily must have good reasons for not letting her in on any of this." *I know I do*, he adds silently, thinking of his own parents.

"You could've just said that."

Albert waits for the rest of whatever she has to say, and after a moment, Olivia goes on.

"My mom chose Perry because he was able to create for her—for us, too, but mostly her—the kind of family she thought we needed to be. *Our* family didn't have that devoted father and husband, so she went out and got us one. A doctor, too—unlike the rat bastard who ran out on her and two little girls." Albert sees her make a face in the darkness. "I'm just reciting here—I don't remember 'the rat bastard' well enough to actually hate him."

"That sucks."

She shrugs. "My point is, she's really wrapped up in the good doctor because she's built this whole *thing* around him—tennis lessons for her, piano for us, new clothes whenever we need them, vacations and dinners at good restaurants and cable television and a nice house. I've heard over and over about what Perry has done for us. 'Your father'—she doesn't mean the sperm donor, she always calls Perry our father—'pulled us out of the *gutter*. Without him, we'd be back in that one-room on the far side of Walker Avenue, with no braces or buttons or bows.'" Olivia bites absently at the tip of her middle finger, as Albert has noticed she often does when she's thinking. "She's said *that* one a million times, too."

"Buttons or bows?" Albert asks.

"Exactly. What the hell does that mean? She's always telling us how lucky we are that he's such an upstanding guy, willing to be daddy to two girls who aren't even his. He's tight with the cops, plays golf with the mayor, and will probably run for city council next year. Let me ask you," she says to Albert, her voice wavering, "do you think she'd want to believe her sainted husband is a perv? And lose everything?"

"I guess not. It doesn't sound like it."

"After the crap Lily put them through ... she's been a kind of nightmare ever since she hit thirteen, seriously. Drinking, smoking, and running around, not to mention everything last year. Mom *isn't* going to believe it." Olivia goes on as if she's convincing herself. "And even if I told her ... I'm afraid if she did come around, it would be too late. She wouldn't be able to protect Lily from Perry, even if she did believe Perry was the problem. And I couldn't protect either of them."

"Or yourself," Albert says, because that matters, too, and he wants her to know. "Maybe being worried out of her mind isn't the worst thing that could happen."

"Yeah. Well. I just know I'm not going to give her a chance to let us down. It's too important."

He doesn't know what to say to this last thing, so he ignores it. "Everything would be so much easier if we had Lily's journal."

Olivia slaps him on the back, two strong blows that sort of hurt. "True. But it's kind of late to worry about that, isn't it?"

They fall silent. Albert draws a deep breath of sharp winter cold into his lungs and is grateful for how easy it is.

He thinks about what Olivia said about not giving her mother a chance to let down her daughters. It had sounded harsh to him—the words themselves, but also the absolute, emotionless way she'd said it. Olivia isn't sure she can turn to her mother in a crisis involving her stepfather and sister, with all that's happened, so she isn't about to take a chance. He wonders what the woman has done to make Olivia so sure it isn't worth the risk, that their mother won't come through when it matters.

While Albert is thinking about all this, he can avoid the fact that he's done the same thing with his parents, and for similar reasons. He knows very well that his parents strongly believe that people in authority are to be trusted and obeyed—this goes for cops and teachers and priests, and doctors, too. If Albert had given them the whole story, he's positive they would have told him he was mistaken about what he thought he knew and insisted he go to the authorities.

(And if he'd still had Lily's firsthand version of what had happened, the one that only she possessed? Even confronted with *that*, Albert's big fear is that his mother would probably slap his face in disgust and call Lily a liar, and that his father would go with whatever his mother said. It seems like it would be too much to expect them to believe Lily's word over her successful, friendly, handsome stepfather. Like Olivia, Albert isn't willing to risk finding out. Olivia's right—it's too important.)

They would have pushed him to tell everything to the same authorities whose head investigator on the case is Andersen, a friend of Kogen's, part of his regular Saturday golf foursome. After seeing what Kogen was willing to do in order to keep Lily's story buried, Albert has a bad feeling that if any of these responsible adults find out where Lily might be before he and Olivia can get to her, Kogen will go to Lily and make sure she never comes back to tattle on him.

As they walk, they pass a phone booth. Albert feels a twinge of guilt and thinks briefly of calling his parents, just to tell them he's okay. Then he remembers about things like wiretaps and line traces, and he can't think what he'd say that would make it worth the risk.

Eleven

On Monday morning, Albert found out that breaking into Lily's house was just as easy as he had imagined. And once he was actually keying open the door and no guard dogs attacked him, and no alarm sounded and no cops jumped out of the bushes led by his new best friend Detective Andersen, Albert let out a relieved sigh.

After Andersen had dropped him off at school on Friday morning, the rest of the day had been painfully slow. At lunch, which Albert had been eating alone as usual, a senior came up to his empty table and rested his hands on the back of a chair. The guy didn't sit, just looked at Albert. Albert recognized him as one of the guys who'd laughed while his lunch tray went flying to the floor in front of the whole school. Patrick MacLennan, that was his name.

"You want to throw my lunch on the floor again?"

Albert asked, holding up what was left of his square of pizza.

"Depends," MacLennan said.

It wasn't the answer he'd expected. And the guy was acting like he had some reason to be pissed at Albert instead of the other way around.

"On what?" Albert asked.

"On if you had anything to do with whatever happened to Lily Odilon," MacLennan said, squeezing the chair to make his muscles flex.

"Aren't you the guy who left her to die on the floor of a dental clinic?"

Albert didn't get MacLennan. They'd had a gym period together last fall, and he remembered thinking the guy was actually okay for a jock. MacLennan was good at everything the coach made them do, of course, but he did it without any of the flack some of the other guys threw at their less-than-athletic classmates, those guys who yelled at fat girls for striking out at softball or at clumsy nerds for tripping over their feet in soccer. But then there was the other thing—the vivid mental picture Albert had of MacLennan laughing with his buddies while Albert's food tray clattered to the lunchroom floor. And then he'd found out that MacLennan was one of the friends who left Lily behind the night of her accident.

"You don't know—" MacLennan began.

"I don't care, either," Albert said. He stood, grabbing his backpack and his tray. "*You* don't know anything about me, or Lily. The last thing she needs is help from an ass-hole like you." Then he hurried away, hoping MacLennan wouldn't punch him in the back of his head as he went.

The weekend that followed had been endless. Albert felt trapped in his house, like a big animal in a small cage. He wanted to escape so he could follow his new hunch about where Lily had run away to ... where, if still not *why* she had gone to that summer cabin they visited every year until their mother remarried and those trips were over.

If he'd known exactly where the cabin and the lake were located, he would've left town immediately to chase after Lily. Though the word that came to his mind first wasn't "chase" but "hunt." It disturbed Albert to think of Lily as some kind of game and himself as her hunter. More exactly, if he was honest with himself, what was disturbing was that he *could* think about her that way. His uneasiness only made him more restless.

While Albert tried to put Lily out of his mind and think about anything besides what he planned to do, some-thing deep in his brain was still busy working things out.

Leave it until Monday, he kept telling himself. There was nothing he could do until after the weekend, when the rest of the world would be back to work and school and he could search Lily's bedroom for a way to help them both.

In the meantime, as the hours crawled by, Albert made sure the word "Lily" never crossed his lips. His parents really didn't want to hear her name and he didn't want to rile them up.

The one bit of good luck Albert could see was that for

some reason, Detective Andersen hadn't followed through on the threat to call his parents about catching him skipping school. All weekend, Albert's nerves were tensed for a phone call—and the parental nuclear fallout—that never came.

At first he couldn't understand this bit of luck, but gradually, as he obsessed over it, the cop's discretion began to make a kind of sense. If Albert's parents found out he wasn't where he was supposed to be, Andersen would expect them to pull Albert's leash even tighter, to punish him. And if they did that, the cops would have even less chance of catching Albert in whatever criminal involvement they thought was related to Lily's missing persons case. Andersen was obviously following him, and he wanted Albert to have plenty of rope with which to hang himself. Albert was supposed to lead them to the sex cult where she was being held, or maybe to where he'd hidden her body.

Picturing the envelope hidden in the back of his bookcase, Albert figured the cops and his parents would be pretty pissed off if they knew he had it but hadn't told anyone. It definitely made things more complicated, but he was pretty sure he was better off knowing the little bit Lily had written to him than knowing nothing. Mostly sure.

When Monday morning finally rolled around, Albert found that now that the day had come, he almost wished it hadn't. He really didn't know how carefully the local cops were watching him or how much was just Andersen trying to frighten him on behalf of the cop's great personal friends, Lily's parents. Not to mention the risk he was taking if his own parents found out. Whichever way he looked at it, Albert knew he was pushing his luck by again not heading straight to school.

He also knew that as much as he didn't understand Lily's reasoning, he had caught her urgency like a sickness. She thought her stepfather was out to get her—fine. She thought she couldn't take her problems to the authorities—fine. The question he had to ask himself was, should he believe her take on things? He knew he had a choice; he hadn't done anything yet. He could reject Lily's trust in him and unload the decision and the responsibility for what to do next. He didn't have to go through with what he was planning—all he had to do was take her letter to the police station and let *them* figure it out.

And hope that she was wrong about whose side they would be on.

Except, because he did believe her and because he wanted desperately to help her, the idea of choice was only an illusion. He would do what he could to find her, by himself, with no one to help or share the responsibility for however the rest unraveled.

He'd been the only person she'd felt she could confide in, and fair or not, she was relying on him. For something. Not yet identified.

So he took the second option, which was really the only one, telling himself it was probably the stupid choice but not quite believing it.

When Albert cut school this time, he was a lot more careful. As he skimmed alleys and willed himself to disappear, he kept a constant eye ahead and behind for what detective novels called a tail. And what the hell, he thought, feeling like he might vomit from nerves—it was still better than geometry.

Now he was inside Lily's house. After shutting the door softly behind him, Albert shoved the key into his pocket without really thinking about it. He found himself standing in a darkened laundry room. He'd only been in this part of the house a couple of times, and the last time he'd been very distracted. He stopped to remember where he was in relation to the rest of the house, specifically Lily's bedroom. After a moment he took a cautious step out of the laundry room, his sneaker squeaking as he lifted it from the linoleum and placed it on the thick beige carpet of the hallway.

He made his way carefully down the short hall and into the dining area, which was between the kitchen on one side and a sunken living room on the other. The formal living room was more toward the front of the house. Across from him was the hall that led to three bedrooms: Lily's sister's room, then the spare room that was the den, then, at the end, the master suite. Though the sun had risen, everything around him was gloomy and dark. All the shades were drawn. Even in the half-light, Albert could see that everything was white: the walls, the tiles around the gas fireplace, the furniture, the vase on the table, and the pillows on the low sofa that lined the edge of the sunken room Lily called "the pit." There weren't any family pictures on the walls, but instead a couple of largish abstract canvases in the dining room and hanging above the fireplace—paintings belonging to Lily's stepfather, paintings she'd told Albert she thought looked like smeared bloody nose. The house had a lifeless smell to match its colors. To Albert it was a mix of school glue and watered-down lemons.

Lily's room was apart from the other three bedrooms, through the kitchen and on the other side, a storage room that hadn't originally been a bedroom. Lily had wanted it anyway, she'd told him once, because it was the farthest bedroom from her parents'. Albert hurried through the dead house to this familiar place. He hesitated in front of her closed door for a moment, wondering if it was really all right if he went in.

Of course anyone who found him here would obviously say it was *not* at all okay that he was in this house. Technically, it was a crime.

On the other hand...he figured that Lily would trust him to enter her bedroom uninvited. Chances were that her privacy here had already been ignored by her parents and the police.

So he opened the door and stepped inside.

Lily's room always seemed to have been ripped from another house and reattached here by accident. The walls—what was visible beneath the posters and pictures Lily had papered up everywhere—were a deep purplish pink. Every bit of space was filled with mismatched furniture, and, between the bed and the tall dresser and the desk and the bookshelves and Lily's prized vintage steamer trunk, very little of the scuffed hardwood floor was visible. The last time Albert had been here, the room had been in a state of restrained chaos—there was stuff everywhere with no obvious organizing system except for a bunch of neat piles. Lily was a fan of tidy random piles for her stuff. Now what Albert was seeing was merely a mess. One that had been made in an impatient hurry and then left that way. He bent over and picked up an orange scarf from the floor, the one that had been draped over the bedside lamp on the night Lily'd gone.

Another word from detective-story jargon popped into his head: this room had been tossed. Of course the police had been through it, more than once probably, looking for anything that would tell them what had happened to Lily. The shades were drawn in here, too. Lily's desk and dresser drawers were open, her clothes still hanging out like they'd been frozen in the act of crawling away; papers and notebooks were dropped wherever. The closet door was barely ajar and a small box, flaps open, blocked the opening. Stepping farther into the room, Albert saw a mountain on the bed, as if someone had dumped several boxes of random stuff there to sift through. The bedding was all gone, the pretty coverlet and the fresh sheets that Lily had left him dozing in; the bare mattress that stared back at him seemed to have a crude, violated look. Albert didn't like to think why the sheets and blankets had been removed.

He dropped to his knees and looked under the bed— the stuff under there had been raked out and left where it ended up.

Albert's stomach sank, and he knew: he wasn't going to find anything that the police hadn't already found. Which meant he wasn't going to find anything helpful at all. He sat on the edge of the bed, the mattress springs squealing under his weight, and cursed himself for not focusing better on what she'd told him about her Last Good Place. He didn't even know where the house was on the lake, or if the lake was even in this *state*. He couldn't quite remember its name—something about trees, maybe—not even enough for an Internet search. And if he could absolve himself with the knowledge that there was no way he could've known there'd be an important test on it later…well, that wasn't much comfort, was it?

"Damn," he whispered, the words hanging in the stillness.

He hadn't come here expecting to find a nice map laid out on the bed with a big red X Marks The Spot, but what *had* he been expecting? If she'd had a diary, that would have been the first thing they'd take. She'd flipped through her photo album with him once, and while he didn't remember any pictures from the lake cabin, he wasn't sure. Even if there had been pictures, there was no reason they'd hold any useful information. He didn't see the album anywhere, anyway.

At the rate he was going, he was going to have to get maps of this and every neighboring state and search them all until the name of a body of water sparked his memory. Not a very promising scheme.

It was a full five minutes before Albert was able to

shake himself out of a state of self-pity and paralysis. He was here, and he was almost certainly going to catch hell for skipping school anyway, so he might as well make something of it. As tempting as it was to sink into the bed and bury his face in the naked pillows to try to catch the scent of Lily's hair, he needed to focus his attention. He needed to find something that would help him find her.

The only thing to do was just what the police had probably done: sift through everything and see if anything helpful turned up. Maybe they'd missed something significant. Obviously they had no idea that she was lying low at that lakeside cabin of her best childhood memories, or they'd have gone after her already, as Albert was planning to do. A nagging voice asked whether it was just a matter of time before they figured it out, too.

The next couple of hours were frustrating and useless. He began his search in the obvious places: under the mattress, behind the drawers of her desk, and on the mirror over the dresser. The rather mysterious nature of another person's collected belongings hit him—how much junk people save, the meaning known only to them. But there was nothing about The Last Good Place—no pictures, no notes, not even a restaurant matchbook or a souvenir map. He flipped through Lily's school notebooks, the sight of her tight, private scrawl doing funny things to his stomach. It was like catching a glimpse of her in her underwear when she didn't know anyone was looking—something he wouldn't want to be caught doing. One by one he pulled the books from her shelves and shook them, hoping for something to flutter out, but nothing did.

After giving up on the room itself, Albert kicked aside the open box blocking the closet and stepped inside. It was a small walk-in and when he opened the door wider, a light went on over his head, startling him. About half of Lily's clothes had been pulled from the rod, hangers and all, and left in a pile on the closet floor. He could see the back wall, a dingy off-white that had probably matched the rest of the room at one time. He ran his hand over the shelves above his head, even though the shoeboxes and other junk that had been on them were all now on the floor just outside the door and the shelves were empty.

He dropped to the floor and sat in the pile that had been scattered there. No box or bag had been left unopened, and even the shoes from her shoe rack had been pulled from their cubbies. Albert could imagine cops poking rubber-gloved fingers into the toes of each pair. It occurred to him that he was leaving fingerprints everywhere, but he supposed it didn't matter much now. He continued to feel the wall, down below the line of clothes left hanging, for a cubby or some secret passageway to the land of Narnia for all he knew. But all he found was the nothing he expected.

Since the shoe rack was flush with the wall, Albert couldn't get his hand behind it. He decided to be thorough, though he knew it was pointless, so he shouldered the rack aside in order to finish his ridiculous pat-down of the walls. The floor back here was the only bare spot in the closet, which pulled his eyes down.

After a moment, he looked down again. This time it was more than a glance, as his brain struggled to catch up with whatever had caught his eye.

Two of those boards did look a little bit, well, *different* from the others—their lines were slightly off, and the color was off as well.

He reached down and gave one a test push. He thought he felt a slight give under his palm, but it was so slight he could have imagined it. These boards were pretty tight after all.

Rocking from his heels to his knees, he bent down for a closer look. He pushed again, and again he couldn't tell. It really would have been too easy. If he expected this to be anything, then he probably really was dumb enough to think there was the map with the big red X Marks The Spot on it. All that and Narnia, too.

But still. He couldn't quite let it go.

He left the closet long enough to find something he could use as a lever, and came back with a letter opener he'd found in the desk. He stuck the point of it in where the boards looked off and pressed down on the end.

With a small squeak the board came up, pretty easily, he felt. Trying to keep down his excitement, he pulled at the boards around it. Only one came loose, exposing an opening that was barely wide enough for him to get his hand through. He hesitated very briefly, then pushed aside the deep disgust he felt at sticking his hand into a place he couldn't see. He put his hand through the hole in the floor and felt around. His fingers got only air. Grunting, he lowered himself more, in order to get his arm farther in. His face was on the floor and he could smell the cool, almost damp smell coming from the hole. Slowly he extended his arm more, not want to whack it on anything he couldn't see.

When his elbow was about half bent, his fingers touched something solid, like concrete, maybe two feet down. His hand crept farther along and found something hard and rough, then another something, soft and papery. He pulled the soft thing out first: it was a crumpled old paper bag. When he went back for the second thing, he came up with a book.

He felt like he'd won something—obviously no one had discovered Lily's clever little hiding place.

Moving the book and the bag out of the way, Albert carefully replaced the shoe rack and tried to settle the mess back the way he'd found it, as best he could. Then he turned his attention to what he'd found. Unrolling the top of the small paper bag, Albert wasn't surprised to see a lighter, an empty bottle of airline-sized vodka, and a nearly empty baggie of what looked like very old weed. He smiled at this trace of Lily's party-girl persona, the ghost of whom he'd rarely seen since he'd met her. Nothing useful there, so he dropped the bag and turned his attention to the other discovery. The book was smallish and plain, a brown color not much darker than the paper bag.

Barely hesitating, he pulled at the little lock—more for show than a real lock—and it gave easily. He flipped the pages and saw steady handwriting across unlined paper. The script filled less than a quarter of the book and most of the pages were still crisp and blank. The first page was dated in November, over a year before. Though it was more crabbed and dark than usual, as if she'd been trying to push the pen right through the paper, he recognized Lily's handwriting.

Thinking perhaps he shouldn't, he read the first lines anyway:

Perry was sleepwalking last night and he came to my room. I'm so embarrassed. I can't tell anyone.

Twelve

Albert stood on Lily's doorstep, waiting for someone to answer the door after he rang the bell. It was only the second time he'd been to Lily's house that her parents knew about, the second thing you could actually call a date: two concert tickets and a car, rare mercy from his dad. Also, the second time he'd used the front door to get in.

The word "date" was possibly the skin-crawlingest word Albert could think of for hanging out with a girl. "Date" made him think of things like ironed slacks and corsages and polite chitchat with adults ... and that joking-but-still-serious "have her home by eleven!" command of the sitcom dad following them out the door.

"Date" made Albert think of some douchy sport coat, and actually a very real sport coat was balled up in the backseat of his car at that very moment. A sport coat that his parents had insisted on buying for him when he made the mistake of asking for the car for his and Lily's first date, and that they insisted he take tonight, even though (a) his parents had already decided this Albert/Lily thing was a temporary annoyance to be put up with until it ran its course, and (b) only a complete dork would wear a sport coat to an all-ages show, anyway. But it wasn't worth arguing about and risking the loss of the car for the night, so Albert wore the jacket right up until the time he tossed it in the backseat while he drove, about a block from home.

"Date" was formal and old-fashioned, and he didn't think those things applied to Lily.

As he was getting himself all worked up and wondering if he should ring again, the door finally opened. His nervous stomach flopped, but it was Lily on the other side, looking as uncomfortable as he felt.

"Come in," she muttered, pulling him inside, "and let's get this over with so we can go."

There was a tiny flash of light at her throat as she turned, and he saw she was wearing the little heart necklace he'd given her.

The first time he'd picked Lily up to take her out, her mother had been on her way out the door; he'd met the woman only in passing and she didn't seem too interested in her daughter's boyfriend. The husband had been waiting for her in their car, and Albert's introduction to him had been his brief wave as he drove away.

Lily led Albert into the kitchen. He'd prepared himself to have to meet the whole family, but now that he was here it didn't actually look too bad. There was no sign of the sister or stepfather, only Lily's mother. Her back was turned as she stood tiptoe on a little step stool so she could water the plant that was hanging above the sink.

"Mom, you remember Albert," Lily recited quickly as she grabbed her bag from the counter. "We have to jet if we're going to make it before the show starts."

Her mother stepped gracefully from the stool and set her watering can on the counter, running her hands over the non-existent creases in her pants. "Honey, it's barely six. What time does this concert begin?"

"We're going to grab a quick bite first," Lily replied. To Albert she said, "Say 'hi' fast, because we're out of here."

"Wait a minute," said Lily's mother, smiling at her daughter and wagging a finger at her. "I didn't get a good look at the boy the first time around. Let me give him the once-over, at least."

Albert stood between the two females, an afterthought to them both in this moment, and he was unsure of what was safe to do. So he said, "Nice to see you again, ma'am."

"*Encantado! Estás en tu casa*," Lily's mother said, brushing his arm with one hand. Albert just smiled and nodded, and before he could think of what to say, she rapid-fired another string of words in what sounded to Albert like pretty good Spanish. Though he couldn't be sure, since he didn't speak the language.

Lily's mom looked at him, and her smile stopped before it got to her eyes, which were probing. She was taller than Lily, and her hair was dark blonde and pulled up away from her face. And though she was a very pretty older version of her very pretty daughter, Albert noticed she was wearing more makeup at home than his mother put on for even the fanciest going out.

"Mom," Lily said, laughing, "he doesn't know what you're saying. He does speak English, though."

Albert's face was starting to hurt from fake-smiling and he wished they could leave already.

Her mother looked confused for a moment, but recovered quickly. "Run along, then, and have a good time. But don't stay out too late, all right?"

Albert could see Lily stifling an eye-roll as she gave her mother a quick kiss on the cheek and then tugged his hand. They were almost to the front door when her mother's voice stopped them.

"Before I forget," she said from the kitchen doorway, "your father—"

Lily turned her head sharply. "You mean Perry?"

"Honestly, Lily," her mother said, her voice sounding a lot more brittle than it had a moment ago. "I don't know why you have to be so combative about everything. Your stepfather, then, wanted me to remind you to leave your car keys on the table so he can check the fluid levels when he gets home. He does so much for you"—her voice rose a pitch—"and honestly, you have so little appreciation."

"Mom …" Lily pleaded, looking from her mother to Albert and back again. After no one said anything, she said, "I'm sorry, okay?" She didn't sound very sorry.

Her mother sighed. "I'm sorry, too, honey, that I snapped at you. I'm just so tired, and I have fifty thousand things to do and not enough hours in the day, you know? I don't mean to take it out on you."

The fact of Lily's apology, if not how she said it, must have been enough to smooth things back out, because she and Albert were finally free, almost racing to the car to get away from the claustrophobic scene in the immaculate white house.

Later, on the drive home after the show, their ears still ringing from the amps, Albert took the long way, as best as he could remember it in this new town with roads he was still learning. Avoiding the freeway that would shoot them pretty much straight back to Lily's doorstep in about thirty minutes, Albert found the two-lane highway and the back roads. He tried to stretch the evening out as long as he could, going nowhere in particular, just prolonging the ride as much as possible. He drove faster than he should have, because Lily laughed wildly whenever they had to lean into the turns and her hand crept up his thigh. He himself felt a pleasant sense of being close to out of control.

Later still, after they came to the unspoken agreement that they couldn't put it off any longer, Albert slowed his driving down and finally turned the car toward Lily's house.

They approached the familiar roads of the neighborhoods close to Lily's, and as they did, something in their mood was disappearing. Lily turned her face to the window and rolled it all the way down. She rested her arm on the metal frame, letting her fingers dangle outside, and the rest of the evening seemed to be rushing out the window, too. The incoming air was cold, and cleared the last of the giddiness from the car along with the heat.

"I don't want this night to end," she said after a moment. "I don't want to go home."

"Me either," Albert said. The engine shuddered when he said it, as if in sympathy. He snaked a hand across the space between them and found her hand.

"Let's just pretend," she said, "that we're not going home at all. Let's say we're just going to keep driving forever."

Thirteen

*H*e kissed me, not a fatherly kiss.

The first entry in Lily's diary ended after four short, matter-of-fact sentences. Albert turned the page, in spite of himself, in spite of preferring to slam the little journal shut and put it back in the closet, buried under the floorboards.

The next entry was dated three days later:

I thought before was a one-time thing, he was a little drunk and so maybe it was just a little too much. But he came back tonight. I got in late and he stayed up for me. Mom and Liv were asleep. He followed me to my room. He said I was growing up, that I was beautiful, that he was confused. That kind of total bullshit. I didn't know what to say, so I just told him I was tired and wanted to go to

bed. Like: hint, dude—leave. He had this weird look
on his face, he was kind of puffy and breathless.
He wouldn't leave me alone until I gave him a hug.
It was a long one and that's all I can write for now
without puking.

   Talk to Liv about it, maybe? Hard to describe
how creepy and bad a hug can be. Have to think
about it.

Albert made himself keep reading. It became clear to
him very soon that this journal had just one theme. The
tone changed from a kind of on-purpose detached irritation, to mushrooming anger, and then sharp fear. Feeling
like a coward for being frightened by words written on a
page, Albert waded through Lily's account of the relationship with her stepfather as it turned toxic. The kisses and
hugs he forced on her grew more frequent and less shy, as
Lily told it, and she wrote about how she was searching for
ways to stay out of the house while her stepfather was finding more excuses to be alone with her. Several pages in, she
wrote about a morning when her mom and sister left early
to go to an eye appointment for Liv. Her stepfather walked
in on her in the bathroom, right after she'd gotten out of
the shower.

He just laughed like it was some hilarious mistake
and wouldn't leave. I guess now he was testing and
deciding.

Later in the journal, Lily described her parents' discussion of whether she should work at Perry's dental office—filing, setting appointments and stuff—after school and maybe weekends.

> They think I need to "buckle down." But if she makes me work with him, I don't know what I'll do. I can't stand to be around him at all, and I'm afraid when we're alone. I hate the way he looks at me.
>
> I don't think he's bothering Liv, though—that's something. I just don't know what to do to keep him from stepping further over the line. He says rude things to me all the time. When I see him, I want to punch him in his stupid smug face.

After maybe a couple dozen entries, most of them short, Albert came to the last one, just a couple months after the journal had begun. It ended on the day before Lily's accident. The cheap paper was stained with dark drops that wrinkled the pages of dark, hasty script.

> I hate myself. I hate my mother. I HATE HIM.
>
> He thinks he can get away with it, just does whatever, that it's my word against his. Slutty little crazy teenage liar versus him. Said I'd get to like it. It's not like you're a virgin, he said. He said he could tell.
>
> But you're not really good at it yet, he said. I'm going to teach you about screwing.

He was drunk—barely drunk—as he always is when he's bothering me. I don't blame the alcohol, though. I think he drinks for courage, for something to blame it on. So he can forget why he shouldn't be doing what he's doing while he's doing it. Maybe so he can look us all in the face the next day, I don't know. I don't know how he could this time, though.

It's driving me crazy to think it might not have happened if we hadn't been alone in the house. I want to die. But I won't give him the satisfaction.

Guess what, you fucking asshole: you shouldn't have been so hot to have the lights on. I can remember everything from the size and shape of your tiny little dick to the birthmark on your ass. I was looking, because I knew I had to remember every bit. Now I'm going to crucify you with it.

Mom, if you find this and read it: Hope you had fun at your girls' weekend.

I have to make this quick because I have to get the hell out of here before I lose it. He thinks I'm in here sleeping, not sitting on the floor of my closet writing it all down. He's probably passed out by now and if I'm lucky he won't hear me shut the window when I leave.

So:

At seven-thirty this evening I was getting ready to go out. My stepfather, Perry Kogen, came into my room without knocking. He was wearing ...

Albert was spared the more graphic details, maybe because there were things about that night Lily couldn't bring herself to write. But there was enough he could hardly stand to read, though he read it anyway because he knew, from the way the letters wavered, that it had to have been almost more than she could bear to put on the page.

Albert was caught in Lily's words and it was like being tangled in a nightmare. The Bad Thing That Happened wasn't the accident at Dr. Perry Kogen's dental practice, but the revolting thing that happened right here in her bedroom. His skin was clammy, and his breath short. He thought he might vomit. He thought he might cry. He wondered what a panic attack was like, and if he was about to have one.

Lily, Lily, Lily, he thought, as if repeating her name enough times could take back what happened.

Albert was so unaware of anything outside of Lily's journal that he actually jumped when he heard a voice above him.

"What the hell are you doing in my sister's room?"

Every muscle in his body seemed to be vibrating. He looked up to see Olivia Odilon standing in the closet doorway. He knew that this must look bad, and perhaps he was infected by Lily's acid writings. As he watched Olivia's eyes flit from his face to the journal and back up again, demanding an explanation, he felt dirty and awkward and guilty.

He asked, "Are you going to call the cops?"

She crossed her arms over her chest. "It depends on if

you have a really *spectacular* reason for sitting on the floor of my missing sister's closet and reading what looks like a diary. You have about ten seconds before I start screaming and dial 911."

A flood of words rushed, panicked, from Albert's mouth. "I think I know where Lily is."

From the look on Olivia's face, of all the things she expected him to say, it wasn't this. But her expression of surprise gave way to suspicion almost immediately. "How do you know? Did you do something?" She backed away a couple of feet, tripping over the mess on the floor.

He scrambled to his feet, an awkward thing given his size and the cramped space. "No! I can explain. Like this— I found it in the back of the closet."

She snatched the journal from his outstretched hand, keeping her distance. "I thought there'd be nothing left here at all, between the cops and my parents. To say they've been through this room thoroughly is an understatement. They took her cell phone, her computer … and a bunch of stuff I don't even get why they need."

"I guess they didn't find the space under the floorboards in her closet." Albert was shocked at his own pale joke and he felt like he might just lose it.

Still not understanding, Olivia was surprised into a grudging bray of a laugh. "I'm not going to say I'm not creeped out—and a little concerned for my safety—but I guess I'm sort of impressed."

He hesitated, trying to figure out how to tell her. "You should probably read it."

She snorted. "It's that good, huh?"

He reached out and put his hand on her shoulder, then immediately regretted it. She reached up and slapped his hand away. He said, "You really don't know anything about what happened with Lily and your stepfather...?"

"I guess you're going to tell me." She sighed heavily and covered her face with her free hand.

"He raped her," Albert said. The words were evil and poisonous in his mouth. It was too raw a topic to be discussed by two people who barely knew each other, but he couldn't help that. He was acutely aware of the grim absurdity of this moment: the location, the players, the reason these things had all come together. It wasn't a scene he could have imagined just a few days ago, and the thought made him even sadder.

"What?" Olivia said, holding the book up like a prop. "It says that?"

He nodded. "She wrote it right before her accident. Read it yourself—it's on the last page."

She read it quickly, her eyes darting across the page. When she was done, she closed the journal, her head still hanging. She mumbled into her chest, "I can't take this. I really can't."

"I know." His eyes welled and he brushed them roughly with the back of his hand. Lily had never given him the slightest indication of what had happened to her, so it made her words—angry and raw—even more of a punch in the gut.

"Why didn't she ever say anything?" Olivia asked, not really asking Albert.

But this was a question he thought he maybe had an answer for. Or at least a working theory, which had popped into his head as a fully formed idea. "She didn't say anything because she didn't know," he said. "It's the only thing that makes sense. I think … it … happened, and she wrote about it, obviously planning to turn him in to the cops or whoever. Then I think she put the journal back in the closet, and that same night there was the accident, and everything that happened with that. She lost all those months, including the memory of—that," he said, pointing to the book. He couldn't bring himself to say it again.

"There's no way she could have stayed here, otherwise," Olivia said, thinking out loud. Pretty soon Albert saw her thin shoulders shake. She was so much smaller that Lily. Whenever Albert saw her at school—if he ever noticed her—she looked like a dark, scowling twelve-year-old. These thoughts crossed his mind and he felt low and mean for thinking them while she was right in front of him, crying for her sister.

"Look, this is all really overwhelming—" Albert began.

"It's a nightmare, is what it is," Olivia interrupted fiercely.

"Maybe I should go. I can put the journal back for now—I'll show you the hiding place—and when you think you're ready, we can—"

"God, stop treating me like a—I don't even know what." She rubbed her eyes, and the tears were gone and the scowl was back. "I don't like it. While you're handing out answers, maybe you can tell me why she's gone, then, if she doesn't remember anything."

To him it was obvious, but then he remembered that Olivia didn't know about Lily's letter. "Because she was starting to remember. And your stepfather knew it. Somehow. The police have witnesses who say the night she left she was fighting with someone. They think—everyone thinks—it was with me. I think the fight was with him."

"How did you get all that?"

"She sent me a letter."

Olivia held out her hand. "Why didn't you say so? Let me see it."

"It's at my house, hidden." But he was able to recite it pretty much word for word from his memory. He felt self-conscious as he did so. When he was done, he was amazed at how successfully Lily's sister fought another storm of tears. He said, "I'll show it to you later, but you can't tell *anyone* about it. Not until I figure it out—"

"Didn't I tell you to stop being an idiot? Who the fuck am I going to tell?" Olivia sat on the edge of her sister's bed. "We can't leave this journal here, either. It's evidence. You have to get out of here, and you have to take it with you and hide it. I'll sneak out later to meet you and you can show me Lily's letter. Then we'll take both to the cops." She was almost smiling, now that she had a strategy. "To keep things simple, I'll tell them it was me who found the journal in her closet."

Albert didn't have the same confidence in the police

that Olivia seemed to have. "Do you think they'll believe it, though? Lily didn't think so."

"Shouldn't this be enough to make them open an investigation of Perry, at least?" She barked out another humorless laugh, holding up the book. "And since Lily obviously doesn't even remember what's written here, we have to keep it safe. It's the only proof left from that night." She stopped abruptly, biting off the word.

"What?" Albert asked.

"This stuff about... Perry." She spat out the name as if it tasted bad. "If she really did forget, I'm glad that for her it doesn't exist."

Except she hadn't forgotten, not completely. Albert shivered, the thought of these things that hadn't stayed buried making him feel ill, and with that feeling was something darker. Then another thought occurred to him, and it was so strange that he spoke it out loud without even meaning to. "It's funny—you and I are the only two people she has who really want to help her, and we hardly know each other."

"Yeah, it's just hilarious. I feel like I'm trapped in a nightmare and if I could just wake up..." Olivia trailed off. "But I can't, and I don't know what to *do*."

"Like you said, we take it to the police. If we can make them understand, make them believe Lily's story, he'll go to jail. And then she'll be able to come home. Simple." He hoped.

"I'm thinking that maybe we—"

But she never finished the sentence, this time because

just then a voice called from the front of the house, "Olivia? Are you home?" There was a pause, then louder and closer: "Olivia?"

Olivia and Albert exchanged a terrified glance, and then Olivia was shoving him into Lily's closet and closing the door on him.

"Hide the journal," she breathed intensely, almost too soft to qualify as a whisper, before the closet door latched with a tiny click.

Not knowing what else to do, he tucked the book down the back of his pants and held his breath.

He heard her scramble away from the door, but before she could get out of Lily's room, Perry Kogen must have walked in through the open door. Even with the closet door closed, Albert could hear everything clearly.

"What are you doing in here?"

"Oh, you know," Olivia said. "Just thinking."

Albert heard a step. "Honey, have you been crying?" The concern in Kogen's voice sounded genuine, and Albert wanted to pinch the bastard's windpipe shut. He had no right to care. "Come here."

"No!" she said, too sharp. "I mean, I just kind of want to be alone, you know?"

"Sure," her stepfather replied after a moment. "I just came in because I thought I heard talking. I thought maybe Lily—"

Albert was suddenly sure both Olivia and Kogen could hear the rabbit-kicking of his heart.

"—No," she interrupted, "it's just me. You caught me

talking to myself." Nervous chuckle. Albert winced. "What are you doing home, anyway? It's barely three o'clock."

There was a sound like someone fiddling with a drawer, then Perry said, "Phil called asked me to play some racquetball. My last appointment was at two, so I thought I'd squeeze a game or two in before dinner. I was just coming home to change my clothes. Hey, you want to come down to the club with me? Swim some laps or something?"

"No," Olivia said again. "But thanks. I just want to be alone. You understand, right?"

"Fine, honey. I'll see you in a couple of hours then, all right?"

"Sure."

Albert heard footsteps and the door shutting. Seconds later, Olivia's face appeared in the crack in the closet doorway. *Stay there*, she mouthed to him. Albert shot her a thumbs-up to indicate he understood he should stay in the closet until Kogen left the house again. He heard the bedsprings creak as Olivia sat on her sister's bed.

After a few long minutes, Albert heard Olivia get up and go to the bedroom door, closing it. Then the closet light went on and she was looking up at Albert.

"Is he gone?" Albert whispered.

"I think so. I heard the front door close." Olivia was whispering, too. "You have to get out of here. Go out the window and cut through the back yard." She had him by the arm and was pulling him from the closet toward the window.

"But—"

She stopped trying to hustle him out of the room and whirled on him, her eyes snapping more than ever. "Look, do you want him to come back and find you here? To find her *journal*? It's the only proof we have—and the best chance we have to help my sister."

"Fine," he said after a moment.

She opened the window blinds with an abrupt jerk. As she was struggling to open the latch, she said, "I'll call you tonight after dinner when Mom and Perry aren't around. Maybe we can ditch tomorrow morning and turn the journal over to the police then."

Albert shouldered her aside and lifted the sash. He wasn't sure about Olivia's plan, and even now the weight of Lily's journal was almost more responsibility than he could bear. He wasn't eager to argue with her, either. Suddenly it was all too much, and he was afraid that if he pushed her, even just a little, they might both break. All he could say was, "I guess I can't think of anything better."

"You really are an idiot, you know that? You do know who Phil, is, right?"

Albert was confused. "What?"

"Phil *Andersen*. Perry's workout buddy and best friend. As in, *Detective* Andersen, the guy who is investigating Lily's case."

A light was beginning to dawn. "Ah."

"So we have to be careful and do this right, because Perry has Andersen's ear."

Albert swung one leg out the window, bending awkwardly at the middle. "You have my number?"

Olivia gestured toward a small, silver feather-rimmed bulletin board hanging next to the mirror. Her voice was too calm, too steady. "It's tacked up over there. Cell phone?"

Embarrassed, he shook his head. "Nah. My parents won't let me get one. But don't worry—when the phone rings, I'll pick it up. Just don't forget to call."

"I won't," she said, and pushed him the rest of the way out the window. As he darted around the side of the house toward the back he thought he heard the wet rasp of a sob, right before the window sash thudded shut behind him.

The sound of that lonely, angry cry echoing in his ears was like a sharp kick. He could hardly stand the sound of it.

Now he was across the back yard and in the alley, where he could cut across to the road and then home. Albert picked up his pace, his long legs covering the ground at not quite a run.

Olivia's sob still rattled in his head—a surprise from a girl he'd already come to view as brittle, sarcastic, and tough. Though he'd formed this impression in a very short time, he'd thought he had her pegged. Then it occurred to him that in the few months he'd known Lily, he hadn't seen her cry, not really. She was quick to laugh, loud, energetic... and tough.

When Lily cried—as the droplet stains on the pages of her journal told him she had—had it been anything, Albert wondered, like that angry, reluctant sound her sister made?

How long had these memories been threatening to

surface? How long had the situation with Kogen been simmering before whatever happened between them, on the night Lily left, sent her running? And why, Albert asked himself, hadn't he noticed anything *wrong*? He really couldn't remember anything that seemed strange. Either Lily was very good at hiding it, or he had been unforgivably blind. He suspected there was something he should have seen, and this made him really pathetic as a boyfriend.

The only thing he could do about it was stop being a dumbass and try to help her now that he *did* know.

Even as he promised himself he would be a man of action instead of a boy of angst, a picture of Lily crept into his head and refused to be pushed away. He saw her crying in her sleep, half-buried memories surfacing as nightmares, not knowing exactly what had happened to her but knowing it was bad; he saw her paralyzed with guilt and fear, retreating, wounded, from the memory her brain was trying to recover.

But he was done being lost and powerless and stupid. Now, he had what the adults—his parents, Lily's parents, their teachers, the cops—didn't have: the key to the puzzle. He only had to deliver it safely, and Olivia Odilon would help him make that happen. Then Kogen would be locked up and Lily could safely come home.

It was funny how both devastation and hope could come at the same time in the same afternoon. When Lily had first slipped away, it had been impossible for Albert to understand *why*, but now he had more of the story, including the identity of the villain, and he planned to take a hangman's pleasure in bringing Kogen down before he could hurt Lily again. Cook the bastard's goose.

It was a phrase Albert's mother used—usually a gleeful "his goose is cooked!" as the family car passed another car getting pulled over, or when a contestant hit "bankrupt" on *Wheel of Fortune*. As when watching the *Wheel*, Albert found the phrase totally square. Yet it was a phrase stuck in his vocabulary, maybe because he'd heard it a million times over the last seventeen years. When it popped into his head, it was in his mother's voice. Square or not, the mental picture was a satisfying one: Kogen's face turning tomato-red, popping beads of sweat and then big, wet blisters, as he sat stewing, cartoon-style, in a big pot of boiling water.

"Hello there, Albert." A pleasant voice got Albert's attention. "Got a minute?"

By now Albert was a few blocks from Lily's house. He was so intent on picturing Kogen's slow, torturous death as he walked along the curb, teetering between people's lawns and the gutter, that he didn't hear the low hum of the expensive import car that pulled up alongside him.

Startled, he looked up to see Kogen, steering his car at about three miles per hour and leaning on his elbow out the open window. It was as if just thinking about the guy had brought him forth, like Satan. Looking at him smiling from the window, Albert found it extra offensive that this creep looked so ... *harmless*. Friendly, even. He was like some handsome, middle-aged catalog model.

"Did I startle you?" The guy laughed, as if reading Albert's mind.

"Yeah, actually," Albert replied, possibly a bit sharper than was wise. Trying to dial back the hostility, he added, "What's up, Dr. Kogen?"

The smile stayed on Kogen's lips. "Give you a ride somewhere?"

"No thank you. But thanks." Albert walked a little faster.

Kogen steered closer to the curb, forcing Albert into someone's juniper bush. He stopped the car. "Come over here, then, and let's chat a minute."

Albert picked himself out of the bush and stood at Kogen's open window. The journal—Lily's journal—was still nestled awkwardly in his waistband, its spine poking into his spine right at the small of his back. It felt like a little dagger back there. As he began to sweat, Albert was sure the journal was sending out some sonar or radar or magnetic resonance that Kogen would pick up on.

"You seem like a stand-up fella, Albert, despite rumors around town to the contrary. But I'm curious: what were you doing this afternoon in my daughter's room with my other daughter?"

Albert gaped at him, surprised. He spluttered for some appropriate response.

"I only ask because she seemed upset. What did you do to her?"

"I didn't do anything to her! And we weren't doing anything, either. We were just talking."

"Talking." Kogen repeated the word as if it tasted sour. By now the smile was gone from his mouth, too, and suddenly he was the catalog guy no more; now he was getting down to some business.

"We're friends," Albert said. It wasn't really true, but the truth—the real nature of their (non)relationship—was nothing he could tell this guy. He almost added, *Got any more dumb questions?* but instead managed to spit out a terse, "Anything else?"

"There is, actually," Kogen said. He opened his car door and got out, a trail of leather upholstery smell coming with him. He stood very close to Albert. Though Albert was taller, Kogen had presence.

Now Albert was seriously alarmed. He was losing his sense of the situation and wondered if perhaps they'd at last arrived at the place where Kogen had been directing this conversation all along. Albert refused to prompt him, determined to wait for Kogen to say whatever he had to say on his own.

"I don't think you're being quite truthful with me. I'd really like to know what you were doing in my house. *My* house. Invited, were you?"

"What?"

"Did your friend Olivia invite you over?" Kogen studied Albert's face, and whatever he saw made him smirk. "Don't bother lying. I heard part of your conversation, and I'm pretty sure you know something about where Lily might be."

"You're wrong," Albert told him, wondering exactly what Kogen had heard or if he was bluffing.

Kogen went on as if Albert hadn't spoken. "So, I followed you. And here we are." He spread his hands.

"Guess you wasted your time, then," Albert said. He wondered if the man was going to hit him or something. "I have nothing to tell you. I don't know anything."

Kogen stepped closer. They were now nose-to-nose. Albert rocked his body forward just barely, determined not to give any ground.

"Don't you?" Kogen asked. Albert could smell the mint he'd probably just eaten.

"Well," Albert said, dropping his voice and forcing Lily's stepfather to strain to catch his words, "I do know *one* thing. And there's not a hell of a lot you can do about *that*, is there? You see, I *know*, you got it? And soon, so will *everyone*."

Kogen's eyes were dead. Albert really expected the guy to take a swing at him now. But Kogen's fists stayed down, even though they were white-knuckled. "Tell me what you *think* you know, and tell me where my goddamn daughter is."

"*Step*daughter."

"I don't make that distinction."

"You have a funny way of showing it." Albert reached behind his back and skimmed a hand over the book under his shirt for courage.

Kogen changed his approach. "You've been seeing Lily for a couple of months now, haven't you? So you must be aware that the poor girl isn't quite right up here." He pointed at his own head. "She is, in fact, quite troubled. Well before the accident that caused her head injury—the accident she had at my clinic with a bunch of her delinquent friends where they almost burned the place down. Everyone knows I was a victim there. Being a stepparent is a thankless job, sometimes."

"Don't you *dare*—"

Kogen held up a hand. "Can we talk reasonably? Think about how things look—which is what matters. I don't think the police are going to look favorably on my delinquent stepdaughter's delinquent boyfriend breaking into *my* house to cause this family more trouble in an already difficult time. You're already looking pretty bad in their eyes, *mi amigo*. Whatever you think you know doesn't matter. Nobody is going to believe anything you say, being some nobody punk kid, while I'm a somebody with plenty of friends in high places. As for Lily... she has been a wild, unpredictable embarrassment to both her mother and myself. *Any* accusation, even if the little runaway turned up to make it herself, would look like the horrible girl was trying to cause her poor family even more grief." He paused to let it sink in. "Do you get the position you're in?"

"I know exactly how things stand. I'm not sure you do. Let's wait and see who's right, yeah?"

Kogen jabbed a finger into the middle of Albert's chest. "Drop it, or I'm going to make your life unbearable. And I can." He reached into the interior pocket of his jacket and Albert flinched, until he saw that Kogen held a cell phone.

"Maybe I'll just call the cops right now and report a break-in. Twenty dollars missing off my kitchen table."

Albert thought he was bluffing. He wished the guy would just do it ... Olivia would back him up anyway. They could lay all their cards out right now. "Go ahead."

"Show me what you're hiding," Kogen said suddenly, grabbing Albert by the forearms. He lowered his voice. "I know you took something."

"Albert Luis Morales!"

Albert heard his name, called in a furious bellow, even before he heard the growl of his mother's beat-up old Ford as it rattled up behind Kogen's sweet ride. His arms were suddenly free and Kogen backed up a pace. Albert's mother's face was furiously peering through the windshield, but he was still glad to see it under the circumstances. She was motioning for him to come to the car. He did. To his dismay, Kogen followed him.

"Where have you *been*?" she demanded once Albert was within scolding range. "The school called me at work to ask why you weren't there today. I had to take time off and I've been driving around looking for you for over an hour!"

Albert's heart sank. "Mom, I—"

She plowed on, really working up a head of steam, "And now I find you out on the street bothering Dr. Kogen!"

Kogen stepped in. "Really, Mrs. Morales, it's fine. We're just having a chat."

Struggling to control her rage at Albert, his mother said, "I'm so sorry if he's done anything distressing. My son is a good boy, but this thing with your daughter—well, you understand. We're all upset about it."

"Please don't waste a moment worrying on my account. Lily has a lot of problems and I think her association with your boy hasn't necessarily been the best for him, in terms of influence."

Albert's mother actually blushed. "She's a lovely girl … I mean, I don't want to speak ill …"

She would have continued sputtering if Kogen hadn't added, "But I think Albert and I understand each other now, don't we, Albert?"

"Go to hell," Albert muttered.

"Albert! That's *it*—get in the car. *Now*. We're going home."

Albert thought about dropping the dime on Kogen right then and there. His mother was so pissed at him right now, though, that if she found out he had skipped school to sneak into the man's house, poke around, and actually steal something too, the last thing she would do before her head actually exploded would be to make Albert turn over Lily's journal, sight unseen, apologizing for Albert's behavior as she did.

"No," he said, letting this vivid picture dissipated. "I feel like walking." He was too close to cornering Kogen to risk it now. He could wait a few hours, take a bit more screaming from his mother. It would be worth it.

He turned on his heel and walked past Kogen, though not without a hard shoulder bump. In a low voice just for

Kogen, he muttered, "Stay away from me unless you want to get hurt."

Lily's stepfather gave him a hard clap on the back as he walked away and said in an equally low voice, "You've started a war you can't win."

But Albert wasn't so sure. Leaving both Kogen and his mother behind, he set off once more toward home, balancing his steps on the curb with a calm he didn't really feel and a confidence that was at least half bluster. He was aware of his mother's car a little ways behind him, where it stayed all the way home. He wasn't looking forward to the next few hours and trying to explain himself to his parents. He'd had to do a lot of that lately, and they were definitely as tired of it as he was. Though he suspected that it wouldn't dampen his mother's enthusiasm for yelling—she had to be fuming as she chugged along behind him at five miles per hour—nor his father's for using the words "unbelievable" and "dink."

It was all too much, and threatened to overwhelm him. His life these days sucked worse than he ever would have believed. But the spine of Lily's journal was still poking him in the small of the back, reminding him what was at stake. And that was something.

Fourteen

1 a.m.

*A*lbert might be the one whose strength is almost tapped by something as stupid as an asthma attack, but Olivia is the first to drain to zero.

"Let's stop a minute," she says when they arrive in the town. They drop themselves onto a bench in the cove of a bus shelter. The best they can say about it as a resting place is that it's dry, at least, and out of the wind. That's good enough for Olivia. Within a few moments of what's supposed to be a short break, she's slumped against Albert, deep in sleep.

He looks down at her upturned face, smashed into his shoulder. Snores and humid breath come from the open hole of her mouth. Placing a hand under her cheek, he lowers her down to the bench while scooting himself out from under her weight. She stirs a bit and tucks her feet up onto the bench, but she doesn't wake up.

Albert is very tired, too, but sleep is about as far away as Antarctica. Watching Olivia drop off like a little kid, he envies her the ability to do that. At least one of them is getting some rest.

Maybe it's because he's tired, or maybe it's an effect of constant worry, but when Albert closes his eyes he can see himself floating up above the bus shelter. He looks down and he sees himself and Olivia below. With their frizzled heads and rounded shoulders they look small and ridiculous, and definitely not what anyone would hope for when expecting the rescue to come riding in. They are just two teenagers slumped on a bench in the middle of the night, far from where they were going and still farther from home.

Albert opens his eyes, and he is himself again. Pathetic.

For a few minutes he lets himself just wallow in his misery. His legs bounce up and down in a jerky, nervous rhythm, and he has that speed-freak adrenaline that surges on the strangely alert other side of exhaustion. Unable to take it any longer, he stands up, and Olivia slumps farther down the bench as he does.

"I'm just going to take a walk up the block and back," he says to her even though she's now asleep, totally beyond the reach of his voice.

Albert has to move, that's all—he's too worked up to sit and watch Olivia sleep. If he just goes up the block and back he'll be able to keep his eye on the bus shelter the entire time, but still work off some of his nervous energy. He's afraid that if he doesn't move his legs will give out on him, like machinery pushed until their springs pop and the whole thing jams.

By this time of night, the town is shut down. Nothing seems to be open, and even the traffic light has gone from timed cycles of red and green to a steady, blinking yellow. Pacing the sidewalk in an unfamiliar town while the rest of the world sleeps, Albert is the loneliest he's ever been.

As he walks, his pace is purposely slow. There's just this block and back to go, and he isn't eager to burn through the only distraction he has while Olivia sleeps awhile. He doesn't have anything to read, not even one of those free newspapers that seem to litter the street until someone actually wants one. He passes a thrift shop storefront with bars on the windows and old manikins in the shadows, and then the front of a narrow Chinese restaurant. When he comes to an alleyway and peers down its dark opening, he sees that all the brick buildings are squatty behind their tall fake fronts. He passes a couple more windows, all of them dark, of course, and comes to the corner. Since there's no traffic, he's able to cross.

The other side of the street isn't much, either. Albert walks by a heavy wood door set back in its building, a neon sign reading *The Prospector* buzzing over the dark entryway. He pauses there a moment, thinking he can hear a faint hum of music from inside. It's a small sign of life that he savors for just a moment, even though he's hoping no one comes staggering out of the place while he's standing there like a dink. He glances toward the bus shelter to make sure Olivia is still fine.

He passes a few more lifeless plate-glass windows, whatever goods inside them completely invisible in the dark, until he comes to a bank of windows that aren't black. He didn't notice it before because the light inside is only a dim gloom. Looking up, he sees a sign that reads *The Rinse Cycle All-Nite Laundromat*. There are banks of molded plastic chairs all along the window, and also opposite the wall of stacked washers and the bank of dryers. The black and white tiled floor looks gray in the bluish gloom of the two fluorescent lights still shining far in the back, next to the vending machines.

The place isn't exactly appealing, but it's probably warm enough, and definitely better than a bus bench in February.

Albert presses his face against the glass and sees just one person in the place—an older guy wrapped in a long scarf and wearing a stocking cap. He looks like he's asleep, and Albert doesn't see any laundry basket near him.

Good enough. Time to retrieve Olivia and regroup somewhere warm.

A flicker and a glow from inside catch his eye, and Albert sees a high wall-mounted television to his left, in the front corner facing the dryers. Onscreen, a man and a woman are sitting behind a desk and he figures the local station is replaying the ten o'clock news. The camera focuses in tight on the woman, a picture-within-the-picture hovering over her left shoulder. There are two still photos in the box next to the woman's head. Albert sees the girl first, and she looks familiar. Next to the photo of the girl, he sees himself, a picture cropped from a framed snapshot of him and his father.

Olivia Odilon and Albert Morales, their pictures right up there on the TV in the all-night laundromat.

He can't read the newswoman's lips and there's no caption under the pictures. And while he should've known people would be looking for them—not the least of which, the police—seeing their likenesses like that is badly startling.

As he stares through the window at the TV screen, Albert has a sudden uncomfortable feeling that someone is right behind him. He whirls around, half-expecting someone to point from the television to him and back and yell for the police to come arrest the fugitive. But when he turns there's no one there, not even a burger wrapper fluttering in the gutter. He is just as alone as he'd been a few minutes before.

Quite jumpy now, Albert hurries away from the laundromat window and cuts a diagonal across the wide street between him and Olivia, a sudden superstitious dread driving him to hurry back to her.

Fifteen

"Get your butt in your room and don't come out until I tell you to."

His mother's command drilled into Albert's back as she followed him through the kitchen door once they'd arrive home—him getting there on foot, her just behind him in the car. When she spoke, her voice was cold. His mother was a no-nonsense type of woman, and although once in a great while she could be surprisingly cool about things, this was not one of those times.

"I've just about had it with you," she said, slamming a cupboard.

Her tone was disgusted, something Albert had gotten used to the past four or five years. When his mother was like this—not just her regular exasperated bluster, but truly pissed off—her eyes became narrow lasers shooting out from under furrowed eyebrows, and her lips were pinched almost out of existence. Then there was her voice. Even though she'd quit smoking two years ago (it was an excruciating couple of months for Albert and his father), her voice still turned sandpapery when she was bitching someone out. Right now she was too angry to hit him with a lecture, but Albert knew that wouldn't last.

Let her be mad, he thought. He was mad at her, too. Tired of her never giving him the benefit of the doubt, and the nagging. He glanced over his shoulder, his glare enough to bore a hole into his mother's back. As if she could feel it, she whirled around and caught his eye. Her expression was poisonous, like she was trying to vaporize him with it. He dropped his gaze first.

"I'm sorry," Albert finally said, taking the safest approach he could think of. There was a lot more he wanted to say; he wanted to yell at her, and the desire to explain himself, to show her she was wrong, was almost unbearable. But he didn't know *how.* They stared at each other—him waiting, her watching, that one muscle under her left eye twitching. He couldn't really do anything with the journal poking him in the small of the back. He had to hold it all in just a bit longer.

"Yeah, you're sorry." His mother reached into a low cupboard and pulled out a frying pan, slamming it onto the stove. "I don't care. In barely more than a week you've been sorry for sneaking out of the house, *sorry* you were pulled out of class for police questioning, for god's sake— and sorry *now* for skipping school."

No, now was definitely not the time to add breaking

and entering to the list of complaints she had against him. He was stunned by what he'd learned today, and by the nasty meeting he'd had with Kogen on the street.

"*Sorry* isn't doing your father and me much good, is it? Not doing you any good, either. When you just keep screwing up anyway? But don't worry, we'll definitely discuss it further when your father gets home from work." Now she was rummaging violently in the fridge. "We've already grounded you, but apparently that's about as useful as your *sorry*."

While her back was turned, Albert started toward the hallway and his bedroom, remembering that she'd originally commanded him to get out of her sight.

"Hold it," she said. He stopped and turned around to see her glaring at him, a package of bloody hamburger oozing in her one upraised hand. "On second thought, I heard a mouse in the basement this morning. Make yourself useful and go get the mousetraps from the garage and set them around down there."

Chores as a prelude to punishment—familiar territory. This one was pretty weak, but it was the middle of February and there weren't any hedges to trim or gutters to be degunked. Though he wouldn't admit it to her, Albert was actually glad to have something to do besides wait in his room for whatever real punishment his parents chose to hand down.

"Can I change my shoes first?" he asked. It was a stupid question, especially since he was only going to the basement, but his mother only rolled her eyes and went back to terrorizing the hamburger. Albert took this for a yes and hurried across the house to his bedroom.

Figuring he only had a few moments before his mother couldn't stand it any longer and came after him to yell a bit more, he pulled Lily's diary from his waistband and looked around for a place to put it.

He felt a pressure to hurry that made him panicky, and he settled for slipping the little book under the pillow of his unmade bed. He wished he didn't have to hide the journal right now, that instead he could just show it to his parents so they could help him. But his mother was so *mad*, and when his father got home, he'd yell at Albert, too, and there'd be a whole lot more of the yelling when he had to explain *how* he got the journal. It would be forever until they calmed down enough to listen to him. And even then, even if they would consent to just *look* at the thing, they would probably think Lily was a liar. "Troubled," as Kogen had said to Albert's mother.

Pulling the covers up a little on the bed, he thought, *screw 'em, then*. His parents could read about Kogen's arrest in the local paper like everyone else. He wouldn't bother them until it was all settled—after he and Olivia had taken the journal to the police as evidence of what had really happened. If the cops believed it, his parents would have to, too.

It was a good thing he'd hidden the diary immediately, because he didn't even have both shoes off before his mother came stomping down the hall to yell at him more. He jumped off his bed, slid his feet into a pair of dorky clogs he'd gotten for Christmas, and left his bedroom. He shut the door tight behind him.

After grabbing the peanut butter and a plastic knife from the kitchen, then the box of traps (after some searching) from the shelf in the garage, Albert hustled downstairs to his chore. As he was baiting the traps and setting them in all the corners around the three rooms of the basement, he tried not to think about the cute little creatures getting themselves squashed by the spring lever when they tried for the peanut-buttery goodness.

He set a loaded trap in the corner behind the water heater. At least these spring-loaded things killed them quickly.

Beyond the furnace and water heater was the back room where his family kept old stuff they couldn't bear to throw away. This was stuff they'd brought here over hundreds of miles. Besides the unmarked cardboard boxes, his dead grandmother's old canning jars, Christmas decorations, a rusty exercise bike, and several pairs of Luis Morales' worn-out work boots, there were several boxes marked *Albert* on a low shelf behind the door. There was *Albert: Schoolwork*, *Albert: Toys* and even *Albert: Baby Clothes*, all written on the boxes with black permanent marker in Vanessa Morales' tight block printing. His mother refused to get rid of the remains of his childhood junk, and the older he got, the more she seemed ready to bring his old Legos and OshKosh overalls upstairs and put Albert down in the basement in a box marked *Albert: Not So Cute Anymore*.

The shock and hostility of the day had drained Albert's

energy, and he slowly crossed to the fruit room at the other end of the basement to set the last mousetrap. Any rodents looking for a snack would get a spring-loaded metal bar through the head instead.

When mice got into their old house a few years ago, his father had bought glue traps, but it had been too horrible. Though it was more humane in theory, in reality, watching the mice—there had been four that time—struggling and slowly dying in the gluey mess was deeply depressing to the eleven-year-old Albert.

He felt like he was wriggling in a giant glue-trap himself now, some awful place between childhood and adulthood. His parents treated him like a little kid. And when he was around them, he felt like one. When he was with Lily, he felt like a real person. She knew nothing about what he used to be like, and she didn't need to know what he was supposed to become. She just took him as he was, as he took her. That she was wrapped up in something worse than he could have imagined didn't change the way Albert felt about her—didn't change the fact that life seemed exciting and somehow open when they were together.

He wanted to save her.

He wanted to save her, because that would prove he loved her better than anyone, prove he was worthy of her love.

He would never admit it, though. It was stupid and desperate. He sat on the bottom step, sighing hard.

As Albert finally stood to shuffle up the stairs, his mother appeared at the top, about to shout that he should wash up for dinner. Next to her was his father, just home from work. *Goodie.* Albert dared a look at his father's face, trying to guess how bad his father's mood was after learning about Albert's latest dumb move.

Blank-faced, his father reached out as he walked past and flicked him on the forehead with one thick, callused finger. He said, "You're on your third strike, boy."

Stars in front of his eyes, Albert slumped and looked down at his feet. It felt like there was a mountain of crap threatening to bury him and this was just another shovelful. The mountain menaced from every direction—Lily's disappearance and her terrible secret...the police...his parents...Kogen, too, who was a double problem. Not only was Kogen a danger to Lily and the cause of everything, but he was suspicious of Albert, too. To what degree, Albert wasn't sure—another problem. And of course, if Kogen somehow knew that Albert had taken something from Lily's room because of the conversation he'd overheard, then he must be suspicious of Olivia as well—which put her in danger.

Thwump. Albert could almost feel the dull thud of another load of crap falling on him. He splashed his face with cold water from the bathroom faucet and went to face his parents in the dining room.

Dinner was painful, as he'd known it would be. His parents dropped a tag-team attack on him. The whole meal was an unrelenting barrage of

"—respect our rules as long as you're living under—"

"—don't keep up in school, you'll never get into a good—"

"—think you're in love, but—"

"—have to take care of yourself—"

"—throw your life away for the first girl you—"

Albert knew better than to interrupt either of his parents, so he had to act like he was listening and apologetic for all the trouble he'd been in lately, while eating a plate of spaghetti—two tasks that were actually kind of hard to do at the same time. A constant chorus of *this sucks* marched through his brain while he was sitting there.

"I just don't understand," his mother was saying. He looked up from his plate and saw that she'd put down her fork and was glaring at him. "I thought you were really back on track—you haven't been in any trouble since we moved here. I thought last year's screw-up was firmly in the past."

Albert flinched. He'd known this was going to come up eventually. It had been over a year since he'd gotten into trouble with Chris and Danny and those guys, that weekend they all went upstate without telling their parents. Jake's uncle—the guy they'd boosted the car from—decided not to press charges, so at least he hadn't actually been arrested. Albert really didn't know they didn't have permission to use the car (though his parents never believed that), but still, he'd known it was dumb when they were doing it. He just hadn't cared enough to let that stop him. He'd been paying for that weekend ever since. His parents still wouldn't let him get his own car or a cell phone, and they didn't like to let him go out. Even though he'd kept in line—which was pretty easy to do after they'd moved away—he couldn't get their trust back.

They weren't likely to loosen his leash even an inch now that all this Lily stuff was happening. The fact that he'd sneaked out—although just to see Lily, not to commit some crime—had made them pull the leash even tighter. It was like it proved their distrust of him was completely justified. He didn't know how to tell them he wasn't headed for some kind of criminal life; he could see flashbacks to that stupid weekend in his parents' eyes now, and he knew they weren't likely to trust him again anytime soon.

"…she hasn't been good for you."

Albert dropped his fork and it clattered loudly on his plate. "Just shut up about Lily, okay? Honestly, I can't believe you're talking about her like then when she—" He was talking too loud and too fast. "Did it ever occur to you that it's not Lily? That I just realized that my big goal in life isn't to keep you happy?"

"You're seventeen," his father said. "You don't know what your goal in life is, or what it ought to be. That's why we worry, and why we push, and why we can't let you let some girl screw it all up."

"Bullshit," Albert said. Dropping a swearword at the table was definitely on his father's shortlist of unacceptable dinner conversation, but Albert had become too angry to care.

"Albert! Apologize to your father right now!"

"Forget it, Vanessa," his father said. He stood up, pushed

his chair abruptly back, and began clearing the table. To his son he said quietly, "I don't know what's happening to you."

"May I be excused?" Albert asked. He didn't know what was happening to him either, but whatever it was, he didn't think he could stop it now.

"Just go," said his mother wearily. "I don't know what to do anymore. I'm not even sure how to punish you."

Albert pushed his chair back. "Yeah, it's kind of tough when I already don't have a car or a cell phone, my girl-friend is missing, and the police are keeping tabs on me better than you are, isn't it?"

"If you want a car, then save your money and buy one!"

"You won't let me get a job, either!" The complaint came out like a reflex even though they weren't fighting about whether Albert should have a car. He just couldn't help himself.

Before this stupid side argument could grow, Albert's father called from the kitchen, "Stop it, both of you! Albert, just go to your room!" As he fled the dining room, Albert wondered why he always found a way to make a bad situation worse.

Then he was closing the door to his bedroom, and his eyes found the lump of his pillow under the rumpled bedcovers. Lily's journal was under there, calling to him, reminding him of his responsibility to her.

I can't get away.

He felt like there was an imaginary string stretched

between him and Lily. Imaginary, but still real somehow. And the pressure pulling it was impossible to ignore.

At this point, he was past worrying about getting into trouble. He was tired of not doing anything. He had an impulse.

He made himself wait several minutes, then went to the door and cracked it carefully, listening. He could hear the hum of the TV from the front room. He opened the door a little wider, scanning the hallway. It was empty, so he opened it just wide enough to slip through. The cordless phone was hanging in its base on the wall a few feet from his door. As silently as possible, Albert grabbed the handset. The sound of his father's voice arrested him, but after a moment he realized that he hadn't been busted; the old man was just saying, "…was fifty out yesterday, but look, it's started snowing."

Exhaling his relief, Albert picked up a phone book, too, and slipped back into his room with the phone and the directory.

He pulled Lily's journal from under his pillow and looked at it. It was time to bury Kogen.

With a sudden rush of nerves that covered him in a light sweat and made his hands tremble, Albert dialed the police station's main number from the phone book. His heart beat harder with every electronic ring. He couldn't quite wrap his mind around the size of what he was doing, and how many lives would be changed by it. He hoped this was what Lily would want him to do. And he hoped they cuffed Perry the Perv's wrists nice and tight when they arrested him.

"..."

Albert realized someone had picked up on the other end. He said softly, "Is Detective Andersen there? Phil Andersen?"

"Sir," said the clearly irritated female voice on the other end of the phone, "speak up. *Who* do you want?"

Albert swallowed and said a bit louder, "Detective Phil Andersen."

"Hold on." There was an abrupt click and then there was Lionel Richie singing the hold music. Not the Muzak version, either. After several bars, there was another abrupt click cutting off the music and the voice said, "The detective isn't in."

"What about..." Albert struggled to remember the other cop's name. "Officer Demiola. Is he there?"

"He's not on tonight. You want to leave a message for one of them?"

"When will Detective Andersen be in?" Albert asked, as loudly as he dared.

"Hold on." There was another, shorter, click-music-click transition, then, "Should be here at eight."

Albert looked at his clock radio on the desk; it was just after seven. "No message. I have something kind of important to ... I'll just come in and talk to him in person."

"Suit yourself."

Now, if Olivia would just call and he could figure out a way to sneak out of the house, they could go down to the police station tonight and finish what he'd just started with the phone call. Tonight.

No sooner had he set down the phone than there were three loud, hard knocks to his bedroom door. His heart jerked painfully at the abrupt interruption.

The door opened and his mother poked her head through. "You have a guest out here." She was gone again as soon as she said it.

Albert glanced at the pile in the middle of his bed—the phone, the directory covering the journal—and was glad his mother hadn't noticed it. But in the next moment his relief was gone, because he knew who his "guest" had to be: Kogen.

It was becoming clear to Albert just how much he was afraid of this man. The memory of Kogen's vague threats, and even more, the calculating look on his face, terrified him. Kogen's expression had been a mix of cold hate under a layer of smugness; it was a face that said, "I'm not worried—I always get my way."

Albert had a feeling that he was about to be steamrolled by an older, more powerful, and smarter enemy. Hastily, he pushed the pile up to the head of the bed and pulled his pillow over it, then went out to face Kogen with very little hope.

When he reached the living room Albert saw three people standing there awkwardly, all of them waiting for him. His parents stood on either side of a third guy, but the guy wasn't Lily and Olivia's stepfather. Albert found himself looking into the vaguely familiar face of a guy in a clichéd small-town high school letterman's jacket and wearing a nervous look on his face. The guy's gaze darted around the Morales' living room, and when it landed on Albert, bounced off again. Trying to figure out what Patrick MacLennan was doing at his house, Albert waited for him to speak; meanwhile, his parents were looking expectantly at Albert.

"Sorry to bug you," the guy finally said. "But you're in my chemistry class and I..." He stopped. "I wondered if you had the reading assignment for the test tomorrow? Somebody said Mrs. Yost gave us chapters last week, but I wasn't there."

"Um..." Albert said. "We're in the same chemistry class?"

"I miss a lot of class during basketball season. And baseball. And football."

"Oh," said Albert. He looked over at his parents, waiting for them to either excuse themselves or tell MacLennan to leave because Widdle Albert was grounded. But they just smiled stiffly, kind of confused, and stood there, the both of them. "Isn't there anyone else you can ask? I've seen you with your friends in the lunchroom. Don't any of them go to chem class, either?"

MacLennan looked down at his scuffed sneakers. "Dude, some of my friends are jerks. They don't mean anything by it."

"Whatever," Albert said abruptly. It didn't make sense that this guy would have the stones to look up Albert's address, come over, and actually ask for *help* with his home-work. They were never going to be friends. Albert couldn't believe he was the only guy MacLennan could think of to ask, and he'd better not have come here to talk about Lily. He didn't say any of this, though—not in front of his parents.

"So, do you have the assignment?" MacLennan asked. "Can I look at your notes?"

The guy was definitely sweating. Albert didn't know what to say. He looked at his parents to see what *they* would say. One look and he could see that they were torn between the fact that they were still pretty pissed at Albert, and the fact that when there was a stranger in their living room they had to be civil. One of the core tenets of the Morales life strategy was that you never aired dirty laundry in front of company.

Albert's father, clearly not understanding what was happening between this kid and his son, said, "Well, go on, Albert. Take the boy to your room and give him the reading assignment."

"Come on," Albert said, gesturing for MacLennan to follow him to his room. Since getting rid of him would be difficult without embarrassing explanations, he decided to just give him what he wanted so he would leave. Time was passing quickly, and he still needed to figure out how he and Olivia were going to sneak out.

He left MacLennan standing in the middle of his room while he searched his desk for his stupid chemistry note-book, wondering if that was even the real reason the guy was here. When he found it, he flipped to Friday's notes and the reading assignment he hadn't even thought of doing, and handed the notebook to MacLennan. "That's it," he said. "Knock yourself out."

MacLennan grabbed a pen off Albert's desk and sat on the edge of his bed with the notebook in his lap. After a moment, and without even looking down at the notes, he said to Albert, "Hey, do you think you could get me a glass of water? My mouth is really dry." MacLennan cleared his throat as if to demonstrate how dry it was in there. He did look a little sick.

Albert didn't care. "Are you kidding? It will take you ten seconds to jot down the assignment. I'll even do it for you. And then you can get the hell out of here." The half-buried phone on his bed gave a ring and they both jumped. Someone picked up another extension after two rings.

MacLennan continued as if they hadn't been interrupted. "What's the big deal, dude? I told you before that I was sorry about... the thing in the lunchroom. We were messing around, that's all. It wasn't even my idea."

Even if he'd wanted to bother explaining, Albert didn't know how to tell the guy it wasn't the lunchroom thing. He just couldn't get past the fact that MacLennan, who had supposedly been Lily's friend, abandoned her the night of the accident. And *then* tried to act all tough-guy-protector about her in the lunchroom. As if MacLennan thought *he* was Lily's worried boyfriend, not Albert. As if MacLennan was actually doing anything to help her.

MacLennan smiled, and Albert guessed it was the same

supposedly charming grin he flashed at teachers when his homework was late. "It's just water."

"Is there something else you want to say to me?" Albert said. It seemed like MacLennan was angling at something and Albert thought maybe just asking him point-blank would surprise him into spitting out whatever it was. "I don't want to talk about her with you any more now than I did before."

But MacLennan just shook his head. They stared at each other, the energy in the room crackling.

"Albert." They both glanced at the door where Albert's mother was standing, her lips pursed. "There's a girl on the phone, says it's about an English assignment." Her tone was doubtful.

Not wanting to admit he had the portable phone in his room, Albert thought for a second. It had to be Olivia calling, in what was about the world's worst timing. "Um…" he said again. He looked at MacLennan. "Are you done yet?"

"No."

Now there were two people looking expectantly at him. Albert didn't know what else to do, so he reached into the pile and retrieved the portable phone. He figured he had no choice, even if it meant he'd be getting another lecture later.

His mother's eyes flashed. "Damn it, Albert." She jerked the receiver from his hand with catlike speed. "You know damn well 'grounded' means 'grounded from the phone,' too. You can take the call in the kitchen, and make it fast." She turned her glance to MacLennan, for a moment seeming to want to say more.

"It'll only take a second," Albert said, reaching to get the phone back.

"It will only take a second in the kitchen, then," his mother said, turning abruptly and taking the portable with her.

Albert knew there was no point arguing over which phone he could use. It would be faster just to get rid of Olivia. He didn't like to leave this jerk MacLennan alone in his bedroom—it creeped him out, actually—even if it was only for a minute.

"Be right back," he said finally, and MacLennan nodded without looking up from the chemistry notebook.

"This had better actually be about school," his mother said as he busted into the kitchen. "All of this had better be about school."

Albert ignored her and picked the phone up from where it rested on the counter, its cord hanging down like coiled rope. His mother made a big show of ignoring him and fussing with the dishwasher, but he knew better—she was eavesdropping, enforcing the whole grounded-from-the-phone policy.

"Hello?" he said, his voice coming out kind of breathless. He cleared his throat into the receiver.

"Gross," came Olivia's irritated voice on the other end. "Hey—I thought you were going to pick up the phone when I called? I had to make up some lie about homework."

"Yeah," Albert said. "I think I have my notes from *The*

Canterbury Tales. If I can find them, I'd be happy to lend them to you."

"Can't talk right now, huh?"

"Totally. Listen, can I just call you back after I find them?"

"Sure," Olivia said, "but don't call before nine, okay? Perry and my mom are watching TV in bed by then. Usually. Perry's acting weird tonight, really restless, and when he thinks I'm not looking he's been staring at me. He knows something. Or suspects something, anyway."

"He definitely *does*," Albert said, hoping she understood his meaning. "But there's nothing he can do about it right now? I think I brought my notes from class home—I'll call you back after I check." Without waiting for her reply, he disconnected and hurried back toward his bedroom. He was still expecting MacLennan to threaten him again about Lily.

Before he got there, he met MacLennan coming down the hall.

"Thanks, Allen," MacLennan said, holding up a piece of notebook paper with a few lines written on it. "You saved my ass."

"It's Albert."

"Right." MacLennan went straight to the door and paused for just a second before leaving the house. "Thanks again." Now that he had what he wanted, he seemed in a hurry to leave. That was fine with Albert.

Then it was just Albert and his parents alone again in the living room, and Albert's parents were back to their active and hostile ignoring. They stared at the television and made no comment as he went back to his room. Also fine by Albert.

The door to his room was wide open, and his chemistry notebook lay open in the middle of the bed. A heavy musky scent, probably MacLennan's aftershave, crawled up Albert's nose. He wasn't pleased to have the guy's smell lingering in his personal space. It was revolting. Waving the door a couple of times to drive away the odor, Albert gave up and shut his door instead. He sat down heavily, brushing the notebook to the floor and wondering how much time he would have to give his parents before trying to call Olivia back.

He reached under the pillow for Lily's journal. As his fingers searched but didn't find it, all the blood drained from Albert's face. He pushed the pillow away. The thick yellow phone directory was there, but the thing he cared about was gone.

He tore the bed apart, peeling away the cover and the sheets and reaching down to feel between the headboard and the wall, in case it had somehow fallen. Panicked now, he checked under the bed and under the mattress and pulled the bed a few inches away from the wall. Nothing.

It dawned on him what had to have happened, if not yet *why*.

Son of a bitch.

MacLennan had gone, and with him, Lily's notebook.

Sixteen

*T*he first time Lily asked Albert to sneak over to her house at night, he agreed without thinking about it first for even a moment.

After she'd asked and he'd said yes, she added, "Unless you'd rather I came to you?"

"No," he said quickly, picturing his family's small house and the extreme likelihood that his parents would bust them if she did. "I mean, how could I let you go sneaking around at night alone?"

"Then I'll see you tonight at my house, around twelve," she said, giving him a quick kiss on the corner of his mouth. "Come to the window and I'll let you in." Then they separated to go to their afternoon classes.

Albert had the rest of the long afternoon to daydream about Lily, and after school and during the even-longer evening he suffered through dinner, then prime-time TV, then waiting for his parents to finally go to bed. He also had time to think about the hundred things that could go wrong with the plan—that he might get caught by his parents sneaking out, or even worse, caught by Lily's parents in her room.

Then he thought about Lily again, and tried to imagine what it would be like to be alone with her in the dark of her bedroom, and the thought made him stop worrying about the rest.

As it turned out, sneaking out of his house was easy. His parents went to bed around ten-thirty, after the local news was over. After that, he gave them an hour—a tedious, watchful hour—to get to sleep before he slid open his window and slipped out of the house. No sirens or dogs or cries of alarm stopped him. There was just a sliver of moon and the shadows to watch him hurry out across the yard to the street.

Little Solace was a quiet town even during the day, something Albert had figured out about the place quickly. When he found he had the streets to himself, Albert relaxed a little. He still had a tight ball of nerves lodged somewhere between his heart and his lungs, pushing, and he had to force himself not to run all the way to Lily.

He was relieved to see that the windows of Lily's house were all dark. All of them except hers, he discovered when he cut around the dark yard to the back of the house. The shade was up and as he got closer, he could see the glow coming from the bedside and desk lamps. Lily was lying on her stomach, propped up on her elbows and facing the end of the bed, a book in front of her. Her bare feet kicked absently at the pillows as she read. Albert stood in the dark yard, leaning against the tall tree that shaded her room and watching her for a moment through the glass.

He was nervous as hell, standing out there all sweaty-palmed and cold, with an optimistic condom in his wallet. Lily, on the other hand, was calm and looked like a princess in a tower to Albert. He felt like he didn't belong in the scene. But for some reason she actually wanted him here, so here he was. After a moment, he left the cover of the tree and went to the window. He raised his hand to knock but before he could touch his knuckles to the glass, Lily looked up. Getting to her feet in one fluid motion, she put a finger to her lips as she came to the window. She lifted the sash and motioned him inside.

"It'll be fine as long as we keep our voices low," she said.

Albert climbed through the window and pulled it down softly behind himself. When he turned around, Lily put her arms around him and pulled him farther into the room.

"Brrr," she said, trying to peel his sweatshirt from his body. "The cold came in on your clothes." He helped her with the sweatshirt and her hands were pleasantly warm on his bare arms.

"I've been thinking about you all day," he said. "I wanted to bring you something nice, like flowers, but I didn't know where to get them this late and I was afraid they'd die before I got here, anyway."

"Who cares about flowers," she said. "I'm glad you came." She pulled the shade over the window, blocking out the night, and switched off the desk lamp. "What do you want to do?"

He sat on the edge of her bed but she stayed where she was, standing by her desk. "I want to kiss you."

"One track mind," she said. "How long can you stay?"

"As long as it's dark, my parents won't even know I left. Come here." He leaned forward and caught her wrists, pulling her closer.

She fell forward willingly, knocking them both back onto the bed in a pile. While she had him pinned, she took the first kiss. Then she reached over him toward the lamp.

"Don't," he said. "I want to look at you for a while."

She rolled away from him and sat up. "I don't want anyone to get up and see the light under the door." She reached up again to turn out the light.

Then Albert noticed a huge bruise on her wrist, one he hadn't noticed earlier that day. He put a hand on her shoulder to stop her for a moment. "How'd you get that?" he asked.

She looked down where he was looking and gave an embarrassed-sounding low laugh. "That's what happens when you take out your frustrations on a chair," she said.

Turning her arm over gently, Albert looked more closely at her wrist. The spot was a couple of inches wide and an ugly reddish-purple color, with a dark bluish knot at its center.

"Are you going to say anything more than that?" he asked.

"Can't we just talk about something more interesting? I thought we were going to make out," she said.

"I won't be able to think of anything else until you tell me how you got that thing."

"I told you; I punched a chair." She looked at the expression on his face and sighed. "It's just my stupid mother and her stupid husband. They piss me off sometimes, and since I can't punch them . . . well, you know. It's nothing."

"Why were you pissed at them?" He kicked off his shoes and leaned back against the mound of pillows at the headboard.

She curled up under his arm and rested her head on his chest. "They found out about a couple of classes I blew off, and the D I got on my last English paper—which, by the way, I totally could have done better on if I'd read the book. And so they were lecturing me, you know, teaming up in the kitchen, trading off lectures or whatever, and of course my sister was probably lurking in the hall enjoying the whole thing. So it was bad enough, but not more than I was expecting, you know? But then Perry starts yelling at me about my attitude. And he grabs my chin in his hand and his nose is this far"—she held up her thumb and forefinger with an inch of space between them—"from mine. And he says, 'You must like high school a lot, since you're going for a third try at your senior year.' And he laughed."

Picturing her parents, Albert felt a hot tingling in his face and neck.

Lily rubbed absently at her wrist, eyes alert and on Albert. "Your face is all red. Please don't get mad. I just want to forget about it." Now she did switch out the light, and this time Albert didn't object. The room went black.

Ignoring her, he said, "I can't believe he would say that, and that your mom would let him." He was trying to keep his voice down. "I'd like to squeeze his face, see how he likes it. Maybe I could make his jawbone crack."

Arms snaked around him and when he heard her voice again, it came from where her face was now cradled in the crook of his neck. Her breath was feathers against his skin. "She probably thinks they're helping me. And maybe she's right, at least a little."

Albert said nothing. Part of him knew there was some truth to what she said, but he didn't want to admit it. His anger at her parents was pure and he didn't want it complicated. Picturing her stepfather grabbing her face did the trick to keep it going. His arm tightened around her.

"I think I'm going to try harder," she said after a moment. "If only because I can't wait to get out of here."

He said, "I don't like anyone hurting you."

"But I'm the one that did it," she said.

"You know what I mean."

"I could take off now," she said. "I'm eighteen. Sometimes I think I should just clear out."

"Great idea. You can be a dropout. Or you can finish school, and then get as far away as you need to from these—"

"—assholes. Whatever."

"Just don't do anything stupid that you'll regret later." He knew how he sounded, but he didn't know what else to say. Of course he didn't want her to leave.

She sighed. "I didn't ask you to come over to talk about my stupid problems."

"Then why did you ask me to come over?" he asked.

"I'll show you."

And she did, and Albert forgot about his anger and his worry as little starbursts of pleasure went off in his head.

Seventeen

By the time Albert realized, sickly, what had happened, MacLennan was long gone in his truck and Albert was stuck pursuing him on foot. As he hurried frantically down the dark pavement toward MacLennan's house, he realized two things.

First, that ever since this mess with Lily started—about the time the police started to pretty much accuse him of doing something to her—he'd wanted to punch someone. After he'd found Lily's journal and had a run-in first with Kogen and then with his mother, that desire had only gotten stronger.

And second, he was planning on finally taking a swing at someone as soon as he had that bastard MacLennan's face in front of him. When his knuckles connected with MacLennan's nose and turned it to hamburger, it was going to be the sweetest moment of his life. He was too pissed to worry anymore about the exact reason why MacLennan thought he'd had to butt in. As long as he recovered Lily's journal and smashed MacLennan one, Albert was going to be satisfied.

Then after that, Albert planned to go straight to the police station. He wouldn't stop until he forced Lily's journal into Andersen's hands and it was officially evidence in the case.

When he was still standing in his bedroom, right after MacLennan had left, the first thing Albert experienced— after the initial shock of discovering the journal was gone— was blind and complete panic. It was all he could do not to scream once he was sure it was really gone.

He couldn't wrap his mind around it: this guy he hardly knew showed up out of the blue and took the most important thing he had, but why? What did he think Albert was planning to do with the journal except turn it over to the cops? And how the hell had he known Albert *had* it? He couldn't understand what MacLennan thought he was doing.

The only thing that *was* clear to Albert was that he had to confront MacLennan and he had to do it immediately. All that mattered was getting that book back and getting it to the cops. He cursed himself for losing Lily's journal—no matter how it had happened—in the first place.

But he couldn't get to MacLennan unless he could get out of the house first, and he couldn't leave unless he could sneak past his parents. And though he was willing to find out if it came down to it, Albert was pretty sure his father was still strong enough to restrain him physically. So leaving by the front door when they were in the living room, or even by the kitchen door, since he had to pass through the living room to get to it, was out. That left the old standby, the bedroom window.

Pulling on a heavy sweatshirt, Albert crept out of his room and down the hall to check on his parents. He hung back far enough to stay hidden. He heard a laugh track from the TV and, over that, the sound of his parents' voices. They were settled in, Albert decided, so he could make his exit and they wouldn't know he'd gone. That was no guarantee they wouldn't lift the silent treatment, come to his room to continue lecturing, and find him gone, but he could think about that later. Satisfied enough, he back-tracked to his bedroom.

His mind racing, Albert opened a dresser drawer and scooped the contents into his arms. He lumped the pile of clothes under his bedcovers in what he hoped was the shape of his body. As he examined his work, he decided that stuffing his bed was kind of an obvious move, but this was the best he could do. He didn't have time to make it perfect.

Albert turned off the light. Leaning, tense, against the windowsill, he took a deep breath, then flipped the lock on the window and lifted the sash, wincing at the squeaky groan the glass made. He stuck a leg through the opening and dropped to the ground, landing with a frosty crunch on the grass. Then he reached up and pulled the window closed behind him as quietly as he could.

Now Albert was hurrying away from his own house toward MacLennan's, with a page ripped from the phone book in the pocket of his jeans. There were only two MacLennans listed, and only one of them in Little Solace. He couldn't be sure that the address was the right one, or that MacLennan had actually gone home, but he was hopeful—if only because it seemed like it was about time he caught a break. His lungs ached from panting in cold air but he barely noticed, only enough to hope his mild asthma wouldn't choose now to pop up.

The address from the phone book was on Holly Street, right next to the community college and probably at least a mile from Albert's house, so he had some time to think as he half walked, half ran through the dark. His thoughts wavered between fantasizing about kicking Patrick MacLennan's ass and worrying about what might go wrong when he got to Holly Street.

A couple blocks from his destination, Albert slowed from a run to a jog and from a jog to a walk. Now that he was nearly there, he wasn't sure what he was actually going to do. His breath came out in harsh gusts, a ghostly vapor in the streetlight. It hit him—a dull, surprising blow like an elbow to the forehead—that he could have saved a lot of time and effort if he'd just taken an extra couple minutes to get his bicycle. It was frustrating to think that once again he'd screwed up by missing the most obvious thing.

The realization didn't do much for his belief that he might actually be able to help Lily instead of making everything worse.

The light snow had stopped. He left the street and stepped onto the uneven sidewalks of this older part of town. His mind grasped for a plan as he drew closer to MacLennan's house. Shoving his hands into his pockets, he tried to walk as if he belonged on this street. He scanned the house numbers in the dark until he saw the one he wanted. Two doors away, he stooped down to tie his shoe, buying himself a moment to think. He couldn't just stand out here and stare without drawing the attention of someone who belonged in this neighborhood and knew that he didn't.

Finally Albert straightened up, having untied and tied the same shoelace a ridiculous number of times. He'd been in a major hurry to get here, but now he was stalled out before the actual confrontation. *Just go*, said the furious voice in his head. *Go bang on the door until MacLennan comes out... tell him to give it back*. Heart pumping hard, he held on to his anger, willing it to suffocate any fear he felt over the stand he was about to make.

MacLennan's house was an old two-story, and even in the dark, from across the street, Albert could see that it was a run-down place with flaking paint and a seedy yard. The lights were off on the first floor even though it was early, and there was a mini-pickup in the driveway. Patrick MacLennan's pickup, Albert was sure—he'd seen this same yellow truck with its teal racing stripe in the parking lot at school.

There was nothing to do but go up to the house and knock. And if that didn't work, he would pound on the door until MacLennan came out.

Albert was not a naturally confrontational person. Most of the time he preferred to fade into the background, unnoticed. That's just how he was built. But nothing in the past few days had been normal, so his stepping out of character—skipping school, breaking into someone's house, sneaking out to face a thief—made a weird kind of sense. But he wasn't thinking about any of that. He gave himself the distance between one side of the road and the other to get ready, no hesitation and no excuses allowed.

Just as Albert made it as far as MacLennan's driveway, the front door opened and someone stepped outside. Instinctively, Albert ducked down behind the first big thing he found—the truck, just a few feet away. Inches from his face was MacLennan's *Gas, Grass, or Ass: Nobody Rides For Free* bumper sticker. His first thought was a disgusted *Do girls really go for that?* followed immediately by the thought that in this town, they probably did. Most of the girls Albert saw seemed to go for athletic guys and pickup trucks; what was more, any guy in school who wasn't like that—who was bookish, maybe, or didn't go out for a team—was a fag. At least, that was the name Albert had been called a few times since his family moved here. MacLennan and his stupid bumper sticker were just a couple of the reasons why Albert hated this stupid town—reasons Lily hated it, too.

Hunkered down behind the tailgate of the pickup, Albert peered around the back tire, trying to see who was coming out of the house and which direction they were going. The figure was coming closer—right toward the truck, in fact—and Albert was able to make out Patrick MacLennan's face. He was headed for the driver's side door of the truck, and two thoughts ran through Albert's head in an instant. First, that he had to confront the guy right now before he got away again; and second, if he didn't move *somewhere* and quickly, he would likely be backed over.

But instead of getting into the truck, MacLennan just leaned against the door. His cell phone was against his ear. "I can't," he said in a low voice. "My parents think I'm in my room and if they hear me start my truck, they'll be pissed."

Albert strained to catch the words.

"Yeah, I got it." Pause. "No, I don't think he noticed. I gave him a story about homework." Another pause, then, in an indignant voice, "Why would I want to read it? I'm not a freak like her boyfriend."

Albert's ears turned red as he listened to MacLennan talk about him, and he felt a fresh rush of anger.

"How many times do I have to tell you?" There was a soft metallic echo as MacLennan gave the side of his truck a frustrated thump. "I did what you asked, to help her. We're even now, right? Like you promised?"

There was a pause and whoever was on the other end did all the talking. And loudly, Albert judged, from the way MacLennan shuffled and winced and held the phone away from his face. Finally MacLennan said, "Can't you pick me up on the corner of—" He stopped. "Fine. I'll meet you at … where? How about Federated Oil by the stockyards? I'll see you in a few. But this is the last—" He stopped talking again and jammed his phone into his pocket with an angry grunt.

Albert just had time to roll away from the wheel and into the hedge along the driveway before the engine roared and MacLennan was backing down the driveway. No sooner had Albert pulled himself from the greenery than he was, once again, chasing Patrick MacLennan.

The railroad tracks were two blocks away from MacLennan's house. Cutting away from the road, Albert made his way straight to the tracks themselves. By moving along them he could make good time, going straight through to where the trains ran by the stockyards across from Federated Oil. Albert's lungs were exploding as he hurried over the uneven ground, focusing on the movement of his legs and not twisting his ankle.

By now he was past being surprised by anything that happened or that he was doing. In the span of one day, his understanding of Lily had changed and his perception of her had changed with it. So far, everything that had happened today had come on fast, and he hadn't needed to process things, only to react to them. Like now. He had no idea of the time or how long he'd been gone, or what he planned to do when he got to Federated Oil except maybe wait and see which one of MacLennan's stupid friends was waiting for him. He wasn't even sure what day it was anymore … the way this one stretched on and on without ending seemed impossible for just one day. All Albert wanted was to get Lily's journal back, and though he was exhausted and scared and confused, he promised himself that once he had the little book in his hands, he would go directly to the police station and stop for nothing.

Ten minutes after he began racing MacLennan to the gas station, Albert was almost there. He slowed his run and cut away from the train tracks and down toward the stockyards. A dirt lane cut between two giant pens of cattle, and, at the end of the lane just before the paved road that ran in front of the station, there was a windowless shed. Hunkered down low, Albert scuttled as best he could over the uneven ground, feeling ridiculously conspicuous. He was thankful, at least, that he was wearing dark jeans and a black sweatshirt.

He arrived at the little building with the crazy expectation of hearing angry shouts of recognition from MacLennan, but the only sound was the wind in the Russian olives along the ditch and the lowing of the cows in the stockyards.

The shingled outer wall of the shed was rough under Albert's palms as he leaned against it, watching the gas station from the shadows. He could see MacLennan's truck idling next to the gray cinderblock Federated Oil office, which was closed at this time of night. Albert couldn't see anyone else in the parking lot.

Pressed against the wall, he watched MacLennan with a curiously light head and found he was holding his breath. The sense of "what next?" drew out as nothing happened—

MacLennan just sat, unmoving, behind the wheel of his truck, his head down so far his chin seemed to be on his chest. No one showed up to share the stage. The air felt thick and hard to breathe, and Albert felt like the world was paused in this moment. The only proof of reality and time was the cattle, their shifting and bellowing making Albert think they knew he was there. Nothing more happened; the scene was frozen.

With a jolt, Albert realized that when something did begin to happen—when the other guy showed up and MacLennan was no longer alone in his truck—he would be too far away to hear what was happening. Too far away to act. What he planned to do, Albert didn't exactly yet know, but he had no intention of letting Lily's journal get any farther than it already had in MacLennan's grubby, thieving hands. So he had to get closer, closer to the parking lot where MacLennan sat waiting.

And with his heart in his throat, terrified of getting caught, terrified of missing something, terrified of failing Lily, Albert bent low again and left the company and smell of the cows and the cover of the building.

Glancing in all directions, he quickly backtracked up the dirt road to the shallow ditch that ran behind the stockyards, then made his way toward the road. When the ditch narrowed into a culvert, he scuttled out of its groove and farther away from Federated Oil, up the dark hill below the highway and away from the floodlights that were lighting the pumps and casting the tanks and the parking lot into half-light. Albert darted across the road and into the darkness of the scrub that choked the large, triangular slope between the gas station below and the highway above.

Hoping his rustling in the weeds wasn't loud enough to draw attention, Albert circled closer to his target destination: a vantage point near MacLennan's truck on the other side of the parking lot. As he struggled to find his way quietly in the darkness of the parking lot's outer edges, he saw the appeal of the Federated Oil station as a meeting place. It was on the other side of the freeway, down the hill in a quiet little spot. The station mainly served truckers who all seemed to pay with gas cards, so there was usually no one around at night except the cattle in the stockyards across the street. It was a quiet, private place.

Albert decided to hunker down behind the dumpster, along the back side of the gas station, because it put him just a few feet away from MacLennan's truck. Crouched on the ground against a big blue trash bin, Albert could hear the radio in MacLennan's truck very clearly. He hoped that the sound of voices would carry half as well.

He also hoped he would know what to do and when to do it. At this point, he was still winging it. The anger he'd been feeling had calmed to a hard, hot coal in his stomach, and Albert concentrated on bringing it back to full flame. He would need it for courage.

The sound of MacLennan singing tunelessly along with a new song on the radio was as clear as Albert could have hoped. He ignored the cold blacktop digging into his hands and knees and gazed up the long, weedy hill. There was a green, decaying smell that may have come from the dead, damp weeds or from the cattle feed, and with it was the manure smell of the feedlots and the sharp tinge of the dumpster beside him. The horizon at the top of the hill was a low, straight line, broken only by the silhouette of the old Odd Fellow's Home and a dark sky with a few darker clouds. It was beautiful in a heartbreaking kind of way, Albert thought. It was the first time he'd found any view in this town worth appreciating, and it struck him what an odd time this was for that to happen. But the view and the silence sucked him in.

The tinny sound of the radio cut abruptly and Albert heard a car door open and shut, echoed by another car door opening and shutting. The sound of metal on metal hung in the air. He hadn't heard another engine. He leaned as far back against the gas station wall as he could, trying to see between it and the dumpster, but the space was barely a slit and it was too dark to see. He crawled to the outer edge of his cover, wondering if he should risk a glance around the edge.

"I've been waiting forever, man," he heard MacLennan grumble. His voice was coming from very close by and Albert hung back, staying completely out of sight. He heard MacLennan ask, "My parents are going to freak if they heard me leave. What took you so long?"

The person MacLennan had been waiting for ignored the question, demanding instead, "Do you have it?"

At the sound of the voice, Albert felt like his chest would cave in. He didn't need to see the speaker to know him. That voice belonged to Kogen.

Eighteen
5 a.m.

"Thought you said you knew the way," Albert gripes as Olivia brings them to an unsure halt. "Don't tell me we're lost."

"I got us this far, didn't I?" Olivia snaps back at him. "I just need make sure we're on track. I'm pretty sure we are, but I want to be completely sure when we're this close."

Albert smacks his hand against his forehead but manages to hold his tongue. It's hard to hold back with Olivia glaring up at him from under her thick fringe of bangs.

After he'd returned to where Olivia slept on the bus bench, Albert hadn't known what to do. Seeing their faces on the laundromat TV had shocked him more than it should have. After all, what was so surprising about it? They were missing minors or fugitives or something, connected to the Lily Odilon story, so it was bound to make the news.

He'd sat next to Olivia, waiting for her to wake up so they could move on, and after a while his eyes had dropped and the next thing he'd known, it was maybe an hour before dawn. The sky had gotten light and it was bitterly cold and Albert was stiff from sleeping on a bench.

He'd shaken Olivia awake, and as they walked the cold and stiffness from their limbs, Albert filled Olivia in on what he'd seen through the laundromat window. She'd taken it with less surprise and more pessimism than he had, shrugging and saying little.

Now here they are, desperate to get through the last leg of their journey. Olivia leads them, since it's on her memory alone that they will find the lakeside house where she and Lily spent so many summers of their childhood.

Neither of them speaks of what comes after that, or what they will do if Lily isn't there or if she's been forced to move on. Albert can't stand to think of the possibility, much less say it out loud.

"We need a map," Olivia says after another pause. "I need to check a map, just to make sure."

Trying to hold in his frustration, Albert thinks. "We can get one at the gas station back that way," he says, gesturing back over his shoulder. "I'm pretty sure they have a bunch of road maps for sale."

She sighs. "One problem. We have less than two bucks left."

He claps his hands together, a startling noise that reverberates in the clear, cold air. "Then we'll just have to steal one." He sounds way more confident than he feels; he's never shoplifted anything in his life.

"Perfect." Olivia adopts the plan so quickly that Albert wonders if this is something she's done before. "You distract the clerk by trying to buy cigarettes, and I'll grab it while they're dealing with you."

"We don't have enough money for a pack of cigarettes. If we did—"

Olivia rolls her eyes. "That's the point, dummy. They won't sell them to you anyway, not without ID. Which you don't have. I just need you to distract the clerk for a few seconds while I grab what we need. Can you handle that, Morales?"

"Whatever," he says, still not overconfident. "Let's just get it over with."

"Right," she says. "I just have a bad feeling, that jumpy, looking-around-corners feeling. I won't feel good until we find my sister and I know she's safe."

Albert agrees but says nothing. He has the same uncomfortable feeling and doesn't like it. Seeing their pictures on TV hasn't helped.

"Funny," Olivia says as they backtrack to the convenience store, "this isn't the first time we've worked together on a theft."

This brings to Albert's mind how he'd found Lily's journal and taken it home hidden in the waistband of his pants. This memory, of course, leads him to the memory of how he'd *lost* Lily's journal—and that part makes him feel sick.

He shivers, but not from the cold. "I hope things turn out better this time." He doesn't just mean stealing the map.

Olivia's plan does work out, though, and they have their map, if by shady means. Albert has started to feel better when Olivia gives a little cry at his elbow and startles him with a shove that almost knocks him off his tired feet.

"What the—?" he begins, irritated.

"Just hide over there," Olivia hisses as a police cruiser coasts toward them, the siren off but the lights flashing.

Albert stumbles to right himself against the mailbox she's just pushed him into. "Over where?" he asks.

"Wherever! Just get lost before they get closer and see us together."

Annoyed by the way she says it but still seeing that she's right, Albert drifts from her side in what he hopes is a nonchalant manner. There aren't many places to hide where they are, but as he glances up and down the sidewalk, he sees the narrow crack of an alley between two old, brick buildings just a few paces away. A rank whiff of damp garbage greets him as he slips into the darkness, just before the police car slows nearby. He's tired of always hiding.

Albert wonders if these cops are just cruising around, or if they're looking for a couple of missing teenagers. Or two recent shoplifters. *Take your pick.*

Olivia keeps walking, passing Albert's hiding place without a glance in his direction. She ignores the police car until they give the siren one long whoop and glide to the curb beside her. She stands there looking bored, her hands buried in her pockets, head cocked, watching the cops get out of the car. *If you didn't know better*, Albert is thinking as he watches her, *you'd guess she wasn't worried about a thing.*

From his vantage point in that narrow alley, Albert can see Olivia—a small girl flanked by two big, uniformed officers—but he can't hear what any of them are saying. All he can hear is some mechanical pulsation from deeper down the alley and the nearby splash of water into water from snow melting on the roof three stories above. He watches as Olivia pulls something from her pocket and hands it to one of the cops, who examines it, then takes it back to the car. After what seems like forever, the cop returns to Olivia and the other cop and gives the thing she handed to him back to her. The three of them appear to be having a conversation and Albert sees Olivia nod her head a couple of times, as well as shrug once. As Olivia is talking with the first cop, the other one looks around, up and down the street and over toward Albert's general location. He doesn't dare move or even breathe as the cop's gaze lingers. Narrowing his eyes, he hopes they don't reflect the dim glow of the streetlight at the corner, like an animal's eyes catch the glow of a headlight.

There's a loud thump and a crash behind him, then an echo from a dumpster, and the second cop's shoulders tense. He takes a step toward the alley, one hand reaching for the heavy-duty flashlight on his belt. Unsure whether to wait it out or to run, Albert is saved having to decide when a streak of fur flies past him and out onto the sidewalk— one hissing, yowling cat chasing another into the street, nearly colliding with the shins of the cop heading for the alley. Feeling faint, Albert watches as the first cop touches the second on the elbow and leads him back to their cruiser. The cop who hasn't just been nearly run down by a cat fight is clearly amused by his partner's jumpiness, and the sound of deep laughter reaches Albert. Olivia is smiling, too, and she gives a kind of half-nod as the cops pull away.

After the car has gone, she drops her lazy pose and hurries over to where Albert is hiding in the alley.

"That was lucky," she says. Her smile is gone and her face is pinched and tired. With a shaking hand she pats down her pockets, saying, "I really wish I had a smoke right now. I can hardly walk, I'm so tired."

"What happened?" Albert asks.

"They just wanted to make sure I wasn't out past curfew."

"But you were. Why didn't they take you in?"

She pulls a small rectangle from her back pocket and flashes it at him. "Saved by the fake ID!" Her smile returns— the mischievous one that echoes her older sister's—at the warring admiration and surprise written on Albert's face, and she adds, "I have a few secrets, too."

"Good thing."

"You're telling me," she says, turning the little rectangle over in her fingers a few times before putting it in her pocket again. "I thought I was toast when he took off back to his car with my ID, but he didn't say anything when he gave it back. I don't think he even bothered to run it."

This time Albert's legs really do feel too weak to hold him, and he slides down the brick wall to the alley floor. "Jesus."

Olivia nudges him with her foot. "Plus, one of them gave me ten bucks. Let's get out of here."

Albert gets slowly to his feet. "You are amazing."

"Yeah?" She's still smiling from her victory over the cops.

"Yeah. You're so good at taking care of yourself."

Her face loses that gleeful kidlike expression, falling into its more familiar scowl. "It's a good thing I am," she says. "No one else is going to do it."

Albert doesn't know what to say.

"I mean, you're so devoted to her. When we were really little, it was my dad. After the accident, it was my mom— for a while, anyway. Now you're the one she has looking out for her." Olivia walks fast now, and Albert wants to pull her back, slow her down.

"What's wrong with devotion? What else can you do when you love someone?" he asks, the words coming out sharp.

"It just never matters what she does…Lily always has someone running to her rescue. I think you're really stupid, actually…and you'll end up with a broken heart no matter what you do for her. It's never enough."

"But you're right here with me!" He grabs her arm to stop her.

She shakes his hand from her arm. "I'm stupid, too!"

"Are you ... jealous of her or something?"

"You are so ... stupid." Something like hatred shoots out of her eyes at him.

"Yeah, you already said that." Now it's Albert who's walking away, and Olivia is left trying to catch up.

"*Fuck* you, Morales," she spits at his back.

After that, she keeps several paces away from him as they walk, and she won't speak to him at all. He finds that he's fine with that.

Nineteen

There in the surreal, theatrical glow of Federated Oil's floodlights, MacLennan slowly got out of his truck while Kogen waited a couple yards away.

When Albert was eavesdropping on MacLennan's conversation in the driveway, he'd assumed the person on the other end of the line was one of MacLennan's asshole friends. But it was Kogen who was behind MacLennan stealing Lily's journal—it had nothing to do with MacLennan wanting to help the girl who had once been his friend. Once again, Albert had missed the point, and once again, he'd let Lily down—badly, this time. His body shook as he risked it to watch MacLennan approach the spot where Kogen, looking relaxed, stood waiting.

Albert couldn't figure out how these two even knew each other. What was a grown man doing sneaking around at night with a teenager? Knowing as he now did how screwed up Kogen was, Albert was afraid he wasn't going to want to find out.

When he thought about the people that came in and out of his daily life—his parents, the other kids at school, his teachers, even the cops—it seemed impossible that someone he knew could really be such a ... the word "villain" came to mind. Albert knew this was an incredibly naïve attitude. Of course, he knew that people did bad things—horrible, unspeakable things sometimes—but it was still hard for him to really believe that such viciousness could ever touch his life, or the life of someone he loved. That he would ever face real danger from another person.

Now he was facing danger from two people, and not only did he not understand how or why they'd come together, he didn't have a clue what he was supposed to do about it. He watched, hoping an idea would come to him.

From where he was hiding behind the dumpster, Albert's view of MacLennan was mostly of his back; Kogen was almost directly across from him, his calm, unreadable face very clear in the electric light. If Albert shifted even just a few inches, he knew his movement would catch Kogen's eye.

It's too much, he thought in a panic. *I'm sorry, Lily.*

"Be smart," were the first words Lily's stepfather said to MacLennan.

It was as if the those flat, reasonable words were really directed at Albert, and that flame of anger blazed up and made him stronger. Whatever he had to do, he would do it.

"Just give me the book, then we can both get out of

this godforsaken cold and go home." Taking another step forward, Kogen smiled slightly at MacLennan, an expression meant to be friendly and reassuring, but failing. His normally handsome face was cut with deep shadows.

Albert's anger gave him courage. He waited to see what MacLennan would do before making his own move, but now that they were about to make the exchange—Lily's journal for what?—MacLennan seemed to hesitate.

"Go on, then," Kogen said, closing the gap and holding out his hand. "I've had enough teenage angst for today." His words were harsher than they'd been before.

He's losing patience, thought Albert. It was as if he could read Kogen's mind—Kogen knew it was about time to make a move for the journal, and he was about to do it. At that moment Albert would have given one of his limbs for a cell phone, and he had to push black and hateful thoughts about his control-freak parents out of his head.

Despite Kogen's obvious impatience, MacLennan was still holding on to Lily's journal, the little book prized by all three people in the gas station parking lot that night. "Why did that fag she was dating steal this thing in the first place?" he asked, still holding the book.

"Because he's a very disturbed young man—one who quite possible knows where my daughter is and may be responsible for her disappearance."

Stepdaughter, Albert shouted at Kogen in his brain. His head was burning.

MacLennan turned his head and Albert could see that his expression was uncertain. "Then why make me steal it back for you? He was acting suspicious . . . he probably knows by now that I took it. If he's crazy, why didn't you just call the police?"

Kogen's hand rested on his hip. "I needed some proof first, which is what's in my daughter's journal."

Which was true, but not in the way Kogen was implying.

"They're not going to just arrest the little creep on my say-so, are they? Use your head, Patrick. It doesn't matter what my reasons are, anyway. I'm fairly certain you're not in a position to question me."

"That's another thing that's bugging me," MacLennan said, his voice carrying as it rose. "What guarantee do I have that you won't call the cops on me after I give you this?" He held up Lily's journal as if he were going to hurl it at something.

That smile was back and Albert thought Kogen seemed relaxed again, as if he'd gotten back control of the situation. He said, "You have my word on it."

Before he could catch himself, Albert snorted. Fortunately, MacLennan snorted at the same time. But why the hell, Albert wondered, would Kogen call the cops on MacLennan? It didn't seem possible that the police would arrest MacLennan, a seventeen-year-old boy, for the theft of a diary that had been stolen in the first place by Albert, while *not* arresting the adult man who asked him to do it. And how could Kogen even prove anybody stole anything when he had Lily's diary back in his possession? The conversation wasn't making any sense.

"My word is going to have to do," Kogen said, ignoring MacLennan's disbelief. "I'm not the one who broke into my friend's father's dental office after hours to steal a controlled substance and probably money, if I could find it—"

"We weren't after any money," MacLennan protested.

"—and probably money," Kogen went on as if MacLennan hadn't spoken. "I'm painting a picture here. As I was saying, *I'm* not the one who was then foolish enough to let my idiot friend overdose on said controlled substance, stupid enough to let the rest of our friends leave her there to die, then *stupid* enough to come back and get caught by the dentist he was trying to rip off. Now am I?"

"No, sir," MacLennan mumbled.

"Right," said Kogen. "I did you a favor by not turning you in—"

"A favor? That didn't have anything to do with me," MacLennan objected angrily. "You just didn't want to get Lily in trouble because it would embarrass you and your family and might be bad for business. I mean, who would go to a dentist who'd put his own daughter in jail?"

He was right, Albert thought. There was no way Kogen was doing anyone any favors but himself. It was just luck— really shitty luck for Lily—that he could use that "favor" against MacLennan all this time later.

"—and all I want is a favor in return," Kogen continued, his words rolling over the top of MacLennan's. "One good turn deserves another. I'm not looking for anything else, except that you keep your mouth shut. If you say anything to anyone, I will be forced to mention your part in the crime that was committed against me. Maybe it would go away, or maybe you'd go to jail for assaulting my daughter. Maybe you'd just lose your scholarship, I don't know." He managed to sound both aggrieved and regretful at the same time. "Nod if you understand what I'm saying."

Looking humiliated, MacLennan nodded as Albert watched from behind the dumpster.

"Now that everything is just oh-so-clear, give me Lily's journal and let's both go home."

"I didn't have a problem helping you because Lily's cool, and if this helps her, I want to do it," MacLennan said. "But I have to be sure that you're not going to come back and hold that night over my head again the next time you need something shady done."

To Albert, MacLennan sounded like he was trying hard to convince himself that helping Kogen was helping Lily. If MacLennan found himself questioning Kogen's motives, Kogen's actions, Kogen's creepy attitude, then he would have to stand up to the guy. He would have to make a choice between sticking up for Lily and pissing Kogen off, or keeping himself out of serious trouble by choosing to believe Kogen and letting his doubts go. But he was waffling; Albert could tell that MacLennan was waffling. Now was the time to show himself, before Kogen had the diary in hand. If he did it just right, it could be two against one.

As Albert was about to shout out, he heard MacLennan give a startled cry—

What is he—?

—and then Albert saw that Kogen was holding a gun on MacLennan. His pulse racing, amazed at the very bad moment at which he'd almost thrown himself into this little drama, Albert hung back, unable to look away. He was as grateful for the cover of the dumpster as he'd ever been for anything.

"You gotta be kidding me," MacLennan said, his voice breathless and cracking.

"I really am done with you," Kogen said. "Give me my daughter's diary. Now."

Terrified, Albert watched MacLennan reach out as far as he could to hand the little book over; he saw MacLennan flinch when Kogen took it roughly from his outstretched hand. There was a moment of complete stillness as Kogen and MacLennan regarded one another across just a few feet of space. In that moment, Albert was convinced that Kogen was going to shoot MacLennan anyway, no matter how absurd the idea was.

Time stretched out as nothing happened, but anything might. And then Kogen began backing away, his eye and his aim still focused on MacLennan. As for MacLennan, he just held his hands up and shrugged. He muttered something that Albert didn't entirely catch, but which sounded like *it's cool.* After putting some distance between himself and the kid he was blackmailing, Kogen made an abrupt turn and moved quickly across the parking lot toward his car. It roared to life, and then Albert and MacLennan were left alone.

A voice in the back of Albert's head was screaming for

him to catch Kogen while he still could, to attack him at a dead run, whatever might happened after that. And he was angry with himself when he found that he wasn't man enough to do it. His legs wouldn't do what he told them, so he stayed where he was. And even if he might rationalize it by saying that he would be hurt or worse if he tried to interfere with Kogen at this moment, that he couldn't help Lily if he ignored his judgment, he knew that the rationalization didn't matter. What was really happening was that he'd seen how serious Kogen was, and he was too afraid.

Legs aching from squatting on the blacktop, Albert wished MacLennan would hurry up and leave, too. He crawled back from the edge of the dumpster and sat all the way down with his back against the dented blue metal. He wanted to scream and curse and kick the dumpster until it rang with the same frustration he himself was suffering. Not only had he completely *failed* to get Lily's journal back, he'd been forced to watch it go to the last person on earth who should have it.

There was no doubt in Albert's mind that now that Kogen knew the diary existed—*thanks to me and my brilliant detective work*—and had it in hand, he would destroy it immediately.

And when he did, there went the best proof they had of Kogen's crimes. Actually, the second-best proof, but what would've been the first best—Lily herself—was nowhere to be found, and half of what she'd endured was probably stilled locked in her brain anyway. What details there were existed only on the pages of her journal.

Gone with it was any protection Albert could promise to Lily, so that he could convince her it was safe to come home. She'd left because she was terrified of her stepfather, but had she recovered from that buried place in her mind the full reason why? *Did* she remember the details, or did her journal really hold the sole story behind the gruesome night of her accident? There was no way right now to know. Albert felt as if he'd been running forward in the dark and just bounced off of a particularly hard brick wall.

Several minutes passed as he struggled under the growing weight of his gloom. He tried to think of what to do next. It took him a while to notice that the night was once again dead silent, except for the cattle and the distant buzz of freeway traffic on the other side of the hill. He didn't hear MacLennan, nor had he heard MacLennan's truck drive away.

Once again Albert edged to the corner of the dumpster, ignoring the pain in his calves. He peered around the corner and came almost face-to-knee with MacLennan's legs, barely a foot away. The breath startled out of him, Albert leapt to his feet and scrambled back a bit. He gave an involuntary yell.

"What the hell?" MacLennan cried, his words echoing loudly.

Albert looked from MacLennan's face to his clenching fists and back up to his clenched jaw, and realized in that fraction of a second that MacLennan was liable to be dangerous as well, now that he knew that Albert knew his part in this dirty business.

After a split second of startled hesitation, Albert sprang into the sprint of his life before MacLennan had a chance to recover from his own surprise. Knowing he was pushing his luck, Albert ran as fast as he could anyway and hoped his lungs continued to cooperate.

His body was thin and wiry where MacLennan's was a beefy football player's, and with his head start, Albert was able to accelerate out of MacLennan's sight and, more frightened than ever, zigag his way home.

Twenty

7 a.m.

Almost there, Albert keeps saying to himself as he tries to ignore his sore body's desire to curl up somewhere and shut down. His muscles are aching and his feet feel like they're collapsing. The mountain lakeside resort where he and Olivia hope to find Lily is only a few more miles up the road. Feeling the pressure of time and pursuit, they've agreed wordlessly to keep going until they get there.

Once we find her and I know she's safe, he thinks, *then I can stop. Sleep for a week. But not until we find her.*

"How long are you going to ignore me?" he asks Olivia after a while.

Of course, she acts like he hasn't spoken and just keeps walking.

"Whatever it was that pissed you off, I'm sorry." It

isn't the warmest apology, but he's pissed at her for being a drama queen when the last thing they need is more drama.

She ignores him.

"We both love her. No matter how much she makes us worry."

"She holds us hostage with it," Olivia mutters.

Albert guesses he's glad that Olivia is speaking to him again, so he ignores what she actually says. He has a strong urge to point out to her that she uses sarcasm and bitchiness to keep people at a distance—then acts hurt and bewildered when it works.

Instead he tries changing the subject, now that they're apparently talking again. "We should be happy," he says. "We're almost there and we haven't been caught."

She mutters something under her breath.

"I can't believe our luck," he says. "No cops, and *he* hasn't caught up with us, either. I'll bet they never even knew which way we went."

"What the hell, Morales," she says. "Don't jinx us."

He scoffs.

"What about when I saw Perry?"

"I think we let our paranoia get to us. I'm not sure it was ever really Kogen we saw back there. I mean, if it was, he gave up surprisingly easy."

"Unless he's setting some trap," she says.

They keep walking, but now she lets him fall in step next to her.

He stares down at his feet as they move one in front of the other. Something has been on his mind, but he's afraid to say it and get Olivia riled up again. He finds himself saying it anyway—he can't help it. "Do you ever wonder what would have happened if she'd just said something, back when all this started? Before the accident?"

Olivia says nothing for a while, and just when Albert thinks she isn't going to, she says, "I don't know. Maybe she was going to. But she was so angry. I think she wanted to hurt him first ... maybe herself, too. I guess she did that." Her voice is shaking, and Albert can't tell if the emotion is anger or sadness or a mix. "And then ... well, everything happened and it was all a big gross mess. *Is* a big gross mess."

"I don't want to upset you again. We have different views on what makes Lily do what Lily does. Maybe we should just—"

Giving a half laugh, she wipes the corner of her eye. "Maybe we're both a little wrong. But you don't really know her. I guess I don't get why you're so ... hung up."

Because I do *know her, and I love her, and she needs me.* Needs. He isn't about to say that word to Olivia. *You act like you don't really like her,* he thinks. He doesn't ask, *So what about* you? He wonders why she's pressing him so much now that they're in too deep to back out. He wonders if either of them is up to finishing what they've started.

"Forget it," she says. "I just wish more than anything that she'd told me, straight out, before it got as bad as this. I think she actually tried once, but she couldn't just come out and say it."

"What do you mean, she tried?"

Thinking for a moment first, Olivia says, "I don't even remember what we were doing, just that it was me and Lily and no one else, and we were talking. Maybe that's why I remember it so well—we weren't talking a lot by then. She says to me, something like, I should stay clear of Perry. It was like she'd arranged to be alone with me to tell me that, and something more, but she never got to the something more. She said it twice. And I just thought she was mad at him, as usual—she and my mom and she and Perry and she and both of them were always fighting about something, before the accident. And then a while after the accident, too…until she left."

"And that's all she said? Before that night and the accident and everything—she never said anything after?"

"That's all she said," Olivia repeats. "Come on—Lil never talked to me, not about real stuff. How much really *real* stuff did she talk about with you? Did she ever talk about Perry?"

The question cuts. "Not much," he says.

Twenty-one

"What's this?" Albert asked.

Lily grabbed his paper lunch-sack with one hand and snatched his peanut butter sandwich from him with the other. She stuffed the soggy bread into the bag and tossed it several feet into the trash can in the corner, arcing the throw for a three-pointer. It was lunch period, the forty-five minutes that were Albert's favorite of the day because this was the only time he could see Lily without having to worry about either of their parents. He survived the other sucky minutes and hours of the day thinking of the ones he spent with her. Right now they were sitting at a small table near the door to the kitchen, a table that was always empty because it was down a short "L", a little apart from rest of the lunchroom.

"It's lunch," she said, dropping a small cooler onto the table with a hollow thud. "I wanted to do something nice ... your lunches are usually so pathetic."

"Have you been hauling that thing around all day? Haven't people been staring? Asking if you were carrying organs for transplant?"

"Ha ha," she said. She sat down and took the lid off the cooler. "Shut up. You're going to hurt my feelings, after I went to all this trouble."

"Cool. But why, again?"

She handed him a plate and a fork and a paper party napkin covered in little teal elephants on a pink background. "Because you're sweet and cute and I really like you."

He looked down at his plate, feeling suddenly shy. "I really like you, too—"

"Don't spoil it," she said, waving off his stammering. "Just eat."

There wasn't much time in a school lunch period to sit and savor the stuffed pitas and large slab of bakery chocolate cake Lily had brought for them to eat, and the noise of the student body and the dreariness of the cafeteria wasn't exactly ambience. But Albert ate like it was, because it was sweet of her to try.

When the lunch period was almost over, she said, "I have one other thing to give you."

"I already feel guilty." He wondered what it was.

"Maybe I'm hoping you'll buy me a steak and take me to a movie this weekend," she laughed. "Crafty me."

"By 'steak,' you mean 'hamburger,' right?"

She said, "Ugh. I just realized how dumb this is." But she pulled something from the back pocket of her jeans anyway and handed it to him. "Well, there it is."

He looked at the thing in his hand—a photograph.

"Thank you," he said, meaning it. "I thought you said you didn't have a picture you could give me."

"I know what I said. And I really don't have any pictures I like enough to let you see," she said, "except you keep asking. So I decided I wanted to give this one to you. It's just an old school shot from before my accident. Totally embarrassing. But I hope you like it."

"I do," he said. The picture was a studio snapshot, and didn't look much different from the girl who sat in front of him—though the girl in the picture wore her hair longer than the Lily he knew. Also, the faint pencil-line scar she had on the left side of her forehead wasn't part of the face in the photograph.

They both jumped when the bell rang, Albert looking at Lily's picture, Lily watching Albert.

"Please put that stupid thing away now," she said, getting to her feet. "You can look at it when I'm not around. It's so dorky I can't stand it."

"You're crazy. It's beautiful." He ripped a piece of paper from one of his notebooks and folded it around the picture before tucking it carefully into a book. "You're like the poster girl for self-esteem issues."

He was trying to be funny, but he was shocked to see that her eyes were shiny and her mouth was twisted awkwardly, as if she was trying to hold back tears.

"Oh, don't," he said. "I was joking. Don't cry!"

Even from their corner, he could see that the lunchroom was emptying, everyone headed to their afternoon classes. He didn't know what to do. When you weren't in charge of your own life, there usually wasn't time to figure it out before you were shoved off to the next thing you didn't want to do.

But she took a deep breath and there were no tears. "Give me a break! I'm totally fine," she said. "You're the one person I can count on for that."

He felt like this responsibility she gave him was another gift, weightless.

Twenty-two

Albert's throat tightened, just as he'd been afraid it would. But even as he tried to keep up the pace of his running he expected it to be MacLennan's big hands, not asthma, that pinched his windpipe shut. Then the physical sensation passed and he was able to draw a jagged breath, and another, and he wondered if this was what a panic attack felt like.

His legs kept pumping anyway, barely stumbling, and his mind raced. As he replayed the last few moments at Federated Oil, he knew MacLennan was going to rat him out to Kogen. The two of them had good reason to keep Albert quiet, after what he'd seen tonight. Once Kogen knew Albert had been a witness to that private meeting, he would definitely be coming after him. That's what had Albert terrified—once Kogen had it in for someone, that person disappeared, one way or the other. Despite the cold, sweat poured from Albert's forehead and stung his eyes.

I'm in bad trouble.

In an amazingly short amount of time, Albert's life had fallen apart. The way he saw it, there was no way to hold one piece together without another breaking away. Kogen was after Lily, Albert was sure...and now MacLennan was a new threat and he was after Albert, too, and Kogen already had it in for Albert, and of course Kogen was the reason Lily was gone in the first place. And with that he was back to Lily—who was so afraid of her stepfather she'd fled town, and who, as of this evening, Albert had once again failed to help or protect.

Looking around to make sure MacLennan or his truck weren't lurking nearby, Albert cut through the neighbors' yard and through the narrow breezeway along the side of their house, startling their dog into barking as he hurdled over the back fence into his own yard.

He pictured Olivia sitting in her bedroom, waiting for him to call and tell her that everything was fine and they could go to the police and Kogen would be arrested and Lily brought home safely.

But now going to the cops was out, because of MacLennan—and because of his failure. He wanted to tell the police what was in Lily's journal, but it was such a ludicrous story that no one would believe any of it. He also couldn't tell anyone that he thought he knew where Lily might be, because doing so would send Kogen right to her.

The trouble he and Lily were in was so deep.

As quietly as he could, Albert lifted the sash on his bedroom window and pulled himself inside. He shut the window behind himself and held his breath a moment. Leaving his light off, he sat on the edge of the bed and listened hard. He thought he heard the TV from the living room, but definitely no footsteps. The very smallest bit of his luck had held, anyway—apparently his parents had never known he'd left the house. He let out a silent, humorless laugh that shook his body.

He closed the window and latched it. As he was pulling off his shoes and wondering whether he had enough nerve to call Olivia tonight and tell her what happened, he had an idea. It was something that even a couple of weeks ago he never would have thought of, let alone seriously considered. But he was out of options.

What if he just left town? What if he stopped waiting for the cops to figure it out and *he* found Lily? If she was beginning to remember what her stepfather had done, maybe by now she remembered about her journal and what she'd written there. And if she did, the journal would no longer be the only piece of evidence against Kogen.

If she came back, she could testify, she could talk to the police herself. If she had remembered any part of what happened, they could still crush Kogen. It was worth a shot. Albert was starting to get excited as the idea formed. He would find her and stay with her and they would figure out a way to negotiate with the police from a distance, and they wouldn't come back until Kogen was arrested. Maybe they could take Lily's story to the newspapers, if they had to. The story would be out and Lily would be safe.

And Albert would have helped her after all. She'd be protected because of him.

And even if she still didn't remember everything about that night, if it remained buried, then Albert would go to her anyway and neither of them would be alone anymore.

But then the image of Kogen holding a gun on MacLennan floated in front of his eyes. Things were falling apart for Kogen, too, which would make him even more dangerous. Olivia was currently under the same roof as that man.

Cursing under his breath, Albert tiptoed out of his room and into the hall to grab the telephone. His muffled footsteps seemed to echo throughout the quiet house, but his parents didn't hear.

Back in his room, Albert dialed Olivia's number, hoping as he did that he wasn't making things worse. She picked up after a couple of rings, answering with no preface to her whispered "What happened?"

Also whispering, he said, "You have to get out of there. Is there somewhere you can go?"

As briefly as he could, he told Olivia everything that had happened, beginning with MacLennan showing up at his house and ending with the abrupt confrontation at the gas station. Olivia said nothing as he spoke, only listened.

When he'd finished the story, Albert said, "If your stepfather reads the journal, he'll know we know *everything*. That makes him even more dangerous. And MacLennan will stoke his paranoia if he tells Kogen I was there." There was more silence on her end. "Are you going to say anything?"

When she spoke, it wasn't what he'd expected her to say. "He had a *gun*?"

"Yeah. I mean, I don't know anything about guns—for all I know it was a starter's pistol. But I saw it," Albert said. "MacLennan saw it. He was pissing himself, too."

What she said next startled him again. "Wait. Patrick was there when Lily had her accident? And he just left her alone to die?"

"Not exactly," he said, briefly explaining that MacLennan had gone back and gotten caught. "Kogen's been holding it over him." He didn't understand why she was focusing on this detail instead of the giant freaking problem of Kogen now having Lily's journal. Which he'd probably already destroyed.

"I can't believe this," she murmured.

"Focus!" Albert said, more sharply than he'd meant to, considering his own screw-ups. "Do you understand what I've just told you? Your stepfather took off with Lily's journal. The only evidence we had to take to the police."

"I know … this is bad," she said, her whisper almost a moan. "Jesus, Morales, what are we going to do?"

He hesitated. "I had an idea, probably a massively terrible one." He told her he'd been thinking of leaving town. "I feel like everyone is either against me or after me, especially now. So I need to leave right away. And you"—he stumbled over the words, hoping she would take him seriously—"you need to get out of there. Your stepfather is a lunatic, and you're not safe."

"You're going to Lily?"

"I'm going to try to find her, yeah. But seriously, Olivia, you have to get somewhere safe." Then he asked, "You and Lily and your mom used to rent a house at some lake every summer, right?"

"Yeah. Yellow Pine Lake."

That was it, the name he couldn't remember. "I'm sure that's where she's hiding. If you can tell me where it is, I'll go to Yellow Pine Lake and find her before Kogen does."

"Then I'm definitely going with you."

He didn't know what he should say, though the thought wasn't horrible to him. The idea of help—any company—was welcome right about now when he was feeling completely alone. And she had to get away from Kogen. "I feel like I should try to talk you out of it."

"You're kidding. Do you even know where you're going?" There was contempt in her voice. "You didn't even have the *name* until I gave it to you a second ago."

"I could've figured it out."

She snorted.

"Running away is totally irresponsible," he said, "and crazy and stupid and probably won't do any good."

"We're both already in it deep enough. Perry will be coming after you—maybe through his connections with the cops, or maybe in a more direct, more violent way."

"Same for you."

"Perry doesn't like messes," Olivia said. "Lily was a mess and he couldn't stand her. He has perfectly cut hair, perfectly ironed suits, a perfect career, a perfect wife, and a perfect life. He also has a temper when the perfect gets messed up."

"But running away," Albert interrupted again, unsure of whether he was trying to talk her or himself out of it. "I know I—we—need to get out of here tonight, but I don't have any money. I don't have a plan. I don't even have a car."

"What the hell else can we do? We'll figure it out."

"Your mother really won't listen if you try to go to her?"

A shuddering sigh came through the phone. "She's never taken our side against his on anything. It's like she's brainwashed. He has her convinced that Lily was a psychopath, determined to do nothing but screw up all our lives. I love my mom, and I guess she does her best, but I don't trust her to see things the way they are—especially because Lily has worked really hard at being a pain in the ass. Mom doesn't want to see her choices too clearly. If she did, Lily might be at home right now."

Albert said, "I can't go to my parents either. They never liked her, and they don't like to think that important people like doctors or cops, people they know, can be monsters underneath. It's easier to believe Lily is just bad, I guess."

"So we're on our own." Olivia sounded impatient. "So we … what? Find Lily and see what she remembers? How are we going to do that?"

"That's as far as I've gotten. Told you it was a stupid idea."

"Then it's already a good thing you have me, because

I can improve your shitty plan," she said. "Here's the deal: we're leaving tonight, while we still can … we're just going to sneak out and meet somewhere crowded. Then we'll disappear."

"Just like that?" Albert asked.

"Just like that. Can you be at Frontier Cinemas downtown in half an hour?"

He looked at the clock—it was after eleven already. "I'll do my best. Is Kogen there now?"

"I think he might still be out," she said. "Don't worry, I always lock my door at night."

That wasn't good enough for Albert, after what had just happened. He was afraid of the man, and he was worried about Olivia. "Is your mother there?"

"She's here, my door's locked, and I'm out of here in a few minutes. If he does come home, he won't try anything with her here. I can take care of myself. You just make sure you meet me at the theater."

He was about to hang up when she suddenly said, "Morales?"

"What?"

"Pack light, okay? No bags, nothing to look suspicious. Just grab whatever money you can scrape together and your coat. It's going to be cold, I think."

Twenty-three

4 p.m.

"We're here," Olivia announces, giving the fake-rustic *Welcome to Pine Glen* sign a firm pat.

The road, ever since the turnoff about three miles back, winds steeply up the mountain, and there seem to be more trees here and the pavement is better. It's lucky for Albert and Olivia that there isn't much traffic in late winter—the nearest ski hill is a hundred miles east, she tells him—because there's nowhere to walk but on the slippery shoulder of the road itself. This sign letting them know the location and population of Pine Glen is attached to two posts on the shoulder. Other than the sign, there's no break in the trees, and nothing to show that this is an actual town.

Taking a deep breath and leaning against the sign, Albert pushes his hair off his forehead. It's a lot colder now and there are snow patches on the ground, but the sun feels good on top of his head. At night, he thinks, it probably gets *really* cold—which is a problem for anyone who doesn't have a warm place to sleep.

Olivia's mouth twists into a smile, a rare thing for her, and Albert notices that it makes a pretty break in her normally scowling face.

"So we're here?" Albert echoes. He looks around. "Where are the buildings? Where are the people? Where's the lake?"

"Well, I mean, this road leads into Pine Glen," Olivia says, starting to walk again. "The summer places are around the lake. It's farther up."

He follows her. "It's so quiet."

"Because it's *winter*," Olivia says impatiently. "Trust me, this is the place. I've been here a million times."

Their voices are clear, and carry in the still air as if on a stage.

"Look, you said Lily is hiding at the lake house," Olivia adds. "Well, Yellow Pine Lake is above Pine Glen." She gestures ahead. "I wouldn't steer you wrong, Morales."

Just as Olivia promises, the actual town of Pine Glen is just up the road. It seems to Albert, legs and chest aching, that nothing they're looking for is ever *here*—it's always farther up the road from wherever they are.

"Sisyphus," he mutters, thinking of the story of the Greek guy who pissed Zeus off and ended up doomed to roll a rock up the same hill over and over for eternity.

"How's that?" Olivia asks, turning her head to look at Albert.

"What?" he says, not realizing he's said anything out loud.

Her eyes narrowing, she says, "There are people over there, so try to be cool, all right?"

"I'm like ice, baby," he says, the words coming out slurred. He knows he's acting weird but can't help it. The tight, itching feeling in his chest is getting tighter and itchier and he's finding it hard to think. Lily might be nearby... he might see her within hours... minutes...

After a while, the wall of evergreen trees thin and Albert and Olivia can now see the little town's few buildings—a basic diner restaurant, a tiny gas and grocery, a very rundown motel—all right along the road, as if they would stop existing if they were built any farther back. Albert notices a couple sitting by the window of the diner, and just two cars parked by the grocery store.

"This place is really dead," he says. It's too quiet, like a Western right after the bad guys ride into town and right before Clint Eastwood jumps out of hiding to take them down. It's quiet like a set. Like a trap. But that's impossible... he knows it's impossible.

"You should see it in the summer," Olivia says. "It's crawling with people and traffic on their way to and from the lake. Or at least that's how I remember it."

"I wish there were more people around. I feel like everyone is looking at us."

"What everyone?"

He jerks his head toward the restaurant window. "Well, them, for instance. You know we stick out like crazy." He hopes Lily didn't stick out as much when she came through town.

Olivia moves closer to him and says in a low voice, "If anyone asks, our car broke down on our way to meet our parents at the lake, and we're lost. Don't lose it now."

But no one bothers them as they walk through town, such as it is, and out toward the lake, which they can kind of see through the trees well before they get near it.

Albert has never thought that this time of day—dull, flat afternoon in late February—could feel so dangerous. But words like *ominous* and *oppressive* keep coming to his mind, even though the late-winter sun is shining and he can smell pine trees and see piles of snow in the shade and Yellow Pine Lake is probably sparkling away somewhere up ahead. Albert is now thinking about how bad, bad things can go down in broad daylight just as well as in the middle of night. He pictures again those empty streets in the spaghetti Westerns, right before the gunfight.

"Quiet on the set," Albert mutters to himself.

"What?"

He rubs his eyes, hard. "Nothing." Everything that's happened lately is so out of his frame of reference that he keeps turning his life into the plot of a bad movie, with himself as the confused lead—sometimes he's a gumshoe, sometimes he's a shooter, but he's always a step behind.

As they leave the center of town behind them, Albert tries to calm his nerves. They're almost to the lake and so, he hopes, almost to Lily. He's been worried about finding her and protecting her for what seems like forever. Now looking at himself like a critical outsider, inspecting his feelings, he finds it strange that he feels more dread than anticipation. He should be crazy with excitement, now that he's so close to her for the first time since that night she slipped away. She's the bright spot in the darkness that had dropped over his life. But instead, he has this enormous and growing sense that something bad is coming to screw it all up.

Albert can tell Olivia is feeling that bad thing, too, though neither of them say anything to the other about it. Things are still a little tense between them and now they don't talk about anything at all. They keep on, silent and on edge, spooked like a couple of dogs right before a thunderstorm hits.

After a while longer, Albert thinks he knows what the bad feeling is. Pine Glen and Yellow Pine Lake may be pretty much deserted for the winter, but they aren't alone. Someone is definitely following them.

Twenty-four

After he and Olivia hung up, Albert realized he was still winded from the panicked run back home from Federated Oil. Or maybe it was just nerves. He looked at the clock, thinking he had *maybe* five minutes before he had to sneak back out again if he was going to make it to the theater in half an hour. He sat on the edge of his bed in the dark. He knew he'd been lucky to make it back inside without his parents noticing, and he hoped his luck would hold. His eyes wandered around the dark room, finally resting on the unshaded window and the glare from the streetlight coming through it.

He wasn't tired, and he kept telling himself *I'm leaving in five minutes* as if repeating it enough times would make it seem more believable—or less insane. Whether he believed it or not, the plan was to take off, and by tomorrow morning—no sooner, he hoped—his parents would be looking for him. Maybe frantic, definitely pissed.

Kogen's good friend and Albert's nemesis, Detective Andersen, would also definitely notice his absence—and Olivia's. Maybe, Albert thought, Andersen might even suspect that Lily's sister hadn't gone with him willingly. Maybe he'd think she'd been Albert's second victim … maybe that's what they'd print in the newspapers. Lily and Olivia's mother would have two missing daughters. And Kogen … Albert didn't know how the guy would react. Except badly.

And by this time the day after tomorrow, there might even been an arrest warrant out there with Albert Morales' name on it. Maybe sooner, he couldn't say.

He stood, pacing, psyching himself up. He felt feverish and restless and nervous as hell. Trying to erase the unhappy thoughts from his brain, he imagined the moment that would make the trouble worth it: he closed his eyes and saw Lily smiling at him … then Kogen in the distance, hauled off to jail in handcuffs.

Albert tried not to dwell on the fact that the justice system didn't always work out that way. The image of Kogen cut off by a Plexiglas window from any friends he had left was sweet, but Albert wasn't sure he believed in it. He tried, anyway … he had to.

And still that doubting voice in the back of his head whispered, *You're crazy to go after her*.

But it was Lily who was at stake. He'd seen tonight what Kogen was capable of, and found it all too easy to imagine what Kogen or MacLennan would do if one of them cornered Albert or Lily or Olivia. Albert told himself he didn't have a choice. And the thought of Olivia spending another night under the same roof as her stepfather now was just insane. Running away to find Lily was the only option they had, as extreme as it seemed. Knowing this didn't make him feel much better.

He went to his door and listened—he could hear the sound of the TV from the living room. He went to the window and looked out. He pressed his hot forehead against the cool glass and watched a few snowflakes fall. The flakes turned to icy pellets that weren't going to last long once the sun came up again. *Like me, if I'm not careful.*

He was procrastinating, he knew, and time was passing quickly. It was time to get it together and just go for it. He looked around his bedroom in the dim light. There were only a few things he wouldn't leave behind when he left. He'd take the clothes he was wearing, of course. He looked down at the hooded sweatshirt that covered two layers of T-shirt, his dirty jeans, and his dirtier sneakers. Good enough. He picked up his wallet from the dresser. Inside was his driver's license, nine dollars cash, and a photo of himself and Lily ripped from the top of a photo booth series. In it, they were laughing like idiots, caught that way forever, her mouth wide open and his eyes screwed shut. He couldn't see it well in the dark, but he had the picture memorized.

He took the money and the picture out of the wallet and slipped them into his back pocket, then dropped the wallet back on the dresser. He didn't want any ID on him in case there was trouble, and otherwise the wallet was empty. There was a photo of Lily propped up against an old jar full of incense sticks, a picture she'd given him. It was a good shot of her, her pale blue eyes standing out above her orange sweater. It was carefree and glammy in a way she never was in real life. He picked it up, considering taking this photo rather than the black and white snapshot he'd already put in his pocket. In case they needed a "Have you seen this girl?" photo to show someone. But he set it gently down again. They weren't going to be showing her photo to anyone, he was pretty sure, and if on the off-chance they did need one, he liked the one he'd already put in his pocket better.

See, the photomat picture said, *this guy was lucky enough to get that girl.*

He paused, considering both pictures, then picked up the glam shot, too, and placed them both in his back pocket. Knowing it was stupid.

There was one other thing. Kneeling in front of his bookcase, Albert pulled *Treasure Island* off the shelf and felt around until he found the envelope with Lily's letter. He took the postcard out and tucked it back into *Treasure Island*, then folded the envelope with the letter into his other back pocket. Obviously there was no way he was leaving it behind.

That was the limit of Albert's packing.

Stop screwing around and just go.

Albert went to his door and opened it quietly, just a crack. His parents were talking in voices that drifted down the hall over the sound of the television. Not for the first time, their topic of discussion was Albert and Lily. It was like they thought they were alone in the house, or that Albert was deaf. Snatches of their conversation reached his ears.

"... was never this bad before he met that girl." This was Albert's mother speaking.

"Oh, Van ... he's a teenager."

"No. That girl has him bewitched. She's going to ruin his life! Even when she's not here, she's ruining his life."

That girl ...

"I feel for her parents," said Albert's father, "to have a child with so many problems."

"I feel worse for us, if she drags our son down with her," Albert's mother said. Laughter from the TV filled the silence after she spoke.

"I know ... but she needs help. If she were *my* kid, I'd have her put away so she could get it."

An angry snort from Albert's mother. "I just wish Albert would see her for what she is—a millstone."

"You can't say anything to him," said his father, "or you know what will happen. He'll just dig in more, and before you know it, we'll be grandparents."

Ears burning, Albert didn't wait to hear more. It was just the same old crap they'd been saying for a while and he was in too much of a hurry to worry about it now. He shut the door as softly as possible. The important thing was, his parents were parked in front of the TV. He had the sad Albert-shaped lump still stuffed under the covers of his bed, which would probably be fine if all they did was look in on him with the light off. He picked up his coat.

He opened the window just wide enough to slip through. After he dropped to the ground, he hurried across the yard, across the street, and into the alley.

The night seemed really empty. The snow had stopped again and the ground was wet as the flakes melted when they hit the ground. Everyone seemed to be wherever they belonged instead of out here—probably bathrobed-out like his parents in front of the TV. Albert had always found it spooky how shifting a few hours changed the streets from a world of cars on their way home from work, school buses stopped at corners, other kids on their way home for family dinner, to a world of silence and stillness. Everyone was where they were supposed to be for the night; everyone except Albert Morales and—he hoped—Olivia Odilon. Maybe it was because his nerves were tweaked, but Albert found the stillness eerily dreamlike.

Then he remembered he was supposed to be downtown in half an hour, which wasn't going to happen if he kept screwing around. So, as it seemed he'd been doing every time he left the house lately, he broke into a slow jog, as fast as he dared.

Twenty-five

11 p.m.

The sun has long set behind the mountains by the time they make it up to the scattered group of cottages around the lake. In the gloom, the dark water looks like a basin of blood and Albert can hardly make out Olivia's face, even though she's standing right next to him.

"Which house was it?" he asks impatiently. His stomach is doing nervous acrobatics now that they're here. His eagerness isn't just simple excitement at the thought of being reunited with Lily... it's tainted with a superstitious nagging that now that they're here, it was too easy. There's a metallic taste in his mouth he tries to ignore.

"Over there," she says shortly, pointing to a vague shape up by the water. She begins walking and he follows.

"So now we... what? Go up to the house and knock?"

She shrugs. "I don't know any more than you do. Let's just, I don't know, have a look around." Her words are slurred and her steps unsteady.

Albert nods wearily, the dim light from the moon and stars streaking like tracers in front of his eyes. He's so tired he feels he's lost his sense of place...like there's never been a time when he hasn't been walking and searching, and there never will be. His life feels like a permanent, restless middle of the night. The back of his tongue itches.

"Are you coming?" Lily is calling softly to him from up ahead...Lily.

"Dude, are you coming or not?"

Jerking his head up, he realizes that he's spaced off. Then the illusion or dream or whatever it is clears like mist and he can see Olivia's silhouette in the darkness.

The sense of dreaming only grows stronger when Olivia leads them down a long, narrow path to the cottage itself— a tiny, weathered building almost on the edge of the water. By moonlight they search the exterior of the rough, shingle-sided cottage, rustling the bushes and trees and calling out Lily's name softly. There's no sign of her anywhere. The small drifts of snow against the house hold no footprints except the ones Albert and Olivia are making.

The door to the cottage is locked, of course, and the shuttered windows are locked, too. By this time Albert is no longer sure he hasn't crossed over to dreaming; his thoughts and movements are slow and frustrated by air that feels thick and resistant like water. It's like a dream of running desperately toward something and not getting anywhere no matter how hard he pushes the muscles of his legs.

Rattling the door latch again fruitlessly, Albert says to Olivia, "Maybe she figured out a way inside and she's hiding in there."

From somewhere at his back, Olivia makes a noise somewhere between a moan and a protest.

"Lily!" Albert calls suddenly, his voice ringing in the silence. He shakes the locked and deadbolted handle and pounds the surprisingly sturdy door. "Lily, it's me!"

"Albert—" Olivia says, grabbing his wrist.

He shakes her off and charges around to the back of the cottage, repeating his assault against the back door and still calling loudly for Lily.

"Albert!" Olivia says again sharply, slipping under his arm to put herself between him and the door. "This place is a vault. She's not in there."

He drops his hands. "But she has to be," he says stupidly. He pulls out the envelope, worn from riding in his back pocket, and stares at Lily's letter. "It says here she's gone to 'the last good place' and that she'll wait for me here. She must've known I'd remember..." he says, forgetting that he barely did, and that he's had to get the rest from Olivia.

"She said she'd wait as long as she could," Olivia corrects gently. "But hey, there's still the boathouse." She points toward the long shack spanning the beach and the nearby dock.

They leave the house and head down the path to the

boathouse, and what they find there is more nothing. No sign of Lily. The door to the narrow building is unlocked and when they let themselves in, darkness and the sound of lapping water against the dock are what meet them. It takes a few moments for their eyes to adjust to the dark, and then they can make out the vague shapes of the stuff hanging on the wall pegs. The place is empty of life.

"Maybe there's something, though, something left behind," Albert says to Olivia, his voice echoing off the walls and the water. "I wish I had a flashlight."

"I don't know what good it will do," Olivia says, "but I think there should be a light of some sort in here."

She pushes into the gloom, feeling her way carefully along. Albert watches her shadow moving, holding his breath and glad that she's able to make sense of the alien shapes she touches, shapes he sees only as vague question marks. The wet wood smell is strong in here and the air doesn't taste clean.

That funny nagging feeling he's had for the last several hours has come back stronger, a feeling that was briefly asleep but is awake again now. And here he was yelling like an idiot when he has a feeling that someone might be nearby who'd followed them. It isn't a particular sound or smell that makes the feeling so strong...he's not sure what it is. Even so, he's convinced someone else is nearby in the darkness.

Just as Albert has decided, no matter how dumb it sounds, to say something to Olivia before she finds a flashlight and lets anyone who is looking know they're there,

Olivia lets out a cry of triumph and blinds Albert with the light of a battery-operated lantern.

Now that it's lit, the boathouse shows a few signs that someone has been there recently, but those signs aren't at all comforting. The words he's about to say die on Albert's lips, overshadowed by a fresher fear than the one of being caught.

Looking beyond what's supposed to be in the boat-house—the old life jackets and paddles and fishing poles and tarps and buckets—it's clear what's *not* supposed to be there. And from what's not supposed to be there, Albert knows someone has been sleeping here. There's a heap of smelly clothes in the far corner, the odor detectable even from where they stand near the door. These clothes are piled on a tarp with a foam life preserver on top like a makeshift pillow on a foul bed. There are some rotting food scraps, more than a couple of empty booze bottles, and a pile of magazines. Moving closer, Albert prods the glossy stack with his foot. The pile collapses and fans out, *Good Housekeeping* sliding down to reveal *Hustler* and an old issue of *Time* near the top.

"Transients," Olivia says softly. "When we used to come here, I remember hearing adults talking about them coming in the winter. We should get out of here. Don't mess with any of it."

But Albert isn't really listening. He can only think that if Lily has been here, if she'd been surprised into dropping an earring, or a shoe—

—or a chunk of hair, pulled out as she ran away from a stranger sleeping here—

—it would've been the easiest thing in the world for someone to drop whatever it was into the water and watch it sink…

Despair threatens to overwhelm him and Albert pushes these thoughts away, trying to find anything else to hold on to. He can come up with nothing, and feels himself close to sinking into the black pool.

"I'm so tired of Lily making us worry!" Olivia cries, dropping the flashlight and pressing herself suddenly and hard against Albert's skinny chest.

And though he truly doubts whether it is the truth, he says to Olivia, as he's said to himself many times already, "It's going to be fine."

Up until now, confronted with this empty, smelly boathouse and that black water, he hasn't honestly believed in any terrible outcome. In death. Not really.

The flashlight has rolled into the corner, shooting light up at a weird angle.

"I hate her," Olivia says, barely loud enough to be heard.

"No you don't." Albert isn't sure he's right, but he wants to be. He can't understand why Olivia wanted so badly to come with him if she does.

"In some ways I do." A small sigh. "At least, I wish I did."

Albert puts his arms lightly around this girl who clings to him. He pats her back awkwardly and makes shushing noises like she's baby. She lets out a series of hiccuping sobs. It feels weird to hold her, but kind of familiar, too; he notices that Olivia's hair smells like Lily's ... he could almost pretend this *is* Lily, that the last hours have been a bad dream and he's stumbled on Lily after all. But Olivia is smaller, and sharper, and no matter how he wants to hold on to the illusion for a few more moments, he can't. She isn't Lily. Albert feels even more lost and lonely than if he'd been alone.

The itch in his throat grows stronger, tightening his airway, and then Albert is pushing Olivia away and making a jerky course for the door, trying to catch his breath.

Twenty-six

"What was that for?" Albert exclaimed, his hand flying up to the spot where Olivia had kissed his cheek. According to the giant illuminated dial on the face of the movie theater, it was just after midnight. He'd been pacing up and down the sidewalk in front of the building when Olivia appeared out of nowhere and took his hands in hers.

"Shut up, dumbass," she hissed between her teeth as a terrible grin stretched across her mouth. Still holding his hands, she pulled him toward the entrance. "You're late—I was afraid you weren't coming."

"It wasn't that easy—"

She gave his hand a hard squeeze. "Never mind. Remember, we're on a date. Got it? Hold my hand and try to act like you like it."

Maybe it was his nerves, but he disliked being treated like an idiot by this girl. Yet they were together now in the search for Lily, so he decided it was easier to let it go than start something over it. He gave her hand a hard squeeze that she ignored as she led him up to the box office window. She asked for two tickets to the midnight show, which turned out to be a teen slasher pic that had come out two months earlier.

"It's started already," the ticket taker told them. Then he gave Albert a knowing glance and said, "Maybe you don't care."

"Just give us two tickets," Olivia said, sliding four bucks under the little half circle cut in the box office window. The clerk slid the tickets back with a shrug.

Frontier Cinemas was a rundown, second-run theater in a rundown strip mall on the seedy edge of downtown. In all his months living in Little Solace, Albert had passed it a few times on the way to better places, but he had never been inside. The lobby was dim and everything seemed to have a layer of old dust. The air smelled of mildewed carpet and stale popcorn.

Besides the bored-looking guy slouched behind the snack counter and the equally bored-looking woman ripping tickets, the place was empty. Still, Olivia looked around nervously.

"Let's hurry up and get inside," she said, pulling Albert toward the theaters.

The roar of the surround-sound blasted them as they went through the door. It was too loud to talk, so Albert let Olivia lead him through the near-deserted place to a couple of seats in an empty row near the screen.

Once they were seated, Albert put his mouth almost against Olivia's ear and whispered, "Can I talk now?"

By now she'd dropped the grin and his hand as well. Turning on him with her more familiar scowl, she leaned close and whispered, "I think Perry saw me leave the house."

He had to strain to hear her. "When you snuck out?"

He felt her head nodding. He glanced up when the girl on the movie screen let out a shriek and the light's glow turned red with the fake blood soaking the scene.

"Do you think he followed you?"

"I don't know," she said. "Maybe not." Even at a whisper, competing with the blaring movie, her tone was completely unconvincing. After a moment she said, "If he did follow me, then I guess he'll be waiting for us outside the theater."

Albert's stomach sank. "What are we going to do? If he knows you're with me, he's going to put two and two together…"

"Yeah. So we'll wait until this shitty movie is over, then we'll sneak out the back exit during the credits, before the lights come on, and hope we get lucky."

"That's it? Hope for luck—that's your best idea?" The words came out in a breathless squeak that made her flinch away in irritation. "Luck hasn't done much for us so far."

"You have a better idea?" She paused and when he didn't argue, she went on, her breath hot on his ear. "Wonder which of us is parked closer. Where's your car?"

"It doesn't exist. I got here on foot."

"Doesn't matter. Either way, we'd be too obvious wherever we went." She was thinking out loud. "We'd be seen eventually, probably sooner than later. The cops will be looking for you. And Perry will be looking for both of us. Not to mention your parents and my mom. So we can't drive any identifiable vehicles."

"So what—we take the train? A bus?" He wasn't sure what she was saying.

"You really aren't from around here, are you?" Her sentence was cut short by a giant onscreen explosion and more screams. The momentary glare of the fireball illuminated the scornful expression on her face. It was an expression Albert was beginning to think she wore a lot. "There is no train or bus to—"

"Don't say it," Albert said, even though there was no way anyone could hear her besides him. Still, he had to stifle the urge to cover her mouth with his hand. He was sure the dirty look was still there, but at least it was too dark to see it.

"The Last Good Place. So we're going to walk."

"In February? Up in the mountains? How far is it?"

"If I remember, it's less than a hundred miles. Totally doable, I think. It'll only take a few days, and we won't have to worry about cops running our plates." She seemed to be smiling again. "Where's your sense of adventure, Frodo?"

"This isn't a joke." But after his initial surprise at the

idea, it started to make a kind of crazy sense. "They can't follow what they can't find, is that the idea?"

She nodded, her movement a dim blur in the dark.

Albert could almost feel the angry spittle showering his face as he imagined his mother shouting up at him in the aftermath of what she would call "a stunt like this."

"So, what, we're just going to walk a hundred miles?" he said. "Just like that?"

"Going to have to," she said.

"Okay then." Once it was decided, he felt something he wouldn't have expected: he felt relief. They now had something definite they were going to do. No more waiting.

Then they both leaned back into their seats, their necks craned as they gazed at the screen in front of them, neither of them really looking at the flashing images. Albert closed his eyes, not enjoying the movie at all.

After the seemingly endless bloodbath finally ended and the credits started to roll, Olivia leaned over the armrest until her mouth was once again at Albert's ear. "Are we really doing this?"

"I think we are."

The lights were coming up now and people were starting to rise. She tapped his wrist. "Now."

They both stood, walking quickly but trying not to draw attention. Olivia got to the door first and pushed it open, the dim light of the hall seeming to flood the movie theater. Just outside, a right turn led down a winding hall back past the bathrooms to the front of the theater; just to the left was the side door exit. Olivia went for the exit but Albert stopped her.

"If your stepfather did follow you, he'll probably be right behind us."

"Then shouldn't we hurry?" She pushed on the exit and said, "Let's just go."

He followed.

It was a dark night, overcast, but the parking lot lights were bright. Olivia led them on a winding route along the back of the building, through some prickly branches of evergreen shrubbery and into the dark, narrow lanes of the residential neighborhood behind the Frontier property.

"Where are we going?" Albert finally asked.

"To my car."

Before he could say anything else, they were beside a little two-door junker car and Olivia was keying the lock. "Get in already," she snapped, adding, "and don't just sit there with the door open and the dome light on!"

"I thought we decided it was too dangerous to drive?" Albert asked.

Olivia was already pulling away from the curb. "It is," she said, "but a well-placed car is a useful, um, misdirection, don't you think?"

"What?" They'd just begun a life on the run, and already he sucked at it.

"Shit," Olivia breathed, ignoring him as her eyes left the road for the rearview mirror. "Lights just went on back there. Maybe we are being followed."

Albert twisted around to look and saw the pair of lights gaining. His heart collapsed.

"I hope this works," she said.

"Hope what works?"

But there was no need for her to respond as it became very obvious what she meant. She put her foot down on the pedal until they were going about fifteen over the limit. She ran the stop sign at a major intersection, and they were lucky there was no traffic at the moment they blew through. Three blocks on the other side of that road, she made a series of moves in such rapid order it was almost instantaneous: right before a smaller cross street, she flipped on her right turn signal, and still going way too fast to make the turn, she cut the headlights and cranked a hard left. Albert braced himself on the dashboard against the motion, all the time watching the headlights in the rearview mirror. They were still on the other side of that stop sign Olivia had run, maybe far enough away that her Evasive Driving 101 maneuver could actually work.

"Let me know if you see them," she said, barreling down the road in almost total darkness.

"I couldn't even make out a car," Albert said, both exhilarated and terrified at the sensation of speeding into nothingness.

"Then just tell me if you see any headlights at all."

Her eyes fixed firmly ahead, Olivia took several more turns before she slowed down a bit and put the lights back on. It was a miracle that they hadn't hit something or gotten pulled over by a cop. Even then, she didn't slow down much. She seemed to be moving very deliberately.

"I give up," Albert said. "Where are we going?"

"Route 21," Olivia said, "and then Ridgeway. It's about five miles in the wrong direction, south and east. We want to go north. There's a Walmart in Ridgeway where we're going to ditch the car. We'll double back on foot."

"Right. Misdirection," Albert said. "They'll find the car within a day or so, and figure out our direction. Except they'll be wrong."

She pulled out onto Route 21 right in front of a car, gunning the gas to escape a rear-end collision and ignoring the horn. "Well, we have to try, anyway, right?"

Twenty-seven

11:30 p.m.

It's a particularly bad attack—asthma or panic, he doesn't know anymore—but it passes even as Albert begins to fear he will never catch his breath again. Olivia follows him out of the boathouse, trying to make sure he's okay, but he waves her off. So she just stands a few feet away, watching him until the attack seems to finally pass.

"Now what?" she asks.

He shrugs.

After the dead end at the boathouse, there is nothing for Albert and Olivia to do but give up for the night and try to sleep for a few hours. They are exhausted, hungry, and bitterly disappointed. The total effect is that neither of them can stay on their feet any longer. They've hit a dead end in more ways than one.

Although the shelter of the boathouse is the most likely place to camp for the night, neither Albert nor Olivia wants to sleep in that creepy and claustrophobic place. In wordless agreement, they find another tarp and a couple of life preservers and carry them to the back side of the old summer cottage itself, a dark nook protected from the wind and from the moonlight by the peak of the roof. Spreading the tarp out as a double bedroll and using the life preservers as pillows, Olivia and Albert huddle close and wait for sleep.

The tarp is stiff and the ground rocky and cold. Albert wants to toss and turn and find a comfortable position, but he holds himself still for Olivia's sake. He wishes for sleep, but his mind keeps playing over all the things he very much *doesn't* want to think about.

Like: it would be such a supreme joke if Lily got this far way from Kogen just to get herself killed by some random homeless guy who found her hiding spot first.

I'm not going to think that way, he tells himself. At this moment, the only thing is sleep. Then, in the morning, they can begin searching again. Maybe some new idea will take root and grow in his subconscious while he sleeps. By the light of morning, maybe this dead-end campout won't seem like as much of a dead end as it looks right now.

The stiff tarp crinkles as Olivia turns over from her back to her side. She faces Albert, and even in the dimness he can see, by the barest reflection of light in her eyes, that she's looking at him.

"Still awake?" she whispers.

He lets out a sigh that turns into a shiver. "Yeah."

He really, really doesn't feel like talking right now, but apparently Olivia does.

"I didn't realize how positive I was we'd find her here," she says, her words coming out in a sleepy drawl. "This *is* her Last Good Place. So if she's not here, where the hell did she go?"

"We must be missing something. We have to be."

After he speaks, a few beats go by and he decides she must've gone back to sleep.

But then she says, "And even if we do find her…"

"We *will* find her," he says. He doesn't want to consider any other outcome. "She's waiting for us—me, anyway—somewhere. I know she is. I guess I was wrong about where, that's all. I need to keep thinking."

"So we find her. So what? Haven't we been idiotic to think finding Lily will solve everything?" Albert can hear in her voice that thick sound of a person holding back tears. "We don't know what kind of condition she's in…what she remembers. She might be strung out on something, or hiding, or still running, or…I don't know. Even if we find her…the needle in the haystack…and we take her home, that doesn't protect any of us from Perry, does it? We'll be going right back to where we started, won't we, without the journal?"

"Unless Lily remembers," Albert says. It's what he's been clinging to.

"Right. One hell of a thing to hang everything on, though, wouldn't you say? Last time I checked, Lily was running away from Little Solace so she could *stop* remembering anything. That's what Lily does when things are bad. She bails." She sounds angry. "Face it, Morales—she bailed on you. On both of us."

He doesn't like to admit to himself how convincing Olivia's words are, so he rejects them. Instead, he clings tighter to his hope and he isn't letting it go until someone can use something real, something actual, to rip it away.

"She was scared and she thought no one could help her. But that's all changed. *We* know about the diary. *We* can help her remember. We'll convince her to come back and make someone listen to her, and us, about Kogen." The more he talks, the more confidence he feels in what he's saying. "Kogen knows that we know what he did to Lily. So it's not just Lily who's in danger. None of the three of us is safe until we get Lily to go to the police. Until Lily talks, he has some big reasons to shut us up before the story gets out. But if, if she does talk, he's screwed."

"Okay, but when I try to envision everything you've said, I can't see it happening. It's too big. It's too hard."

"We don't have any choice but to try, though, do we?"

She has no answer to this. After a while, what has been a pause and then a lull in the conversation stretches back into silence. Albert slides into this cold quiet as easily as if into water, and soon there's no noise in that protected nook in the back of the house except two sets of long, deep breaths.

And of course, as Albert falls into a real sleep for the first time in days, he dreams of the sole thing that occupies his mind. He dreams of Lily.

It was a warm, sunny day and Albert found himself at a park. It was a park unlike any he'd ever been to before, though—the carpet of bright green grass stretched on forever and there were trees and fountains and statues everywhere and he could see a lake off in one direction and a carousel far away in another direction. Of everything, only the lake gave him a familiar tug of recognition. The rest looked like his idea of the grounds at some big old European palace.

He was walking around this unfamiliar park, astonished at how crowded such a large place had become in such a short time. There were people on the lake, crowding the carousel and crowding the lawn. Albert elbowed his way through many happy clusters, focused on heading in a specific, steady direction, but unsure why it had to be this direction and no other.

As he walked, he scanned the faces around him for one face in particular. Lily had come with him to the park, he remembered that very clearly, but somehow they'd gotten separated and he wanted to find her so they could buy ice cream cones. On such a hot day, cold ice cream sounded really good. He was irritated at Lily for disappearing when she had his wallet and he couldn't have any ice cream until he found her.

The park was vast and although he tried to search it methodically, weaving back and forth toward the carousel, he kept getting turned around. Pretty soon he couldn't tell where he'd been or where he was going. The sun was right overhead, melting hot, and with so many people crowded together there was no air.

Just when he was sure he'd never find her, but instead spend eternity pushing against the flow of the endless crowd,

Albert spotted Lily a few yards away. She was moving quickly away from him, and he had to really push to catch up to her. He was beginning to think this was one of those dreams where you chase and chase what you want without ever catching it—and it was then that he reached out for her arm and actually caught hold of it.

He pulled her toward him, spinning her around somehow. "Why did you run off like—" he began, but the sentence died on his lips.

The person he'd grabbed wasn't Lily at all, but a much older woman—she looks French, *he thought irrelevantly—and she was giving him the dirtiest of looks. She jerked her arm out of his grasp and advanced on him, abusing him in a language he didn't recognize but the meaning of which was obvious. Soon she wasn't just forcing him backward but poking an angry finger into his chest to punctuate her words.*

Shortness of breath, Albert's old friend, settled in his chest and pretty soon he was swooning from stress and heat and claustrophobia into another asthma attack. He felt a fuzzy wave of fresh anger as he remembered that Lily had his inhaler, too . . . that she'd probably left him here in this hot crowd with no inhaler and no money on purpose. Nearly fainting, he looked around for a shady patch to lie in until this horrible suffocation passed, but he was surrounded by people and all of them were Lily, all these Lilies turned away from him.

As soon as this passes, *he thought, still fighting for breath.* She could reject him all she wanted—he wasn't going to stop—

Albert wakes up with a start, sitting up, breathless and

sweating in the cold. He can't have been asleep long, since it's still pitch black out. His throat aches from that soundless screaming people do when they're having a bad dream. When he looks down next to him, he can see that Olivia is curled into a tight ball, sound asleep. It takes him a minute to separate reality from his dream, which had been so vivid. He is breathing just fine, which is good.

Lying back down in the cold dark, Albert moves as close to Olivia's warmth as he can. He feels like sleep is far away again, no matter how tired he still is.

Where is she?

He turns the question over and over in his mind, trying to see what he's missing.

Twenty-eight

*A*lbert sat by himself in the crowded lunchroom, trying to act like he was totally engrossed in his sandwich. It was his first week at this new school and his fifth meal on this plastic bench at a nearly empty table in the far corner of the lunchroom. He couldn't wait until he was finally able to stop counting out the days like hash marks on a prison wall ... until he stopped being the new guy.

But at least there was something different today. There was a girl, and now that he'd really seen her, he couldn't help staring.

Once Albert noticed that he was crushing his soggy peanut butter sandwich as he stared, open-mouthed, at the girl a couple tables over, he ducked his head, feeling himself blush. He was the sole person at his table since the two Korean exchange students and the weird kid who wore a green bow tie every day and drank soup from a thermos had already finished their lunches and left this particular loser table. There was no one around to make fun of how uncool he was. The girl herself hadn't seemed to notice Albert's creepy staring; she was standing a little apart from the crowd around a nearby lunch table, staring at nothing as if she was thinking hard about something.

Albert had seen her a couple of times in the halls. He didn't have any classes with her and he didn't know her name. He had seen her before, but not really noticed her until today. As he was eating his lunch in complete solitude, not cool enough for the Korean girls or Mr. Bow Tie even to hang out with, a loud clattering had startled him to attention. He looked up to see this girl standing perfectly still, face white with two red splotches on her cheeks, after apparently dropping her lunch tray on the table. Albert watched as this part of the room went silent for about one entire second before swallowing up the girl and her loud tray in the general din. He watched as the girl and the girl she was with exchanged a few words before sitting down at the crowded table to eat.

And then it hit him that this girl was very pretty.

He spent the next twenty minutes trying not to look at her. But he found himself searching for a better look at her face among the shoulders and faces of the other people at her table. When he was looking she never seemed to be talking to anyone. She didn't seem to be there at all.

But then, Albert thought, he might have been projecting his own loneliness a little. In the couple of weeks since he and his parents had moved to Little Solace, he'd sent off two postcards and five emails to his friends, and he'd received exactly one return email. He was forced to conclude that his old friends had forgotten him already. And no one here seemed to like him, either. He was shy, he was unsure of himself, he was gawky and geeky and not even knowing what it was about himself that was putting out the gawky, geeky vibe. Whatever it was, people here had picked up on it immediately.

After a week at this school, Albert was still as out of place as if he'd been flown halfway around the world and dropped from an airplane with nothing but a map, a water bottle, and a Swiss Army knife. As it was, he'd come from halfway across the country, from a school of several thousand to one of several hundred. The teachers here knew all the students by name, had had these kids' older siblings in class, or were on a bowling league or in church group with their moms or dads. As for the students … they'd all grown up together and didn't easily let an outsider into their little world. Or at least, not Albert. He'd had a secret hope when he left his real home that he might start his new school as the cool city guy, but after a week he gave that up. He had no idea how he was going to make it through nearly two years to graduate from this stupid school.

"Forgot my handkerchief," said a voice nearby.

Albert turned his attention back to the table and saw that Mr. Bow Tie was back. "What's that?"

Bow Tie waved a tiny white square at Albert. "My handkerchief. It's one of my favorites. Monogrammed."

Albert gave him a neutral nod, thinking, *This guy's a freak* —with an immediate wave of guilt for turning on a fellow freak. "It's nice," he added, turning his attention back to the girl.

"What are we staring at?" Bow Tie asked, actually sitting down at the table again.

"Nothing," Albert said quickly. He turned to see Bow Tie rolling his eyes. "Do you know that girl's name?" he asked.

"Who?"

Albert pointed her out as subtly as he could, which wasn't very, wishing he hadn't asked.

"That's Lily Odilon. She's a dinosaur."

"A what?" Albert couldn't tell if Bow Tie was a weirdo or if he himself was just not up on the local slang. The girl's name seemed to ring a vague bell.

"She's George Washington High's oldest senior. Kind of a local legend, actually. Lily Odilon? You don't know that story?"

"No," Albert said, wishing Bow Tie didn't have such a loud voice.

"She used to be a real party girl, at the cool parties every weekend, Miss Popularity. She partied too hard a while back and apparently it broke her brain. She was out for months and now she's back. Sort of," he added, turning contemplative, as if sorting this out while unaware of Albert's presence. "I mean, it's her, but not the same her. Got to hand it to her for sticking it out, though, right? No one thought she'd come back after all that stuff with the laughing gas and the police and the hospital. She's kind of ..." he said, making a whirling gesture at his temple with his finger.

"Thanks," Albert mumbled, getting to his feet and thinking privately that a seventeen-year-old with a green bow tie and monogrammed hanky probably shouldn't be judging other people's sanity.

He took a couple steps in Lily Odilon's direction before he realized that he didn't know what he intended to do. Introduce himself? Talk to her, in front of all those people? What he did was stop moving toward her before it was too late and he made an ass of himself. He made a sharp turn toward some distant garbage bin instead. He made throwing away his lunch sack into as lengthy a thing as he could manage, just to be doing something.

But he didn't stop watching her. She looked so apart and kind of sad, and he felt drawn to her, misfit to misfit. Then the other girl gave Lily Odilon's shoulder a squeeze and left her at an empty lunch table as the rest of the group left, too.

Albert exhaled gustily, then walked toward her before he could stop himself.

"Hi," he said once he was in front of her. When he spoke, his words came out rushed, not at all smooth. "I'm Albert. I'm new and I don't know anybody here."

Her eyes widened at his voice, and she looked up as if she hadn't really seen him before that moment. Then she smiled. "I'm Lily."

Twenty-nine

3:05 a.m.

*B*efore Albert and Olivia had pretty much collapsed, there was an unspoken understanding that they would just pick the search up again tomorrow. And if they came up with nothing again, then they would search the day after that, and then every tomorrow after that until something changed. The agreement made, they both doze in that feverish limbo between consciousness and unconsciousness.

But there won't be an endless series of tomorrows, that's the thing. Lying on the tarp, conscious but feeling brain-dead, Albert keeps cycling through the same thought: every day they don't find Lily makes it all the more likely they will never find her. They're two points on a graph—Lily is one, Albert and Olivia are the other—with a shrinking chance of ever intersecting.

With the added pressure that he and Olivia aren't the only ones in the race.

He stares up at the starlit sky, wishing his brain would rest long enough for him to catch another scrap of sleep, one without nightmares.

The thought of Lily hurts him again, a physical pain. Where is she, and what is she thinking? He gives the wall at his head a vindictive punch. It's like punching ice; an indifferent shingle scrapes off the skin of his knuckles and does nothing for his frustration.

"Feel better?" Olivia's awake, too.

"No." He shivers in the cold and adjusts the hard life preserver under his head. "I wish I knew what to do."

"That's definitely my sister, in a nutshell," Olivia says.

Silence again. Albert's thoughts fracture and subside. His breathing grows slow and deep.

Some time later, Albert's eyes are popping open again and something is wrong. He's surprised to find that he has slept; it's still dark. He feels a hand at his back. Ignoring the crick in his neck, he rolls over instinctively and catches hold of a slim wrist, pulling himself and the owner of the wrist to a sitting position.

Olivia gives a stifled cry and they glare at each other.

"What the hell?" he says, snatching up the object that's fallen from her fingers. He holds up Lily's letter. "Why'd you pick my pocket while I was asleep?"

"I had a dream." Before he can react to this, she takes the letter back from him and scrambles to her feet, away from him, holding the little piece of paper up in an attempt to catch any light. "I wanted to read it again but I didn't want to wake you up." Her voice is excited.

Catching her excitement, Albert says quickly, "What is it?"

"We were just being *stupid*," she says, ignoring him. "Or maybe just I was. It doesn't matter. Albert," she says, "I was so *scared* when she wasn't here and there was that smelly bum pile in the boat house—but she was only here for a moment, if at all. She was just passing through. I was having a dream, I don't even remember it really, and when I woke up, I remembered that the boat was gone."

"The boat?"

"Shut up. I'm trying to tell you … I know what we missed. I know where she is!"

He staggers up and gives her a happy squeeze, then pulls her arms from around his neck. He's still confused, but her excitement is so genuine it's hard not to feel it too. "What are you talking about? How do you know where she is?"

She takes a deep breath. "When we were in the boathouse, I noticed that the canoe was gone. It *always* hung there when we were here in the summers. Well, whenever we weren't using it, which was all the time. And it was gone this time, but I didn't really think anything of it. It's been so long…"

"You're still not making any sense." He wonders whether shaking her will make the story come spilling out any faster.

"We're so stupid," she says again. "I just hope she'll hold on a little while longer until we get there." Albert's face must show what he's thinking, because Olivia says hastily, "You know Lily and her secrets. She had a secret place here that last summer."

"And you just now thought of it?" But a dim memory reaches him as he says it, and it hovers at the edge of his consciousness, just out of reach.

"I know. But she only had it for an afternoon before I knew about it and it wasn't a secret anymore. And then I forgot, because we never came back. It was almost nothing, except to Lily."

Neither of them can stay still. So they walk around the house in the dark, down to the end of the little dock and back, the lapping water a black pool around them. They make a wide, slow circuit around the cottage and the lake-front while Olivia tells Albert what she'd missed about The Last Good Place.

It was late summer, she explains—the last summer, it turned out, that Rene Odilon and her two daughters would go to the little cabin by the lake. "We'd spent the morning doing something together, I don't even remember what. I remember Mom sending us to our room for a nap while she went to hers for one, too. I fell asleep. When I woke up, Lily wasn't there. I figured she'd gotten up to go play without me, which was something she was always doing—I wanted to play with her and she wanted to play alone.

"I slipped out of bed to find her, all quiet so Mom wouldn't hear me, because I knew Lily would be mad if I got her in trouble. I went all around the house looking for her, and when I couldn't find her I went outside. I couldn't find her there, either. I think I must have decided to go down to the water, because I remember I was walking barefoot in the sand when I looked out on the water and saw Lily out there in the boat. She was so far away I could barely make her out.

"I was terrified—afraid she would drown but also afraid Mom would catch her. I didn't know what to do, so I went back to the house and got into my bed. I guess I fell asleep, and when I woke up, Mom was shaking me and asking me where Lily was."

"Did you tell her?" Albert asks.

Olivia shakes her head. "Not at first. I was more afraid of Lily getting mad at me for tattling than I was of Mom. But after several hours, when Lily still hadn't come back and Mom was upset and crying and worried out of her mind, I told her what I'd seen. I acted like I'd seen it from the window, like I might have thought it was a dream. My mom was frantic when I told her. She was about to call the police when Lily came into the house." Olivia looks toward the black lake as if reliving the day.

"All Lily would say was that she'd been rowing around the lake. Mom was really angry but she believed her. I didn't believe her, though, because I knew that look she had on her face. She was hiding something. When we were alone in our room after Mom sent us both to bed, I asked her where she'd really gone. She didn't want to tell me and at first she told me the same story she'd told Mom. But I told her she had to tell me, that she owed me because she'd gone off without taking me with her. So she started to tell me where she'd gone, but that wasn't good enough, either. I wanted her to take me there. I knew it had to be good if she needed to lie about it.

"So the next morning, right after breakfast, Lily told Mom we were going rowing on the lake. Once we were in the canoe, Lily steered us along the shore until she found what she was looking for—this little stream cutting through an arm of marshy land and flowing toward some other part of the lake. The stream got wider and we floated for a long time, not paddling, not even talking, until we came to this little island-y thing. I guess it was a like a small peninsula. It was crowded with aspen trees and there was this little falling-down house that didn't have any glass or doors and barely even a roof, with plants growing inside and through it. Lily told me it was a miner's shack and that she'd played there all yesterday afternoon. It was tiny, hidden in the trees, and I understood why she'd wanted to keep it a secret. It was perfect."

Albert waits for her to go on, but Olivia is apparently done. "Get it? That's where she is, I'm sure."

"Let's go then."

"No," she says. "I can't find it in the dark. We can't do anything until it gets light. And when it does, *if* I can find the way, maybe we'll finally catch a break."

When Albert doesn't immediately respond, she shrugs, that feigned universal indifference that she seems to have perfected, and leaves him at the edge of the little yard. A moment later he hears the tarp crinkle under her weight.

He follows her, lying down next to her on the cold stiff tarp, but the idea of sleep is ludicrous—he's too excited. Lily might be okay after all. And they might find her after all. And things might work out after all. It's too good to think about directly; like staring into the sun, it hurts.

He tries to calm his racing heart, feeling that dawn has never been as far away as it is right now. After an eternity made up of wakeful minutes, he receives a second shock, which sends sleep flying away for good.

A sharp crack, like a twig breaking, makes his unsleeping eyes fly open, and he's sure he sees a moving shadow just a couple of feet away. Albert blinks and sits up, unsure whether sleep cobwebs are messing up his perception or what. But what he sees isn't a tree, or his imagination, or even a stranger.

It's Patrick MacLennan.

Thirty

On their first date, Albert had scrounged together all the money he had so he could take Lily out. He was as nervous as he'd ever been and unable to believe his luck that she'd agreed to go out with him. He couldn't think of anything cool to do, and the idea of trying to eat while sitting across from this beautiful, fascinating girl made him choke, so he took her to the only vaguely datish place he could think of in Little Solace. He took her bowling. And he had to beg and plead with his parents in order to get the keys to his dad's rusty old Dodge.

Between home and Lily's house and the bowling alley, the car acted like it was about to die at every other intersection. The bowling itself was a disaster. They both sucked at it, and it was so loud in the bowling alley that they couldn't really talk. When they gave up after two games and got back into Albert's dad's car to leave, they both smelled like the cigarette smoke from the crowded lanes and neither of them could think of anything to say.

Wanting to sink into a hole and disappear, Albert steered the car automatically toward Lily's house.

"Hey," she said after a couple of blocks, "do you want to get some pie or something? I don't feel like going home yet."

They ended up going to the twenty-four-hour diner at the truck stop by the freeway and talking over muddy coffee until three hours past Albert's curfew. When he dropped Lily off in front her house, it felt like no time had passed but also like they'd always known each other. Somehow, while they were self-consciously trading bites from a big slab of peach pie, Albert's little crush had turned into lovesickness. He caught major hell from his worried parents when he finally got home, but it had been so worth getting in trouble.

There was a second date, after they were both ungrounded. Inexperienced Albert found out that on a second date, Lily hinted at everything. On the third date, she did almost everything. And Albert—who had done nothing besides making out with a couple of girls and getting oh-so-briefly to second base once with a girl he'd taken to a party—couldn't believe his good luck. For some reason, this awesome and kinda scary girl wanted him as much as he wanted her.

On the fourth date—whether they were dates, exactly, Albert didn't know or really care—they said they loved each other. Albert had been delirious with desire when he'd said it, but he'd meant it.

It wasn't too long before Albert was able to recognize

when "the Other Lily," as he thought of it, came around. When she was the Other Lily, she didn't laugh as much and most definitely didn't want to be touched. At these times she clung to Albert, craving reassurance but still pushing him away. Her vulnerability was a raw, naked thing, hard to witness and harder for Albert, himself lovesick, to understand.

On that fourth whatever, he'd tried to kiss her, a wet and messy consuming kiss, certainly not the first they'd shared, but she turned her face and his mouth met her cheek instead of her lips. They were alone in her basement and no one else knew he was there. They were squeezed together on an old loveseat, the TV playing a movie on mute and a record spinning out soft music they both ignored.

"Did I do something wrong?" he said.

She wouldn't look at him and he could see that her eyes were very shiny.

"Hey," he said, alarmed. "What's the matter?" The Other Lily had shown up, it seemed.

"It's so stupid." She shook her head and laughed, wiping at her eyes with the back of her hand. "Sometimes I'm afraid you'll hurt me."

"I won't," he said breathlessly. "I could never, because—

Thirty-one

6:45 a.m.

Albert's first instinct is to shield Olivia from MacLennan, but she's awake, too, and she's ducking away before he can do much of anything. From the corner of his eye he sees her spring to her feet. He scrambles up as well, never taking his eyes off MacLennan.

Albert's tired brain does a few somersaults as he tries to figure out what to do next. He's been sensing something—someone—for miles, and here that something is. Finally. MacLennan in front of him... not the boogey monster, but a real person. Albert can't quite wrap his mind around the fact that the guy isn't here to knock a lunch tray out of his hands for his buddies' amusement. It's much more serious.

Albert clenches his fists to stop them from shaking. He

wonders what's going to happen. Are they actually going to have to fight?

Bringing him back to the moment and adding to its surrealness is Olivia's voice from over his shoulder. "Look, Morales, it's Perry's little bitch." Her voice is bright but brittle, like it's about to break. As if this is just one setback too many.

"Shut up," Albert says sharply, adding in a softer voice, "If you piss him off he's going to punch me, not you." He glances over at her and sees her biting her lip, her black glare shifting between Albert and MacLennan before settling on MacLennan.

To MacLennan, Albert says, "So?" He wonders how long MacLennan has been hanging around, and what, if anything, he's heard.

MacLennan takes a step forward and Albert puts out a protective arm to push Olivia back. Albert can't see anything in MacLennan's hands, but it's too dark to be sure and he isn't taking any chances. "Stop there."

"You two really know how to make a guy feel welcome," MacLennan says, putting his hands up. It sounds like he's laughing, but he takes a few steps back just the same.

"Are you alone?"

"Completely," MacLennan says. "My truck is about half a mile up the road."

"He's probably lying," Olivia says to Albert. To MacLennan, she says, "Who's back there? The GWHS Wolverines' starting line? The cops? Wait, let me guess, your new best friend, my stepfather?"

"Olivia—" Albert says.

But MacLennan interrupts him. "Well, that's one thing I don't have to wonder about. Yes, folks," he says, as if talking to a crowd, "Liv Odilon is still a huge bitch." Then, to her, "I guess you don't wonder why no one likes you anymore."

"Funny," she says. "I thought it was because you felt guilty for letting my sister almost bleed to death when you idiots were—"

"Stop!" Albert shouts at them both, his voice ringing. "You," he says to MacLennan in what he hopes is a menacing voice. "What are you doing here?"

MacLennan turns his face up to the sky for a moment and sighs. He doesn't act menaced. "Looking for you two."

Afraid to ask the question but asking it anyway, Albert says, "Did Kogen put you up to it?"

"No," MacLennan says. His face is grim. "I'm here because the cops are looking for you. I've been … I guess you could say I'm sort of helping Detective Andersen."

Albert's heart sinks. That isn't much better.

"Then we can assume you're not here to kill us, anyway," Olivia says with a humorless laugh. "How'd you find us?"

"I *followed* you. You're not as stealthy as you think you are."

Before MacLennan can say anything else, Olivia is flying at him. "No matter what, she was your friend!" she screams, her voice echoing in the clear air. "Do you want me to tell you what Perry did to her? What he'll do to *me* if your cop friends come and force me to go home?"

MacLennan catches her wrists easily as she comes at him, pulling her to his chest and tightening his grip on her. Albert moves to pull Olivia out of MacLennan's grasp but MacLennan says, "Stay the hell back, Morales, and let me explain." To Olivia he says, "I don't want to stand here and keep your arms pinned, but if you don't calm down and listen to me for a minute, I will."

"Let go of me, Patrick," she says in a dead tone.

He does. He releases her with a small push and she stumbles away from both him and Albert. She sits on a rock a little bit away.

"Are you going to explain, then," asks Albert, "or are you stalling for time?"

"Why would I be stalling?"

"You're still doing it! Is there a SWAT team waiting nearby or something?"

"You're a weird dude," MacLennan says, shaking his head. "I've been following you by myself. There's no one else."

The meaning of this hits Albert hard, and for a moment he thinks his legs won't hold him up. He's been thinking they've been so clever, and that if they've done nothing else right, at least they've managed to escape the net of Little Solace. But here this mouth-breathing jock itch has been right behind them all along. They've been just that easy to follow—so easy a not-so-bright guy their own age has done it. They've led him along, almost right to Lily.

They haven't escaped at all; they've just been given

enough rope to tie neatly around their own necks for whoever wants to pull. The only thing Albert can't understand is why MacLennan has bothered following them in the first place.

"I don't get it," he says. "What happened? From what I saw at the gas station, you're in pretty deep with Kogen. We're supposed to believe you're not helping him now?"

"And why did the police let us get this far, if you've been behind us all along?" comes Olivia's voice from where she sits.

"The police didn't send me," MacLennan says. "You don't understand anything. You haven't been there."

"I think we understand enough," Olivia says.

MacLennan ignores her, wrapped up in trying to make his explanation. "After that thing at the gas station, I was really freaked. I knew Kogen was intense, but that was..." He trails off, shaking his head. "I tried to catch you when I saw you," he says to Albert, "but you were so fast. I figured you didn't trust me, and it made sense, because up until right before that night I didn't trust you, either. I didn't know what happened to Lily or who might know about it or who was to blame. Then after Kogen got all crazy, waving that gun around—"

"That was you following us at the movies, wasn't it?" Albert says.

"Naw, that was Kogen," MacLennan answers. "I didn't even know you were there. I was following *him*. I found you that night because *he* found you. And when he started chasing you, I stopped following him and started following you. And I've been following you ever since, because I thought you might be going to her. To Lily. I figured you'd found her when you stopped here."

Albert doesn't understand. "Why do you want to find Lily, if you're not helping Kogen?"

"He's lying," Olivia says flatly.

MacLennan drives a fist into his palm. "I'm trying to explain, if you'd just shut up a minute." He pauses, and when neither of them say anything, he goes on. "I know you both think I'm scum. And yeah, at first I *was* helping Kogen. He had me cornered with that shit about the night of Lily's accident, and he threatened to go to the cops if I didn't help him get that diary back. He kept telling me he was trying to help Lily, and he also kept hinting that you"—he's pointing at Albert—"had something to do with Lily being gone. I wanted to believe him. Not just because it was easier. But he started really pressing on me about getting that book back, and it was freaking me out. And then I just started to wonder, what was in that book that he wanted it so bad, you know? So when I stole it from you—"

"You read it," Olivia says. "You knew. The night you gave it back to Perry to *destroy*, you knew. You knew it was evidence."

Albert grabs her by the wrist to stop her from flying at MacLennan again. He wants to hear the rest of the story before they kick the crap out of this asshole, this false friend, this coward. He wants to hear the guy out before they do whatever they have to do to keep him from being a problem, if it isn't already too late.

"Yeah, I read it. Didn't feel good about doing it, and felt even worse about it once I saw what was in there. But Kogen was so strange about it, I had to know. But you have to understand, that guy is crazy dangerous. I couldn't just keep it from him. I was afraid he'd do something to me, or my family."

Olivia snorts. "That would suck, wouldn't it?"

"I didn't have a lot of time to come up with a plan," MacLennan snaps at her. "Kogen was leaning on me hard once he knew I had it. So I took some photos with my cell phone before I gave it to him."

"You did?" Albert has not expected this. It was actually a smart idea, from MacLennan.

"And I called the cops right after I left the gas station and texted them the pictures." By now MacLennan is sitting on the ground, as is Albert. Olivia stays back, now on her feet.

"You know," MacLennan says slowly, "I almost didn't look at her diary before I gave it back to him. I can't stop thinking about what would've happened. What I would've done. It would have been so much easier just to try to believe that Kogen was the good guy and I was helping Lily by helping him." No one says anything. "When I think about it, I feel like I might puke. But I did read it, and now I'm definitely the newest name on your stepfather's shit list, Liv."

Still no one says anything. Albert is by now wide-awake and aware of how cold the air is. "Finish the story," he tells MacLennan. "We need to hear the rest."

"There's not much left to tell," MacLennan says. He tells them briefly how things have changed in Little Solace in the short time since they've left. After the pictures came through, Demiola and then Andersen had a lot of questions and wanted him to come in to make a statement. He didn't want to let Kogen out of his sight, so they had to settle, after making a couple of empty threats, for hearing MacLennan's version—of the long and kind of sordid story of how and why Kogen was blackmailing him—over his cell while he drove. But in light of what the photos showed, even as poor quality as they were, it was too bad to ignore. It seems the police decided to overlook MacLennan's own shady behavior because they brought Kogen in for questioning.

"The cops even thought he might have had something to do with Lily's disappearance," MacLennan tells them. "I don't think the guy's in jail, but he's definitely in deep crap, according to Andersen."

"I thought Andersen and Kogen were friends," Albert says, though it's really a question.

"I guess they were," MacLennan says. "But Andersen's a cop, and the stuff Lily wrote was … bad. Kogen's denying everything, of course, but somehow the TV news and the newspapers got ahold of it, and he had to deny the story to them, too."

Albert wonders if MacLennan had something to do

with that, and how Lily will react to the fact that her private misery is now public.

"If you've been following us, how do you know all this?" he asks.

MacLennan holds up his cell phone in the pre-dawn dark, the little screen glowing. "I've been talking with Andersen, and seriously, if you'd looked at a newspaper or a TV in the last few days, you'd know all this, too. It's all over the place. They've been looking pretty hard for you guys. I told Andersen I knew you guys skipped town and that I thought I could find you. He didn't like it, but I also told him that I thought you might be going to Lily and since he needs Lily's statement before they can charge Kogen, he didn't have much choice. Especially since I didn't tell him where I was looking. He doesn't know I actually found you. Yet."

The first thing to pop into Albert's head is, *It's not too late*. Still, he doesn't get his hopes up yet—not without knowing what MacLennan wants or if he's planning to be a problem. Glancing over at Olivia, he can barely make out her face, though he can see that she's looking back at him and probably having the same thoughts that he is.

"So," MacLennan says, leaning forward. "What was the plan—for the three of you to run away? Where's Lily?"

So he *doesn't* know. Albert silently thanks whatever thin luck they have that MacLennan didn't come across them sooner and overhear them talking about The Last Good Place.

Albert thinks of lying, of telling MacLennan that they

don't know where Lily is, but Olivia speaks first. Albert's heart crawls up into his mouth and he's terrified that in her anger she might blurt out their idea of where to find her sister.

Instead, she demands, "Why are you doing this, Patrick? Why are you stalking us?"

"I'm trying to help," MacLennan says. He sounds sincere, Albert thinks, and that grates on him. Like, who is this guy to help them now, after all he's done that has hurt Lily?

Olivia presses him. "Did the cops promise to cut you a deal if you brought us in?"

MacLennan is on his feet now, clearly angry. "I'm in enough trouble over all this—with my parents, with the cops, with that psycho Kogen. I don't need this shit, too. Just forget it, all right?" He turns and walks away.

Albert follows MacLennan and grabs his shoulder. MacLennan reaches up and clamps his hand around Albert's wrist, then whirls around to look down at him, still crushing his wrist in his grip. Albert is forcefully reminded of the massive size difference between himself and this football player upon whom he's so stupidly laid his hands.

Trying not to flinch, he says, "No, we can't just forget it. Not until we know what you're planning to do after you leave."

MacLennan finally lets go. Ignoring Albert's question, he asks again, suddenly, "Where is Lily hiding?"

"We thought she'd be here," Albert says. "But she isn't. It doesn't look like she ever was." He leaves it at that.

"Don't say anything else," Olivia says. "He's got no reason to want to help us, or Lily."

"That's not true, Liv," MacLennan says. "I feel horrible about ... what Kogen did to Lily, and then there's what I did—the accident, and then I actually helped the piece of garbage. I just want to help find Lily and bring her back, so she can talk to the police herself and make sure the guy's locked up, you know? But if she really isn't here, I'll have to settle for bringing you two back with me. Maybe *you* can help the cops find her."

"I'm not leaving, not now," Olivia says, folding her arms over her chest.

"Me either," says Albert. "Don't you get it? We still haven't found her. It's not over for us. We're not going anywhere without her."

"She ran away because she was afraid of Perry," Olivia adds. "If she knew what you've just told us, that Perry is as good as fried, maybe she'd come back with us and pound that final nail in, instead of just clearing out for good. So, you see why we can't stop?"

"Then I'll come with you," says MacLennan slowly, as if he's speaking before thinking it through. "Maybe I can help."

"No," say Albert and Olivia together. Though MacLennan sounds like he means it, they are far from trusting him. They both just want to get rid of him, so they can salvage their plan before he completely wrecks it.

"None of us knows how she'll react if we do find her," Olivia says. "She's confused, and afraid, and seeing you might send her running again. You can't risk screwing things up worse than they already are because you have a guilty conscience. Just go home, MacLennan. Leave us alone."

Silence on all three sides.

"Fine," MacLennan sighs, the first one to break.

Albert is sure he hears relief in MacLennan's voice that he doesn't have to keep up the chase anymore. The whole twisted mess is partially his fault, and he probably wants to get as far away from it as possible and try to forget what he's done. Albert can't even really blame the guy for allowing Lily's sister and boyfriend to clear him of further responsibility so easily. But he's too tired to worry about it now. Blame might come later, he thinks, once he has the luxury of time.

There's an owl hooting somewhere in the trees, and the three of them, nerves already taught, jump.

"Listen, though—you can't tell anyone where we are," Albert says. "As soon as we find Lily and convince her to come with us, we'll go home. You can sit on this for a few days?"

"Man, Andersen wasn't happy with me for taking off in the first place," MacLennan says, hesitant. His scowl is discernible in the gloom. "But if I don't have information for him, he's probably going to arrest me, too."

"Please," Albert says.

"Forget the cops, then. What am I supposed to tell your parents when they come after me? They're going to want to know where you are."

"Just tell them all the same thing: you made contact with us and we said we'd call with information in, say, three days. That's pretty much the truth. Tell them if they come after us, we'll run, which is also the truth." Desperation. "I don't care what you tell them, honestly. Can't you hold them off for just a couple of days?"

"I don't know … it's going to sound so flimsy …" MacLennan runs his hands through his hair, thinking.

"You owe her," Olivia interrupts quietly. "I know my sister, and I know she was almost at the breaking point when she ran away. If the cops start looking for her, she's going to freak out and maybe never stop running. And then we might never find her at all. Whatever bad things happen to her after that will be *your* fault. So just keep your mouth shut for a few days. And if it gets uncomfortable, just tell yourself it's your punishment for everything you've done to hurt her."

"I never meant to!" MacLennan shouts, his voice echoing on the water. "That's not an excuse, it's the truth. I was scared. I didn't *know*."

"But you know *now*," Olivia insists. "So, are you going to help us, or are you going to keep screwing us over? You won't be able to say you didn't know this time."

Albert watches them—Olivia delivering her harsh judgment, MacLennan deciding what he can and can't live with. Albert is just an observer, holding his breath and waiting for the outcome.

Finally, MacLennan says, "I won't tell anyone where you are. But I don't know how long I can string the cops along. If you haven't called or come home in a couple of days, they're either going to figure out I'm lying or they're going to force me to tell them where I tracked you to."

"A couple of days will be enough," Albert says, privately wondering if that's actually true.

There's nothing more to be said after that. MacLennan starts to stick out his hand like he wants to shake Albert's, then he thinks better of it and shoves both hands in his pockets.

Albert and Olivia stand shoulder to shoulder, watching him. Waiting him out.

"So I guess I'm out of here," MacLennan says finally. "My truck isn't far. You guys need a ride anywhere?" he asks as he turns to go.

They don't.

Albert listens until he can't hear MacLennan's movements anymore. Shivering, he pulls his jacket more tightly around his body. He isn't at all tired anymore. MacLennan's appearance, besides almost causing an adrenaline heart attack, has forced Albert into new awareness of the shortness of time.

"I hope he keeps his promise," Albert sighs. He has no confidence that MacLennan will last more than a day before the police and their parents—and maybe Kogen, too, even after everything—are able to get the whole story out of him. And then they'll come after Albert and Olivia.

And maybe, thinks the superstitious part of Albert, it will drive Lily away forever.

Neither Albert nor Olivia move. They just stand there,

watching the space in the trees where MacLennan disappeared. Some minutes later, they hear the echo of an engine.

Abruptly, Albert begins walking. "We can't wait for the light. We're going now, before he changes his mind and sends the cops after us."

Olivia nods, catching up and taking the lead. "It'll be dawn soon. We don't have the canoe, of course," she says to herself as she walks, "but I think I can find it eventually, if we just follow the shoreline. I hope I'm right, that Lily's waiting for us there. And that she'll listen."

"You have to be right," Albert says, right behind her. "Otherwise it's all just dead ends."

Thirty-two

*B*ecause I love you," he finished lamely.

"Ah." She smiled a little. "You're in the love-means-never-having-to-say-you're-sorry camp? Love conquers all?"

"Something like that," he said. He watched her face, saw it play out in her eyes as she checked out again, as good as a million miles away. She'd been doing that a lot lately. Even her body language spoke of distance as she squeezed herself into the farthest corner of the couch, the farthest away from Albert.

He didn't want to push this Other Lily, so when it was clear she wasn't going to say anything else, he followed her example and turned his eyes back to the forgettable movie playing silently on the TV screen. The pictures flickered and hurt his eyes and he didn't really see them.

"If I took off, you'd follow me, wouldn't you?"

He glanced at her and saw that she'd spoken without taking her eyes from the television. "Don't talk like that."

"But would you?" she insisted.

A little frightened, he reached over and grabbed her around the waist, pulling her body to his until they sort of met in the middle of the couch. Though the gesture was rough, she let him do it. His voice muffled by her hair, where he'd buried his face, he murmured, "Yes. Yes, of course I would."

"And you'd bring me back, no matter what?"

"If that's what you want."

"That's what I want," she said. "Promise me. No matter what, you'd find me."

She pulled away a bit and their eyes met—his searching; hers unblinking, calm. Or at least, that was the effect she was trying for … Lily was often going for an effect. Only the way she gripped his forearms betrayed that this was anything other than idle talk.

"I promise."

Thirty-three
7:30 a.m.

They set out immediately, with the last of the night still clinging to everything. Very soon the gray light grows brighter and they're picking their way over the brushy ground, with Olivia breaking the trail and Albert following. The shore leads them to the little place where the stream flows into the trees, just as Olivia remembers. The way is pathless and thickly overgrown and it's slow going. Frustratingly slow. Albert wants to ask her if this seems right, if this seems like the way, but he forces himself to leave her alone. The only sound is their labored breathing and the snap of frosty twigs and pine needles under their feet.

At first Albert is convinced he's only imagining the stream widening, but after a while it's clear that the water really is getting broader. The trees thin a bit at the water's edge and then they're able to walk more quickly. He's concentrating on his footing, and so, when Olivia stops, he runs into her back and they both stumble.

"There," Olivia says, pointing across the water. "That's the place."

Albert follows her finger with his eyes and sees what looks like an island. The stream has widened back into a larger, stiller body of water and their target seems far away. His heart flutters nervously.

"I can't see much," he says. Squinting, he's able to make out the shack, though whether he would've recognized the rough lines as those of a building without having Olivia's story fresh in his mind, he isn't sure. "How do we get out to the island without a boat?"

"It's a peninsula," she says. "It'll take some walking, but if we just follow the shore to the far side, we'll get around to there eventually."

Albert's stomach lurches and he doesn't want to leave this moment. Anticipation mingles with terror. His fear is that the moment that waits for him up ahead will turn out to be empty. There's a part of him that doesn't want to know how this turns out, in case it should turn out badly.

As if reading his mind, Olivia motions him forward. "We've come too far not to see this all the way through," she says. "Try to think the best will happen." She continues following the bank without waiting to see if he's behind her.

He stares across the rippling water. A pale shimmer

catches his eye and he thinks he can see a thin stream of smoke. Sniffing the air, he thinks yes, he can smell the distinctive, woody smell of a campfire.

Then a movement.

Has he seen movement in the falling-down shack? It's too far away and the evergreens and the trunks of the aspens make it hard to tell if he's seen real movement or just been fooled by the bouncing shadows of the branches in the wind.

"Lily?" he calls, the name falling out of his mouth before he knows it. His voice sounds thin in the gray morning's cold. He steps forward as far as he can, his toes sinking into the soft bank and the frigid water.

This time there is definitely movement. He's almost certain. Albert stretches forward as far as he can, looking hard.

Then he sees a slip of a figure come out of the shack and look back at him through the trees—a lean figure, moving with a familiar taut, darting energy. Finally she emerges from the trees and glides to the edge of the opposite shore.

Their eyes lock across the water.

Albert raises his hand and gives an abrupt, joyful shout. In his peripheral vision, he's aware of Olivia looking at him, but then he completely forgets her.

"What are you—" she begins.

But Albert isn't listening.

Pulling off his shoes and throwing down his coat, he half runs, half stumbles from the shore, plunging into the icy water and the shortest distance between two points.

Acknowledgments

Bringing *The Last Good Place of Lily Odilon* from its first handwritten jots to publication would not have happened without the following people: My better half, Paul, a keen-eyed first reader, my best sounding board, and a tireless champion; my extraordinary agent, Kate Schafer Testerman of kt literary; my fabulous editor, Brian Farrey; as well as production editor Sandy Sullivan, cover designer Ellen Dahl, publicist Marissa Pederson, and the rest of the inimitable Flux corps. Then there are the friends and family who are bound and determined to make sure everyone in the galaxy picks up a copy of this book whether they want to or not. My grateful and superlative-laced thanks to you all.

About the Author

Sara Beitia is the product of a small Western town and is married to artist Paul Marshall. She has worked as, among other things, a staff writer and arts editor for an independent alt-weekly. *The Last Good Place of Lily Odilon* is her debut YA novel. Visit Sara online at www.sarabeitia.com.